I0653850

RUNAWAY ROMANCE

Spoiled Brats Book Series
Book Two
by
Marissa Marchan

RUNAWAY ROMANCE

Spoiled Brats Book Series
Book Two
Copyright © 2020 by Marissa Marchan

First Edition: My Runaway Bride (Book 2)
ISBN-10: 1541142586
ISBN-13: 978-1541142589
Second Edition: Runaway Romance
ISBN-13: 9798644628940
Third Edition: Runaway Romance
ISBN-13: 978-1-953577-09-2 (eBook)
ISBN-13: 978-1-953577-14-6 (Print)

Book Cover Design by Marissa Marchan
Image(s) from Canva
Published by 3 Ways Publishing
https://marissamarchan.com[1]
https://3wayspublishing.wordpress.com[2]

---

1.   https://marissamarchan.com/

2.   https://3wayspublishing.wordpress.com/

THANK YOU

For the love and support

Leo

Ray-Angelo

Haley-Alexis

Kayla Marie

Lesley-Anne and Hardy

Matt-Derek and Maria

PROLOGUE

Beverly Hills Prep Academy was a haven for the wealthy, famous, and spoiled brats. Twelve eighth students traveled to New York City for a two-day educational excursion.

The groups checked into their assigned rooms at the famous Majestic Inn. The teachers separated the students into four groups of three and assigned each team a room, with the instructors sharing the last room. Six of the students—attractive, extremely affluent, vicious girls who felt superior to other cliques—refused to share a room with anybody other than themselves.

Due to their anger, the teachers confined them to a single room. The teenagers resisted, unwilling to share, but their professors insisted they stay together or sleep in the corridor, a notion that made them cringe. Out of desperation, the teens agreed to share a room.

The youngsters recognized their similarities and differences, and the friendships they formed while sharing a room were incredible. Vanessa Florence Grandeville, Stephanie Elaine Lee, Rachel Ann Franchesca Davenport, Alexandra Jane Moore, Samantha Isabella St. James, and Jennifer Clarice Stevens became great friends and supported one another through difficult personal times.

CHAPTER ONE

The airport was especially crowded that morning, with irate travelers waiting for updates on their canceled flights because of mechanical issues. Children running rampant and passengers disembarking just added to the chaos.

Samantha proceeded to a souvenir shop and perused the gift section while waiting for them to depart, before choosing a light reading material. She couldn't find any magazines, so she grabbed a newspaper and handed the cashier a five-dollar bill. Samantha flipped over the pages, but nothing caught her eye. And then she saw it. A full-page wedding announcement was written below her picture in large bold letters: *Artemus St. James of Beverly Hills, California, is pleased to announce the engagement of his daughter, Samantha Isabella St. James, to Robert Chandler Jr., the son of a wealthy industrialist, Robert Chandler Sr., and his wife, Emilia Chandler, of Los Angeles, California. A summer wedding is now on the horizon.*

Samantha's eyes widened. Outraged, she yelled so loudly that everyone turned around to see what was going on. Samantha raised her head and noticed everybody was staring at her. She kicked the chair next to her. Her friends reached out, caressing her back to calm her. They'd never seen her agitated or upset before.

"Sam, what happened?" Stephanie inquired.

Samantha's sniffles and sobs broke the stillness for a few seconds. It took a while for her to calm down. After she had recovered from the first shock, she sat down on a chair, tears welling up in her eyes as she folded the newspaper and handed it to her friends. They snatched it from her grasp and began reading the May 12 society page section of the Los Angeles Times. Their eyes widened. They, too, couldn't believe what they were reading.

Samantha was furious. How could her father have done this to her? He couldn't plan her wedding without telling her. She couldn't believe her happiness just minutes before, when she kissed and held her goddaughter in her arms before saying goodbye, had turned into a nightmare.

"Sam, why would your father announce your wedding without your knowledge and approval?" Rachel wondered.

"I'm not sure, but I need to figure this out. It's unusual for my father to do anything like this. Something must have happened at home for him to make this decision on his own."

Samantha tightened her teeth and fought back her anger. She was upset and confused, and she couldn't wait to get home and talk to her father.

SAMANTHA ISABELLA ST. James, a frivolous twenty-two-year-old Beverly Hills socialite and well-known spoiled brat, was the only child of Angelina and Artemus St. James. Her father was a multimillionaire commercial entrepreneur, a wealthy property developer, and the president and CEO of Artemus Industries, a multimillion-dollar retail corporation. Her mother died just before her seventeenth birthday. Samantha was the only child in line to inherit the family business.

Samantha was in the airport departure area in Honolulu with her friends: Stephanie, Rachel, Jennifer, and Alexandra. They were preparing to board their plane for the flight home after spending a month at Fisherman's Wife Vacation Resort on Towi Island, a charming little village on a small island in the Pacific Ocean. Vanessa Florence Grandeville-Angelo, their best friend and sixth member of the Spoiled Brats Princesses of Beverly Hills, or SBPs, for short, owned the resort. It was a nickname given to them in high school by students and even teachers because of their beauty, money, and popularity. They were in Hawaii to celebrate the first birthday of Clarissa Belle, Vanessa's daughter, and Samantha's first godchild.

Samantha became restless on the plane for the next five hours. She slumped back in her seat and tightened her seat belt, letting out a hard breath she hadn't realized she'd been holding. She tried to pass the time by flipping through magazines that the flight attendant had handed her earlier, but she kept coming back to the wedding announcement. Looking at it made her feel confused and helpless. Something resembling panic made her heart race, as if she had entered the twilight zone. What might have prompted her father to betray her by making such an arrangement without first consulting her?

Samantha phoned her father as soon as they landed at LAX, but she didn't get a response, which was just as well. She was furious at what he had done, and she didn't know what her first words would be.

Samantha hugged her friends after retrieving her luggage, refusing their offer of a ride home in the black stretch limousine waiting at the curb. All she wanted to do was be alone to collect her thoughts.

"We understand, Sam. Just remember that we are here to support you. Promise you'll call if you need us?" Rachel suggested.

Samantha said farewell to her friends as she headed to the car rental counter. Minutes later, she was driving down the Pacific Coast Highway in a rented silver convertible, letting the wind blow over her long black hair. Samantha switched on the radio and listened to hard rock, which she had never listened to before, but thought could console her. She wanted to forget everything, even her father and her imminent marriage to a man she despised. Samantha pounded her fists on the steering wheel until her hands hurt. Tears flowed down her cheeks, and she brushed them away as they blurred her vision. Samantha felt the desire to scream, so she lifted her hands and yelled, much as she would on a roller coaster, but her cry became lodged in her throat. She pulled over to the side of the road, turned off the car, and leaned on the steering wheel. She wanted to weep, but couldn't move or breathe, so she slumped back into her seat.

She restarted the car after a long delay. Strong wind gusts buffeted her convertible as she drove. It hit her hard that there was no place to forget, wander, or hide. It was time to confront her father. She slowed the car, did a U-turn, and returned the way she had come.

The security officer at their gated community saw her coming. He grinned, waved his hand, and opened the security gate, allowing her to enter. Samantha paid no attention to him. She sped up as soon as she passed through the gate and onto their driveway, slamming on the brakes and screeching to a halt in time to miss her father's car parked a few feet away. Her sudden stop left big tire impressions on the driveway. Grabbing the folded paper from the vehicle seat, she rushed out of the car, up the steps, and into the living room, where her father was entertaining a guest.

"Dad, is this true? What it says in the newspaper?" Samantha asked, waving the newspaper.

Her father gave her a quick glance, shrugged, and resumed his attention to his guest.

"You can't do this, Dad! You can't force me to marry someone I despise! I'm not ready to marry yet, and even if I were, I wouldn't marry someone like... RJ. He is the devil's spawn. I'm only twenty-two years old, and if you hadn't noticed, I'm too young to marry. Dad, are you listening?"

Her father's eyes narrowed as he halted his conversation with his guest. He stood from his seat, his worn old face turning scarlet, and paused for a moment, as if indecisive, before heading to his wet bar. He closed his eyes and sighed, before turning to face his daughter and gulping down a glass of his best cognac.

"What the heck is the point of this? What is so important that you feel the need to interrupt my meeting?" he asked as he sat back down.

"This wedding announcement in the newspaper," Samantha asked, waving the paper. "Is this true?"

Artemus just gave her a sidelong glance. He instead inhaled deeply. "I'm sorry to say I'm disappointed in you, Samantha. Since when do you raise your voice in front of a guest?"

"I hope you don't mind, but I need to speak with my father alone." Samantha addressed the guest. She gave him a quick glance.

The guest realized he needed to leave after getting the gist of the girl's impatience. "Um, Mr. St. James, we can reschedule this meeting."

"Humph," Artemus growled back. "Perhaps you're right. Just give my secretary a call, and we'll set up another meeting."

The guest nodded and exited, leaving the father and daughter to their argument.

"Well?" Samantha asked when they were alone.

"So, what exactly are you talking about?" Artemus asked.

"Dad!" Samantha screamed. "Why aren't you telling me what's going on?"

"I have nothing to say. I made the arrangements for your wedding, and that's that," Artemus responded, moving his attention away from her. It terrified him that his daughter would see through him and discover that he was deceiving her.

Samantha felt betrayed when her father admitted what he had done to her. The reality came at her at a dizzying velocity. She later puzzled how she could speak or breathe at all. She should be allowed to make her own future decisions. That should be a basic human right for everyone. She knew her parents had never believed in arranged marriages, whether religious or financial reasons. She had no idea her father would even consider a coerced agreement. Knowing him well, she realized something was wrong.

"But, Dad, why? It's unusual for you to behave in this way. Please help me understand your unexpected decision. Can you tell me what is going on?"

Artemus avoided confrontation, yet he knew he might be passive aggressive.

"Sam, believe me when I say you're the last person I'd ever want to hurt, and you deserve to know the truth. I'm in a lot of trouble. I didn't say anything to you before, believing I could make things right. I didn't want to ruin your vacation in Hawaii with your friends. But I was mistaken. When your mother died, I drank to drown my sadness. I committed myself to expanding my business empire and obtaining a variety of projects. I needed to stay active in order to divert myself long enough to help me deal with the ongoing anguish I felt after your mother's death. Even though she's been gone for a few years now, I still miss her. My acquaintance invited me to meet him at Bayview Casino, about an hour's drive from the office, to explore potential business options. I hadn't seen him in a long time, and he called me completely unexpectedly. I agreed, since I thought I needed a break. We drank a couple cocktails and then went to the high-limit poker area to play a few hands. We later went back to the bar and drank some more."

Samantha focused her attention on her father's narrative. Her father slumped back in his chair, put his hands on his face, and cried, much to her surprise.

"I don't know what transpired after that, Sam. It was all a blur. Something awful happened, and I ended up in a bind. I'm sorry, but I'm unable to provide any other information. I'm too embarrassed."

As Samantha glanced at her father, her eyes widened and she felt perplexed. "What are you keeping from me, Dad? What was the name of the friend you were drinking with? Please help me understand you."

"I'm sorry, Sam, but that's all I have to say. For our sake, trust me when I say it's best for you to marry RJ."

"For our sake?" she said again. "I'm not sure I understand what you're saying. You are one of the country's wealthiest and most successful people, as well as one of the most influential business executives. Why are you putting up with RJ's bullying? Is there something he has against you that makes you feel compelled to comply? You have twice as much money as his father. It's unusual for you to put me in this situation. I know you're hiding something from me. Please, tell me the truth. What makes you want me to marry RJ?"

"I'm sorry, Sam, but I've already decided for the both of us.'

"No, this is not happening!" Samantha demanded under her breath. Her head felt like a bomb had hit it and exploded. She wanted to scream at him. She was enraged, furious, and disappointed. It defied everything she knew about her father's ability to commit such a horrific act. Her entire world had crumbled around her. Samantha could feel all her hopes and dreams shattered.

Samantha was deafeningly quiet, but the sorrow in her eyes was clear. She shook her head, tears streaming down her cheeks.

"So, this marriage is a business transaction, is that it? Did you sell me to pay off your debt? Is it money? How much is it, Dad? How much do you owe them?" Samantha shouted, her chest tightening as she looked at her father.

Artemus couldn't look at his daughter. Instead, he rubbed his hands together and avoided her gaze by glancing at the floor. He remained silent and did not answer.

Samantha was becoming annoyed with her father's silence. She loved him, but she couldn't trust him anymore.

"I will flee if you force me to marry RJ," she said.

Artemus had not expected his daughter to say that. "My decision is final, Samantha, and if you disobey me, I will disown you," Artemus said, hoping to scare his daughter into complying with his decision. He almost burst into tears when he realized how much he had hurt her with what he had said. He walked away without looking back, afraid of falling apart in front of her.

Samantha felt as if she was falling, and there was no solid ground under her as her world crumbled around her. Her father insists on accepting RJ's proposal. He had threatened to disown her, something she had not imagined hearing from him. It infuriated her.

"If my mother were still alive, she would not have allowed you to force me to marry..." Her voice was trembling. "I hate you, Daddy!" she couldn't bring herself to say. Samantha had slumped on the sofa and was on the verge of passing out. Her heart was in excruciating pain, and she was panting for air.

Artemus heard his daughter's voice behind him. He came to a sudden standstill and turned around. "I'm sorry, Samantha. I truly am. I don't want to hurt you, but I don't want to discuss this anymore. You're marrying RJ whether you like it or not."

Samantha waited, as if she had something to say. She gazed at her father, a terrible wrath welling up in her as he returned her gaze, steadfast but not defiant. Samantha's patience had run out. She couldn't go on like this for much longer.

"I'm going to my room!" She screamed, dashed across the hall, and hurried upstairs without looking back.

A few moments later, she heard a knock on her door.

"May I come in, Sam?" said her father.

"No, you may not." Samantha stated. "Please leave me alone."

"We need to talk, Samantha. Open the door, please," Artemus urged.

Samantha remained silent and did not answer. She didn't want to hear anything her father had to say anymore.

"Okay, have it your way, but our discussion is far from over," Artemus said as he walked away.

Samantha didn't care how many times her father knocked and begged her to open the door. She closed her eyes, put her hands over her ears, and ignored his plea.

THE ROOM WAS DARK AND quiet. Samantha rose to her feet and headed to the door on tiptoe. When she turned the door handle, she discovered her father had locked the door from the outside. She shook her head and exhaled deeply.

Maybe if I sleep long enough and wake up tomorrow, I'll realize everything that occurred today was just a dreadful dream.

CHAPTER TWO

S amantha yawned and stretched when she awoke the next morning.

What a strange dream I had last night.

She rose up and stumbled to the door. She turned the doorknob, but it was locked. Memories of the previous night flooded her mind, and she panicked. What she remembered couldn't be real. It couldn't be!

Samantha banged on the door, hoping someone would hear her, but no one came. She leaned against the wall for a minute and turned the doorknob again, but it still didn't open. Samantha slumped to the floor, furious. She sat up on her knees and struggled to her feet a few moments later. Samantha threw herself on the bed and curled up on her side, clutching her pillow. She cried, more out of anger than anything else. It was the first time her father had confined her in her room, raised his voice, and threatened to disown her. Samantha had fallen into deep depression. She knew her father would never change his mind, and she would have to marry RJ.

Samantha knew the day would come when she'd have to marry, but it did not prepare her for it, especially because she hadn't considered herself a lady yet. She still had a lot of growing up to do. Samantha wasn't ready to be RJ's or any other man's wife. She never imagined her life would turn out this way.

Samantha recounted her first meeting with RJ many years ago at his parents' ranch in Texas. She was fourteen, and RJ was sixteen. She and her mother attended a charity gathering hosted by RJ's aristocratic mother. His innuendos both enraged and titillated her.

Sure, everyone knew who Robert Chandler Jr. was. He was handsome, rich, and charming. RJ was every girl's fantasy, but he was also self-centered and rude. He was every inch the young, attractive guy who loved to walk around flaunting his charm and money. RJ had a way of making girls feel special and important, but there was something in his look she couldn't quite fathom. Samantha felt it was because of the way he looked at her, as if he was undressing her, which revolted and violated her. Samantha shook at the thought. It happened many years ago, but she recalled it as if it had happened yesterday. Samantha cried, burying her face in her pillow. She felt unloved and alone without her mother, because of the burden of obligation her father expected her to shoulder.

Samantha had fallen back to sleep before she realized it, and the scent of Irish crème coffee, bacon, eggs, and pancakes—her favorite morning foods—awakened her. She opened her eyes to find Nanny Lorraine standing in the doorway, holding a tray of food.

"Please help me, Nanny Lorraine. I need to get out of this house," she said.

"I'm sorry, Sam. I have strict orders from your father not to let you leave this room. Believe me, child, this is for your own good."

"For my own good?" she asked again. "How can that be if I'm a prisoner in my home?"

"Sam, sweetheart, your father has explained everything to you. Trust him, regardless of his reasons or weaknesses. Don't worry. It'll be OK," Nanny Lorraine reassured her as she held her, wrapping her in soothing warmth.

Samantha clutched her hand, wanting to cry, but she had no tears left in her. She closed her eyes and took a deep breath. Samantha did not know how long it had been since Nanny Lorraine had left her room, or how long she had been sitting by the window, looking blankly into space. She climbed into her bed and curled up in a ball beneath the blankets.

Meanwhile, Artemus was drinking himself to oblivion in the library room. He'd spent many sleepless hours thinking about what he'd done to his daughter. He drank more heavily last night and this morning. Artemus loved Samantha, and he had indulged her much too much since his wife died. It saddened him to force his daughter into a marriage she didn't want. It was all his fault.

Why did I let this get so out of hand? I should have gone straight to the police station.

Artemus was a well-known businessman who was also aggressive. Nothing was enough for him. He was high on power because he wanted more investments and properties. It was his way of dealing with his wife's death. He longed for her. Artemus would never have met with Robert Chandler Sr. if he hadn't been greedy about another business prospect. He would not be in this situation. His only child's chances of marrying someone he loved and spending time with his grandchildren were dwindling. It was now too late for them.

"I'M NOT SURE WHAT I'D do if my parents told me I had to marry a complete stranger. I would absolutely flee." Stephanie added.

She and her friends, Jennifer, Rachel, and Alexandra, were in Samantha's room, trying to console her. Artemus had allowed them to visit Samantha, but he remained outside, guarding the door. He believed keeping a close eye on his daughter was the proper thing to do. Artemus had even boosted security and hired a bodyguard for his daughter. He was afraid Samantha would escape, exactly as she had said.

"I don't know about you, but if I can't live with someone I like, how can I live with someone I despise?" Jennifer stated. "That's why I'm cautious when it comes to dating and starting a relationship. Do you know how demanding I am? I can't date anyone."

"You don't have to tell us, Jen. Remember that we are also members of the SBPs? We all have the same problems," Stephanie said, as everyone burst out laughing.

"Sam, you need to think about this. You don't want to be with some random person your father chose for you. There's no way in hell I'd put up with that," Jennifer said.

"But what should I do? I don't want to defy my father, but I also don't want to marry that pervert," Samantha stated.

"Calm down, Sam. I'm confident we'll come up with something," Alexandra said. "When is the wedding?"

"RJ phoned me the other day and said he wanted us to be married right away. His family wanted us to fly to Paris soon after our wedding. They made all our decisions without consulting with me," Stephanie explained. "RJ also said that once we're married, whatever I do, wherever I go, and whomever I see, I have to check with him beforehand."

"What?" Stephanie asked. "That's like living with a dictator."

Samantha said, "Tell me about it. I told him I was fourteen the last time I saw him. I don't know him that well, and he's insane if he thinks I'd give him power over me."

"What did he say?" Rachel asked. Her eyes widened in disbelief.

"He said, 'We'll see about that,' and hung up."

"He also appears to have a bad temper. You'd best think about it, Sam. He has the potential to be a violent person. What confuses me is why your father would press you to marry him. Can't he see there's something wrong with this union from the start? Something fishy is going on here. There's more to this than meets the eye," Rachel remarked.

Everyone looked at each other, perplexed.

Samantha, tired and worn out, lamented her circumstances. She looked out the window as she watched her friends drive away. Then a grin appeared on her face as she remembered something that could help her situation.

Samantha spent the day locked up in her room, looking for her gold trinket box, where she stored all her treasures and secrets, including a master key she fashioned that opened all the inside and outdoor doors in the house. She had it made when her father forbade her from entering her mother's bedroom after she died. It stayed locked even after they buried her. When her father was away on business, she would sleep in her mother's bed and sometimes smell her mother's clothes as if she were still with her. Her mother was very special to her. She loved her very much.

IT WAS LATE AT NIGHT. Samantha moved slowly. She slung her backpack on her back, tiptoed to her door, and opened it. If she made the slightest sound, her father may have heard her, and her escape plan would be discovered. As she made her way downstairs, a strange combination of emotions rushed over her. Samantha's heart pounded in her chest. She tried to open the front door with much trepidation, only to discover that her key did not work. After a few minutes, she learned her father had installed two new types of key locks, rendering her master key useless. Her father made sure she couldn't leave the house. He was trying to confine her to her home.

Frustrated, she dragged herself back to her room and wept till she had no more tears to shed. Her eyes were heavy, and she fell asleep until she heard a knock at the door, which jolted her awake, confused and disoriented.

"Sam?"

Samantha could hear her father's voice on the other side of the door, but she remained mute.

The door opened slightly.

"RJ and his father are here to see you. Please come downstairs and meet them for a few minutes."

Samantha rubbed her sleepy eyes. She looked at the wall clock. It was nine o'clock. She drew the blanket over her head and tried to sleep again.

"I don't want to see anyone," she mumbled as she drew the covers closer to her.

"Samantha, don't start with me. Don't test my patience. This marriage is the best thing for both of us."

Samantha locked her focus on her father. "I will not marry RJ."

"Of course, you will, God help me."

Samantha glanced over at her father, who was standing at the slightly open door. "And what if I refuse?"

"This is my family, and I make the rules around here. If you defy me, I will disown you," Artemus said, his voice loud.

Samantha was taken aback and blinked. There was no longer use in fighting with her father. She gave up and burst into tears. With a sad heart, she pulled out the black dress she had worn at her mother's funeral and put it on. She trudged to the bathroom, splashed cold water on her face, and pulled her hair into a bun. She walked out the door and down the stairs. The sound of her black high heels rang across the living room, and everyone turned to see her as she entered. Samantha looked at the people seated on the sofa. Mr. Chandler, RJ, and a middle-aged man in a brown suit were there.

"Good morning, Sam," RJ said, kissing her cheek. "I'm surprised you're not wearing black gloves and a black veil to match your mourning outfit," he joked.

Samantha raised her eyebrows and frowned over.

"Sam, don't be rude to our guests," Artemus said.

"It's okay, Artemus. She'll grow to like me in time," RJ replied slyly.

Mr. Chandler stood up. "We seek your consent, Samantha. Do you accept RJ's marriage proposal?"

Samantha gazed at him in silence, uncertain of what to say.

"Before you answer, Samantha, allow me to introduce our attorney, Andrew Tomei," Mr. Chandler said.

Artemus looked at him, concerned. "Your attorney?"

"Yes, Artemus. He will draft our agreement. I'm also offering you a fantastic chance to become partners in your firm. You will keep ownership and control of the company, but you will no longer be the CEO. You will have to step down."

"Step down?" Artemus said angrily. "And what makes you think I would agree to that? I will not enter into such an arrangement. We agreed my daughter would marry your son, but I never discussed giving up my business."

"We'll see," Mr. Chandler said, with a grin.

"Is that a threat, Robert?"

"No, it's only a thought, since we'll be one big family soon, so don't worry. We will stick to our original plan. I'll leave you now, since I have other matters to attend to. I'll see you later, Artemus. Goodbye, Samantha," Mr. Chandler remarked as he walked away.

This revelation was met with a stunned hush. Samantha couldn't believe what she had just heard. She kept hearing the word "agreement" in her head like a broken record. Samantha was right. She felt Mr. Chandler had something against her father. She knew he was being blackmailed more now than ever. Samantha had no doubts in her mind. She needed to play along. She needed some time to mull things through. Samantha took a deep breath to reinforce her courage and sprinted to catch up with Mr. Chandler. RJ, his attorney, and her father followed her.

"Mr. Chandler," Samantha shouted as she caught up with him.

Mr. Chandler came to a halt and turned around, a smile on his face. "What can I do for you, Samantha?"

"I implore you. There has to be a better way to resolve this on whatever arrangement you made with my father. I don't want to marry your son," Samantha begged.

Mr. Chandler gazed at her for a full minute before speaking. "Samantha, please allow me to explain something to you. Your decision will affect the outcome of your father's debt to me. Do you understand what I'm saying?"

"I don't understand. My father is a wealthy businessman, who is also one of the country's richest people. You, however, did not even make the list of the top one hundred entrepreneurs. It smells like blackmail, Mr. Chandler, and I've seen and heard enough to know what's going on. What secret do you have against my father?"

"I think I underestimated you, Samantha. However, as you mentioned, it is a tightly kept secret. I'll repeat: your decision will affect the outcome of your father's debt to me."

Samantha dropped her eyes to hide the tears that threatened to flow. She glared angrily at her father, who was now standing between them. Samantha understood that whatever Mr. Chandler had against her father had to be extremely important to allow this calamity to happen. It was pointless to argue with any of them, so she opted to play along for the time being.

Samantha said, "Yes, I accept marrying your son," in a barely audible voice. She could scarcely speak.

RJ, who was standing behind her, reached out and hugged her.

"I'm happy you agreed, Samantha," Mr. Chandler said. "We'll start planning the wedding as soon as possible. Let's go, RJ. We have a lot of work to do."

RJ grinned and kissed Samantha on the cheek. "Goodbye, Sam. You won't be sorry. I promise to make you the happiest bride in the world."

Samantha clenched her jaw and fixed her attention on him. "Somehow, I doubt that," she said.

RJ's smile had faded, and his expression had become glum. He averted his gaze for a while, then moved in closer and mumbled into her ear. "Don't worry, it's a promise."

Samantha fixed her eyes on him again, her face hard and cold. RJ tightened his teeth, struggling to control his anger. He was still furious as he walked to his car and slammed the door shut.

Artemus waved goodbye as the father and son drove away.

"Thank you, Sam," Artemus mumbled as he briefly hugged his daughter. "You've prevented my reputation from being tarnished."

Samantha stood in the doorway, staring blankly into nothingness as her father left. She was paralyzed, her body heavy as if it had turned to stone. Her eyes welled up as tears spilled down her face. Her entire existence flashed before her eyes. For the first time in her life, it scared her. She had to play along so she could think. She needed to sit down and carefully plan her escape now, more than ever.

CHAPTER THREE

A black Rolls Royce pulled up to the curb, and the driver, dressed in a black uniform, got out and opened the door. Samantha's bodyguard was behind them.

"Here we go, ma'am," the driver remarked.

Samantha took her time exiting the car. She took a deep breath and exhaled while standing in the Chandler mansion's wide, circular driveway. A chill rushed through her as she looked at the house that would be her home for who knows how long after she and RJ got married. Her stomach twisted. She clenched her hands, her nails digging into the skin of her palms.

As she neared the front door, it irritated her to see her father's car parked on the opposite side of the driveway. She kept walking, a churning sickness in her stomach with each stride. Samantha groaned exasperatedly as she approached the front door. She straightened her shoulders, inhaled deeply, and rang the doorbell. RJ grinned as he opened the door for her. Samantha stared at him for a long time, all the intensity she had felt before still there in her eyes.

"Come in," RJ muttered, reaching down to kiss her. Samantha took a step backward from his kiss.

"Why are you torturing me like this, Samantha?" he pleaded, his voice low. He tried to draw her into his arms, but she refused and shrugged.

"You may deceive my father, and we may marry, but you have no right to touch me. We are not yet married. You are not to kiss or touch me until that time. Do you understand?" Her voice was tense, yet controlled.

RJ didn't answer, instead clenching his fist and slamming it against the wall in anger. His eyes were wide open, and his face was flushed. Samantha shivered in terror and gazed at him in fear. She hadn't expected him to respond in that way.

"Samantha," RJ said calmly, as he drew her back in with his arm. "You'll be mine eventually. Take my word for it!"

Samantha's face was expressionless. She wrenched her arm free from his grasp. "Keep your dirty hands away from me!"

RJ clenched his hands again. He started walking away, then came to a halt and returned. He moved in to kiss Samantha's lips, but she was ready and turned her head. RJ reached for her lips, but she moved her head in the opposite direction. It annoyed him, and despite her uncomfortable response, RJ ignored it, threw his arms around her, and drew her close. He tried to kiss her again, but she averted her gaze. He was about to give it another go when he heard a voice behind him.

"Ahem," Artemus interrupted. "Are you coming in?"

"Yes," RJ said as he let go of Samantha. He took her hand in his and brought her to the living room.

His father sat in his favorite comfortable chair, smoking a cigar, while his mother sat across the room, waiting for them.

"Good evening, Samantha," said Mr. Chandler. Mrs. Chandler repeated what her husband had said.

"Good evening, Mr. and Mrs. Chandler," Samantha said softly as she took a seat in one of the empty chairs.

RJ sat beside her. He took a moment to relish being so close to Samantha. He held his breath, but that just heightened his excitement. "Do we have to be here for this meeting, Dad?" "Do you mind if I take Samantha around the garden?" RJ queried as he took Samantha into a close embrace and kissed her on the cheek.

Samantha whacked him across the ribs. RJ shouted and groaned in pain, which his father and Artemus heard.

"RJ, what happened?" his father asked.

"Nothing, Dad. I'm OK." RJ stated, his gaze fixed on Samantha. "Sam, let's go to the garden together."

RJ grabbed Samantha's hand and yanked her to her feet before she could answer. She pushed his hands away and gave him a nasty look. RJ broke out laughing, but only for a split second.

"Come with me," he shouted, clutching her arm, but she jerked it hard enough to get away.

Mr. and Mrs. Chandler watched them in horror.

"It's a pre-wedding jitter," Artemus laughed. "We should leave our children alone, since they need to work out their differences before the wedding."

RJ REACHED OUT AND caressed Samantha's cheek as she sat on the garden bench. She recoiled instinctively, turning her head away. He let out a furious moan and lifted his hands in the air.

"OK, I understand it. I give up, but Samantha, whether you admit it or not, I know you're upset with me. I know it's foolish to get personal with you, but I'll do anything to make you like me."

The change in his manner surprised Samantha. He looked cool and collected now, but she realized it was all a ruse. The way he spoke charmed her, but it wasn't enough for her to like him.

"Did you hear what I said, Samantha?"

"No matter what you say or do, RJ, you can't make me like you, let alone love you," Samantha remarked.

RJ's fists tightened. His jaw clenched so hard that the veins in his neck throbbed, and his anger stretched his entire body.

"You are a headstrong Samantha, but I shall tame you once we marry. And I'm confident I'll have a terrific time doing it."

Samantha looked at him with a blank expression, her face devoid of emotion, which only heightened RJ's yearning for her.

Samantha averted RJ's stare throughout dinner, since the lecherous sight on his face had made her skin crawl. It brought back memories of their adolescence. Her stomach twisted as she remembered how much she disliked him back then.

Before the night was over, Artemus and the Chandlers had agreed on a date and venue for the wedding, but RJ was eager to get married and pushed for it to happen as soon as possible. After considerable consideration, they agreed the wedding would take place in a week.

"Wait a second! Who says we are getting married in a week? We agreed to marry in the summer, in July or August, rather than next week." Samantha clarified. When her father employed a 24-hour security crew at home, a week was not enough time for her to plan her escape.

"We're aware, but RJ doesn't want to waste any time. He intends to start a new life with you as his wife right away." Mr. Chandler elaborated. "Are you with me, Artemus?"

Artemus understood what Mr. Chandler was hinting. He looked at Samantha and felt his heart break for what he was doing to her. But he could not object.

"Don't worry, Samantha and I agreed," he murmured, holding his daughter closer to him. "Isn't that right, Samantha?"

Samantha stayed silent for a long time until she found her voice.

"Yes, it's fine," was all she could say.

Mrs. Chandler didn't waste any time. She wanted a magnificent and luxurious wedding for her only son. With less than a week to prepare, she engaged herself in every aspect of preparation, no matter how big or small, to ensure that no detail was missed. Two wedding planners organized and oversaw the whole affair. Samantha and her father didn't have to do anything to plan the wedding. The Chandlers handled everything, including her wedding gown, reception, ceremony, and even the guest list.

During that time, Samantha felt overwhelmed by RJ's constant phone calls, and his hostile behavior was too much for her to bear. The more she talked to him, the more she loathed him. He continued to be dominant, possessive, and arrogant. She couldn't stand him. Their wedding should not take place, because it would be a disaster.

"What is the point of having a wedding rehearsal? Why can't we just get married at a municipal hall and be done with it?" Samantha explained. She was having a heated argument with her father one morning.

"RJ's family wishes to proceed appropriately. He is their only son and the heir to their empire. They want our family and their family to get to know one another," her father stated. Samantha didn't say anything, but Artemus could hear her sniffling.

"Enough with the sobbing, Samantha. You'd best get accustomed to the reality that you and RJ are getting married. There is no turning back."

Samantha remained silent and fixed her attention to her father. Her anger and disgust for him were unbearable.

SAMANTHA APPEARED UNCOMFORTABLE and overwhelmed at the rehearsal dinner. The Chandlers wanted the most magnificent wedding celebration for their only son that Los Angeles County had seen in a long time. At least fifty people—people she didn't know—were there, and the wedding was to be attended by at least 500 people the next day.

Samantha prayed and hoped her father would change his mind, but she was merely delusory. She was sure her father would not back down from his decision. Samantha focused her attention on her future husband's face. She had to admit that RJ was handsomer than Brad Pitt. He exuded the image of someone who was at ease with himself. RJ oozed masculinity, but she had to tell herself not to stare at him for too long for fear of his misinterpreting it. RJ had a tremendous ego and proved he was a control freak. He was obviously obsessed with his looks, and she noticed he spent more time getting ready than she did. She despised him much more than before.

Following the rehearsal dinner, guests dined on delectable Italian food, which featured handmade pasta and fresh fish grilled over a mesquite wood fire, as well as vine-ripened garden vegetable salads served to perfection. The inventive French desserts were created, and the guests thoroughly enjoyed the excellent wine selections.

"I wish this union a long and fruitful life. To Samantha and Robert," Mr. Chandler said as he gave a toast of the night.

Everyone in the room said the same thing and raised their glasses to the couple in front of them. The toast echoed across Ray's Bistro Ristorante's high-ceilinged room, where the wedding rehearsal dinner was being held. Samantha looked around and saw that everyone was thrilled and delighted. Every female in the room envied her for marrying the handsome and wealthy Robert Chandler Jr., who appeared satisfied and proud of himself the whole night. They were the embodiment of a perfect couple: young, vivacious, and set for marriage in a matter of hours. Her troubled state of mind was unknown to everyone. A shiver went through her body. She'd be Mrs. Robert Chandler Jr. tomorrow afternoon. Samantha turned to face RJ and his father, who were chatting with the guests. She knew what they wanted to do after the wedding. Samantha would be an excellent trophy wife. All she had to do was smile, nod gracefully, and seem happy. Samantha seemed as exhausted as she felt with all the craziness around her. Or maybe she was weary of everyone telling her how lucky she was to have gotten such a gem as RJ, one of the country's most sought-after and desirable bachelors. Samantha would scream if she heard those words again. Her father gave her explicit orders to convince everyone that their union was amicable, and she was not to exhibit any indications of resistance. Samantha could only grin, nod, and agree, no matter how ridiculous it sounded. She was smart enough not to frown in front of her father and the Chandlers.

"RJ, PLEASE STOP!" SAMANTHA begged.

RJ was attempting to kiss her outside in the garden. It was the third time she had stopped him from kissing her, and the third time she had denied his advances. RJ grabbed her arm as she walked away.

"Let me go, RJ. You are hurting me."

He busted out laughing. "Why do you have to be so difficult, Samantha? You'll be my wife in a matter of hours. I'll make love to you anytime I want, day or night," he said as he grabbed her and kissed her.

Samantha pushed him back and smacked him across the face with all her might.

RJ touched the mark on his face where she had struck him. A woman had never before assaulted him. He gave her a cold glare.

"If you do that again, I swear I'll kiss you so hard your mouth will bleed."

Samantha's eyes welled up with tears as she heard RJ's scathing and furious comments.

RJ sighed, trying to appear serious. "Okay, I promise I'll be kind. Is it all right with you?"

Samantha nodded.

"Samantha, you understand, right? To seal this deal, you will kiss me willingly."

Samantha gazed at him, stunned. The thought of kissing him made her shiver.

RJ tensed, and he thought he saw a hint of uncertainty on her face. "I'll be a true gentleman every time we make love."

Before Samantha could respond, RJ took advantage of the opportunity and brought her in as close as possible. His hold on her hips tightened. As his arms suffocated her, his lips found hers and sealed them together. RJ kissed her lips fiercely, hoping to feel the tingling of affection, but there was none. Samantha didn't move. He kissed her again, expecting a response, but it disappointed him that his lips had not affected her at all.

RJ dipped his head and tried to kiss Samantha again, but she resisted. RJ shook his head. He exhaled a frustrated sigh. No woman he'd ever kissed had ever rejected him. Samantha continued to ignore him, although he had always swayed the ladies with a kiss. He couldn't figure out why his million-dollar charm didn't work on her.

"All I can think of, Samantha, is holding you in my arms, feeling you, and making love to you all night long," RJ murmured, his voice strained.

He lowered his head and captured her mouth on his own. He had his hands all over her. RJ grinned and was about to kiss her again when someone interrupted them. RJ snarled menacingly.

"I apologize for interrupting you, sir." A man dressed as a servant approached them. "Mr. St. James is looking for his daughter, sir, but I see you... well, are busy," he said, a grin on his lips.

RJ seized the man's shirt and snarled at him. "You idiot! Tell Mr. St. James—"

Samantha cut RJ off mid-sentence. "Please inform my father that I am on my way."

"Oh, very good, ma'am," the man responded, unaffected by RJ's pushy demeanor. After another glance at RJ, he scurried away.

"I need to get back to the party," Samantha said, straightening and smoothing her dress, but RJ stopped her.

"The heck with that," RJ responded.

As Samantha tried to flee, RJ grabbed her arm, swung her around, and slammed her up against the wall, ravishing her mouth without waiting for a response, as if he'd run out of patience and reached his limit. Samantha begged him to let her go, threatening to scream if he didn't.

RJ came to a halt and raised one hand in the air, worried about a scandal before their wedding. "I've had a lifetime to make you mine, and I'm sure you'll beg me for more," RJ said, winking at her, smiling devilishly, and laughing a bit.

Angry and disgusted, Samantha pulled away from his grasp as quickly as she could and ran away from him.

Samantha raced to her room and slammed the door as soon as she came home. She buried her face in her hands. Her teeth chattered.

Oh, my goodness. RJ would have gotten away with more than a kiss from me out in the garden if the help hadn't interrupted us.

Samantha shivered as she imagined the scary prospect. She wiped her mouth with the back of her hands, trying to get the taste of him out of her mouth. She cringed at the notion. Samantha stumbled across the dimly lit room, her hands extended, finding her way to the bathroom door. She yanked at her clothes hurriedly, ripping them from her body and throwing them into the garbage bin. She intended to burn them the next day. Samantha turned on the shower and adjusted the temperature to the highest setting. She waited for the shower to steam up before entering. She scrubbed every inch of her skin till it hurt, then cleansed her mouth and teeth, gargling and emptying the bottle of mouthwash.

Samantha couldn't sleep that night. She lay in bed, musing over the events of the evening. Samantha trembled every time she remembered RJ. How could she ever make love to him when she felt nauseous whenever she was near him? Samantha despised the prospect of having to commit herself, but she knew she would have to once they were married.

Her brow wrinkled considerably. Samantha took out her phone and dialed Jennifer's number. She needed her friends. She had no choice but to carry out their plan.

It was now or never!

CHAPTER FOUR

Preparations had been hectic for the much-anticipated wedding of the year. The news media had a field day. Photographers and reporters flocked to the opulent Grandeville Resort in Beverly Hills, where the reception would take place.

Meanwhile, the road leading up to the church was closed, and security was tight in and around the surrounding area. The set-up was beautiful. The altar was decorated with 10,000 roses and orchids, one of Samantha's favorite flowers, which filled the church and the arches, as well as the benches.

While everyone else was setting up, Samantha's room was completely dark. There wasn't a single ray of light piercing the curtain. She lay in bed for a while, wishing the day would end. She dragged herself up to get ready. Her wedding day was today. She should have been happy, but it overcame her with sorrow.

Back in the church, the bulk of the guests had arrived and conversed as if they were old friends. How could they not be? They were all affluent, influential people with political clout. It was a gathering of leaders from business, politics, and other spheres of influence. RJ was grinning as he thought about his upcoming honeymoon. He became agitated as he continued to pace.

A few moments later, two limousines arrived in front of the church, and the bridesmaids exited one by one. However, none of them were Samantha's friends. They did not come on purpose. Samantha was in the second limo. When the vehicle slowed to a stop in front of the church's main entrance, several people assisted the bride and her magnificent gown out of the car. Samantha rose to her feet and faced the doors. Her assistants hastily arranged her lengthy train.

The white carpet was unrolled. The music kept playing, and the priest, RJ, and best man took their places to the right of the altar. As his bride approached, RJ was on the verge of tears and pressed his palms together.

The wedding procession started. The flower girl was the first to go down the aisle, dropping red roses on the floor, followed by the ring bearer, bridesmaids, groomsmen, and maid of honor.

The philharmonic orchestra began their music, and the large doors swung open to reveal the lovely bride. Samantha entered the room, her father's arm around her. All eyes turned to her as they stood up, and she dazzled everyone as she walked down the aisle in her white, beautiful, flowing gown. They were all smiling at her, and a few of them were even envious of her extravagant wedding. They did not know that her eyes were all red and puffy from weeping under her veil. Samantha could feel the thumping of her heart in her chest. She stood still, her legs like lead and her feet firmly lodged on the church floor.

RJ smiled at Samantha as she approached the altar. Samantha looked at him, and she couldn't understand how someone with so much going for him—good features, a wonderful body, oozing with sex appeal—could be so boring. RJ lacked personality and had a large ego. By looking at the floor, Samantha avoided eye contact with him. Her anxiety intensified. It drew her attention to her father. She narrowed her eyes and stared at him. Samantha couldn't bring herself to forgive him.

A priest officiated at the wedding. "Dearly Beloved, we are gathered here today in the presence of these witnesses to join Samantha and Robert in matrimony, commended to be honorable among all; and, therefore, it is not to be entered into lightly but reverently, passionately, lovingly, and solemnly. Into this—these two people present now come to be joined. If anyone can show just cause why they may not be joined, let them speak now or forever hold your peace."

Samantha's heart was slamming against the wall of her chest. If she wanted to stop her wedding, now was the time. She moaned as she lowered her head and prayed for courage.

"I'm sorry, RJ, but this is wrong," Samantha said. "I can't marry you because I don't love you." She then turned to her father and said, "I'm sorry, Dad, but you can't choose my life for me."

As soon as she had said that, Samantha lifted her bridal gown, revealing the running shoes she was wearing. She ran down the aisle to the church steps, looking back over her shoulder and worrying about the consequences of her action. Samantha was taking a significant risk, but she didn't care. She knew she had made the right decision.

The guests sat in stunned silence, unable to fathom what was going on. Samantha could hear her father and Mr. Chandler yelling at her to return. RJ froze in front of the altar, speechless. Mrs. Chandler passed out and slumped on the floor. And the priest shook his head in disbelief.

Samantha nearly tripped in her haste to flee. She noticed a tall, attractive man standing next to his red sports car, his hands tucked into his pockets. Samantha averted her gaze for a split second. Her heart pounded as she dashed down the church's side and into the back seat of a waiting van.

Meanwhile, security personnel and Samantha's bodyguard seemed unconcerned about individuals attempting to leave the church. They were more concerned with screening those trying to enter. As part of Mr. Chandler's increased security, staff were busy inspecting all vehicles as they entered the church parking lot. They didn't even see a darkly tinted SUV departing, and the guards had no way of knowing the bride was inside. The guards saw RJ waving his hand and yelling at them to close the gate. RJ thought Samantha was still in the area and hadn't gotten far. Except for the handsome man standing next to his red sports car, no one saw Samantha enter the vehicle. No one cared to question him, and the man didn't want to get involved, so he kept it to himself.

SAMANTHA WAS IN THE back seat of a leased Mercedes-Benz luxury van driven by Jason, Vanessa's brother. Vanessa and the rest of the SBPs orchestrated everything. It was all part of their strategy to help Samantha escape her wedding nightmare. Jason, who was opposed to a forced marriage, readily agreed and supported his sister's decision to assist Samantha.

Jason skidded to a halt as soon as they turned onto the next street. They jumped into his Lexus, where his friend Lionel was waiting for them. Lionel drove the van to confuse anyone who could have been following them.

"Thank you, Jason. This is very kind of you. I can't believe we did it," Samantha said as they entered the freeway.

"I don't agree to an arranged marriage, Sam. I can't let you ruin your life in this way," Jason sought to console her. "Are you going to be all right?"

"You know, Jason, I believe I will be fine. What's the worst that might happen?" Samantha forced a giggle.

"Do you know where you're going? Do you want me to drive you there?"

"No, Jason. The fewer people who knew where I was going, the better. I know my dad. He will stop at nothing. I don't want anyone to know that you helped me. I don't want any ill will between our families."

"I understand. Where should I take you?"

"I'm sure they'll look into the local bus station and airport. Just take me to the next town and drop me off at the bus terminal. I'll figure it out."

"Are you sure? Do you need any cash?"

"Don't worry about me, Jason. I'm OK."

"Okay, so good luck, Sam. If you need anything, please call Vanessa or myself."

"Thank you, Jason." She gave him a kind grin.

Samantha reached behind the driver's seat for her travel bag, which Jennifer had picked up that morning at her place. She snuck it out of her house undetected. Jennifer had entrusted Jason with it.

Jason pulled up at a gas station as they got closer to the bus terminal. Samantha used the restroom and changed into an oversized shirt, a denim jacket, and elastic waist sweatpants.

She took off her makeup and put her hair in a ponytail to blend in. Samantha tossed away her wedding gown in the trash.

SAMANTHA STOOD AT THE Palmdale bus station, glancing at the timetable on the board.

"Las Vegas, New Mexico..." Samantha read the sign.

A bus to Seattle, Washington, was leaving in ten minutes. The next bus departs at five o'clock in the afternoon for San Diego. Samantha looked at her watch. It was 12 p.m. She couldn't wait that long. She needed to get out of town as soon as possible. Samantha lifted her hands in the air without hesitation, requesting the bus driver to wait for her. She hurriedly purchased a ticket for Seattle, handed her luggage to the bus driver, and boarded the bus. Samantha heaved a sigh of relief as she sat down. She looked at her ticket. It was an overnight trip—a day and a half, to be exact. She peeked out the window, happy to see no one suspicious.

The driver started the engine, and they were on their way. Samantha took hold of her purse. It was her first time using public transportation. When she looked around, she spotted an older woman across from her, who she believed was sixty years old. There were a few middle-aged males in the front and men and women in the back. A younger woman in front of her held a newborn and a toddler. She could never understand how someone could go such a long distance with small children in tow.

It was a long drive, and despite her efforts to stay awake, Samantha soon fell asleep, only to be jolted awake by the bus driver's loud voice.

"We're going to take a quick break here. If you want to stretch or grab something to eat, do it now," the driver stated.

The passengers disembarked, leaving Samantha alone on the bus. Samantha rubbed her eyes as she looked around. They stopped at a gas station with a little food shop in the middle of nowhere. Her stomach growled, so she went inside the deli to get something to eat.

A long line of people waited to place their orders. Samantha joined them and waited for her turn. She looked up at the menu board, trying to decide what to order. The selection was mediocre, and she struggled to decide what to buy.

"Where are you going?"

It surprised Samantha when she heard a woman's voice close to her ear.

"Where are you from?"

Samantha heard the voice again. She turned around to see the woman sitting across from her on the bus. Samantha stayed silent and said nothing, only giving her an intense stare and shaking her head. The last thing she needed was to make friends with anyone on the bus.

"Are you not talking right now? It's all right. I, too, dislike speaking on an empty stomach," the woman laughed.

Samantha's lips twitched, as if she was trying to hide a grin.

"I see you get what I'm saying."

Samantha said gently, "I'm not sure yet."

"Not sure what?" the woman responded, picking up a ready-made tuna sandwich and a can of Coca-Cola.

"Well, I'm planning to spend a few days in Seattle before deciding where to go next."

"So, you're a nomad?"

"I suppose you could say that."

"But a lovely wanderer."

Samantha giggled as she raised her head, a twinkle in her eyes.

"You look like you are from a wealthy family. Are you famous?"

Samantha almost choked on her saliva.

"No, I'm not. I was an orphan. My parents passed away a long time ago. I'm visiting my uncle in Seattle. I hoped he'd let me stay with him for a few days before I traveled to see another family in Canada." Samantha was thinking about stories to go along with the fake uncle narrative she had invented.

"Oh, I see." The woman nodded, as if she had comprehended what she had said.

Samantha walked away with the last ready-made tuna sandwich and a bottle of water. She proceeded through the line, handing the cashier a twenty-dollar bill and explaining that she was paying for two tuna sandwiches, a can of coke, and a bottle of water. It was less than ten dollars. Samantha received twelve dollars and fifty cents in change from the cashier.

"No, thank you. Please keep the change," Samantha said.

"Thank you very much," the cashier smiled appreciatively.

The elderly lady was speechless, but expressed gratitude. Samantha said it was her treat. She walked out before the woman could react, leaving her perplexed.

SAMANTHA HAD FALLEN asleep. In her dream, two guys stopped the bus and told everyone to get off. She tried to hide between the seats, but the two men found her and dragged her away. They took her to a dingy building where RJ awaited her.

RJ glanced at Samantha and murmured, "Samantha," with silky smoothness. He extended his hand, inviting her to come up to him.

Samantha walked up to him and placed her hand on his.

"Do you see what I mean?" RJ whispered, a malicious smirk coming across his lips. "You can't get away from me."

"No," Samantha screamed as she awoke from her dream, shaking her head in fear.

The passengers were irritated and raised their eyebrows at her.

"Are you all right, honey?" the woman asked. She had taken her seat next to her.

Samantha apologized and said, "I had a dreadful dream."

The woman gave her a worried look. "Are you positive you're okay? You looked like you had seen a ghost."

"I'm fine, but thank you for asking," Samantha said as she wiped her sweat away with her sleeves.

They became silent as the bus driver sped down the highway, before slamming on the brakes, prompting the passengers to yell and curse at him to slow down. The bus driver apologized as he drove extra cautiously, much to the delight of the passengers.

Samantha cast a glance out the window. She breathed deeply, relieved that her dream had not come true, although she felt as if it had. Samantha closed her eyes and tried to clear her mind of the memories. She wondered whether she had already lost this war.

CHAPTER FIVE

When the bus arrived at the Seattle Transit Station, it was raining. As Samantha followed the passengers out of the bus, a few people raised their umbrellas. Samantha could see the rain pelting the last step, and she could tell it was pouring down hard now, soaking her body. She could feel the squish and water sluicing down her pants into her running shoes, agitated by the torrential rain. She walked down the side of the bus, joining the other passengers waiting for the bus driver to unload their luggage. Samantha shivered from the cold and scowled at her drenched garments.

The driver lifted the side panel, revealing the luggage compartment. He dug through the suitcases and brought out a Hermes suitcase, which he handed to Samantha.

"How did you guess?" she said as she snatched it from him.

"Lucky guess," the driver answered, smiling and staring at her matching purse.

The passengers picked up their belongings as the driver unloaded the rest. He drew the last bag and slammed the compartment door shut. Before returning to the bus for his final destination, the driver saluted everyone.

Samantha zipped up her denim jacket, clutched her purse even tighter, and marched into the bus terminal. She stepped up to the taxi line, dragging her travel bag behind her. Samantha did not know where she was going or what her realistic plans were when her stomach growled. She realized she had eaten nothing since last night, and she was ravenously hungry. Wading in cold water in the pouring rain, she walked a short distance, crossed the street, and entered a coffee shop. The aromas of a home-cooked meal wafted from the kitchen.

"There is nothing better than entering a room and smelling the delicious scent of freshly brewed coffee with a pot roast cooking," she said to herself, closing her eyes and inhaling deeply. The pot roast reminded her of her mother cooking in the kitchen when she wasn't at a function or on a trip with her father. Her stomach growled again.

Samantha took off her jacket and dusted off the excess water. She looked around the café, found an empty table, and made her way across the old and broken wooden floor. She hadn't even taken a seat when a young waitress with purple hair came to take her order. Samantha opted for the traditional pot roast and black coffee. She watched as the waitress walked away. She returned with a pot of coffee and poured her a full cup, before proceeding to another table to take their order. She looked around. There were a few more customers, mostly men. In fact, there was just one other woman, her white hair wrapped in a bun, chattering animatedly with her mouth full.

While Samantha waited for her food, she rummaged through her handbag for her phone. She took it out, didn't bother to close her bag, and carelessly placed it on the next seat. It was exposed and unsecured for a brief moment, long enough for a man to walk out the door to steal her wallet without being seen. He took the cash and slipped it inside his coat pocket. He threw the wallet into the nearest garbage can.

Samantha checked her texts. There were hundreds of SMS and voicemails from her friends, father, and RJ. She erased them without reading or listening to them. Samantha texted her friends to let them know she had arrived safely, but didn't say where she was, only that she would let them know as soon as she settled in. She told them not to worry about her.

Her food had arrived. Samantha was hungry, so she ate quickly, taking huge bites. The pot roast was delicious. She pushed the empty plate away and settled in for another cup of coffee.

Now that she was full, she looked up the Seattle area on Google Maps and planned to spend the night in a beautiful luxury hotel before going to Vancouver. She reasoned that if she had to disappear, leaving the country wasn't such a bad idea. Samantha called her mobile phone provider and suspended her service before turning it off. She cut off her lines of communication. Instead, she intended to buy a prepaid phone.

Samantha was looking for her server to get another cup of coffee when the busboy, in his late forties, saw her. He approached her with a fresh pot of coffee in hand and filled her cup. Samantha smiled appreciatively.

"Are you done eating?" he queried.

"Yes, I am," Samantha said.

The man returned with a cart moments later. "Are you on vacation here?" he asked again, trying to strike up a conversation while clearing the table.

"Yes, I am," Samantha said reluctantly.

"I was born in Seattle. I can't imagine myself anywhere else. The recession hit us hard, but that's okay. My wife works at a nearby factory to help me. Our two children are healthy and doing well in school. I should say we're doing better than others."

Samantha was upset and considered the man unpleasant. She didn't have time to listen to other people's life tales.

"I'd prefer it if you left me alone," she retorted fiercely.

"Enough chit-chat, Felipe. I'm not paying you to talk to our customers. There are several tables that need to be cleaned." The owner yelled across the room at the worker.

Felipe turned to Samantha and gave her the most genuine grin she'd ever seen. As he pushed the cart to the next empty table, he looked at Samantha and apologized for speaking to her. There was a little hollow pinch in her heart. She almost felt awful for mistreating him.

Samantha looked out the window. The rain had stopped. It was getting late, and she wanted to change into dry clothing. It was time to leave. She caught the server's attention and signaled she was ready to pay her bill.

The waitress stepped up to her table. "How did you like the food?"

"Delicious," she said honestly.

"That's Felipe's specialty. He made it this morning."

"Felipe? I thought he was the busboy?"

"Yes, he is the busboy here, but the customers love his pot roast so much that the owner has to add it to the menu. Felipe comes in early in the morning to cook it, but when the restaurant opens, he becomes the busboy for the length of his shift. Unfortunately, the owner never gave him the opportunity to work as a full-time cook here," the server said, looking around to check whether anybody had heard her. "Don't tell the owner

I said that. Felipe is a terrific cook. All of our customers adore him."

Samantha averted her gaze as she felt another pang of guilt.

"Can I get you anything else?" the waitress said.

"No, thank you. I'm OK," she said.

The server gave her a quick smile before handing her the bill. Samantha took it and went to the cashier to pay. She opened her bag to get her money. She hastily placed her handbag on the counter, looking for her wallet. It was no longer there. All she could find was thirty-five cents in loose change.

"Oh, my gosh," she said, horror rising in her voice as she rechecked her bag and luggage. "Where is my wallet?"

Samantha fixed her gaze on the cashier, who didn't appear concerned by anything.

"I'm sorry, but I've lost my wallet," she exclaimed. "I have no money to pay you."

"What? What do you mean you don't have any money to pay?" The cashier repeated herself for everyone to hear. "You and your fancy designer bag!" she sneered. "What a crock. Speak with the owner."

The cashier called the owner, who was similarly unconcerned. He stated he would call the police.

"Oh, mister, please," Samantha begged. The cops were the last thing she needed.

Felipe heard the commotion and approached the owner, telling him, "I'll pay for it. Take it out of my pay."

"What pay?" asked the owner. "I've already paid you for the extra hours you worked. In fact, you still owe me for the advance payment I gave you last week."

Even though the owner's insults humiliated Felipe in front of everyone, he laughed it off and pretended not to be affected by it.

"Oh, that's right. I'd forgotten." Felipe answered, scratching his head. He turned around and looked at Samantha with the saddest eyes she'd ever seen. "I'm sorry, miss. I tried."

Samantha felt sorry for the man she had met and insulted. She couldn't believe that after her prior rudeness to him, he was still trying to help her.

"Thank you for trying, Felipe," she murmured, patting him on the back as he scratched his head again, before turning and walking into the kitchen.

Samantha gave the owner a furious look before speaking. "Would you let me come back and pay for it if I signed an IOU with 100% interest?"

The owner gave her a sarcastic look. "Do you think I'm stupid, lady? I might as well kiss that money goodbye."

"What? Do you think I'll skip town for a pitiful fifteen dollars?"

By this time, a few people had gathered around them, listening to their heated discussion.

"Oh, for God's sake, Hank, give this woman a break," commented a stranger as he handed the owner a twenty-dollar bill to pay for Samantha's tab and entered the washroom to wash up.

"Be grateful, lady," said the owner. "Someone paid for your meal. Otherwise, you'd have to do a lot of dish washing in the kitchen."

Samantha had never met anybody in her life who treated her like a common criminal. "You stupid man!" she yelled. "I'll have you know that as soon as I get my money, I'm going to buy this building and demolish it."

The cashier raised a single brow and looked down at her. "In your dreams," she chuckled.

Samantha heard it. She had never been mocked and humiliated in her life, but there was no use in protesting anymore. She didn't want to make a bigger fuss, since someone could have recognized her. Samantha stormed out of the coffee shop, slamming the door behind her. She could still hear the clerk and the owner laughing.

Samantha sat down on the bench, waiting for the stranger who paid for her meal to thank him. When he finally came out, she ran in front of him, impeding his way. Samantha saw his face for the first time when he looked at her, and it was heavenly. She was smitten at first sight. She stood there, as if in a daze, staring at him.

"I hope you learned your lesson. Pay attention to your surroundings, or at least appear aware of them." The man chastised. "You got lucky this time, since only your wallet was stolen."

Samantha furrowed her brows. Never mind she had a crush on him earlier. Nobody could treat her in such a manner.

"I waited for you so I could thank you for bailing me out at the coffee shop, but you have no right to scold and yell at me." Samantha screamed at him.

"A young, beautiful girl like you shouldn't be traveling alone. You lost your money today. What about tomorrow and the day after that? What are you going to do?" He stated this while ignoring what she had said.

"I'm sorry for inconveniencing you, sir, but I'm not inter-ested in your sermon. Goodbye!" Samantha remarked as she abruptly left. Her thoughts formed stinging criticisms of his pompous behavior.

The stranger shook his head. He broke into a warm smile. He walked over to Samantha, seated in the bus stop shelter.

"Here's some cash for a taxi."

"Thank you, but no. I don't need your money."

"Please take it. It's getting dark. You need to go home."

"I appreciate you paying for my meal, but even if you were the last person on the planet, I don't need your help anymore."

"Suit yourself," the guy mumbled as he tossed the money in-to her lap.

Samantha was still irritated as she observed the man stroll to his red shiny sports car, which was parked nearby, but she couldn't deny she was in a trance as she watched her prince charming.

"Oh, my gosh!" she screamed with pleasure as she picked up four twenty-dollar bills off her lap and stuffed them into her bag.

Benjamin McClain was the handsome stranger, a well-known architect who lived in a beautiful mansion on a private waterfront estate he built himself, with each room offering a view of Lake Washington. He was one of King County's most eligible bachelors. Benjamin McClain was the son of Julius and Jane McClain, two well-known and affluent Santa Barbara res-idents. He had an early flight home from Los Angeles the day before, but when his uncle, the District Court's chief judge, found out he was in town, he insists on staying the night and catching up. Benjamin couldn't say no to his uncle, so he canceled his flight home and rented a red sports car on the spur of the moment. He intended to leave the next day. Benjamin waited for his uncle at the front entrance of Our Lady Mirla in Beverly Hills, where he had gone to a wedding that never took place. The bride changed her mind and fled.

It devastated Samantha as she watched the man drive away, and she stayed there for some time before realizing she was being stupid. She sat on the bench, wondering what to do, because she didn't have an ID, money, or credit or ATM cards. Samantha pondered contacting her friends for help, but she didn't have an active phone. She didn't want to trouble them anyway. It was time for her to grow up and learn how to tackle her own troubles. But how would she do it?

Samantha was sitting with her elbows propped up on her knees when a woman approached her and asked if she was okay. Samantha lifted her head, recognizing her from the bus. It was the same woman who was seated next to her. She went to see a friend who lived in the area before heading home.

"Oh, hello there again," the old woman said. "Are you okay?"

Samantha looked at her with a frown and a grin. It was nice to see a familiar face. "I lost my wallet, and now I don't know where to go."

"Can't you call your uncle and ask him to pick you up?" the woman said.

"M-my uncle?" she stammered. "Oh, yeah, my uncle," Samantha answered, scratching her head. "Regarding that, I merely stated that since I don't know where to go, I made him up."

"You mean you don't know anyone in Seattle, have nowhere to go, and no money?"

"Yes, it pretty much covers it."

"What are you going to do now?"

"I have no idea."

"Child, are you in some kind of trouble?" the woman asked as she took a seat next to her.

Samantha looked down at the ground. She wasn't sure whether she should tell her everything about herself, but she couldn't trust anyone. She had no choice but to lie again. Samantha fabricated a fake story.

"I'm an orphan looking for a fresh start somewhere else," she stated.

The woman felt sorry for her. "In that case, you're coming with me till you figure things out for yourself."

Samantha focused her attention on the woman, trying to read her thoughts and attitude. Her instincts told her she was a good person, but how far could she trust her?

The woman saw her reluctance. "I realize you're afraid to go with a stranger, but believe me when I say you need a place to stay. A beautiful girl like you shouldn't be wandering about the city by herself at night. And there is no safer place for you to be than with me."

The woman was right. It was almost dark, and Samantha knew she had no business out on the street at this hour. She had no idea where she was going or what her plans were. Samantha had no clear thoughts anymore, and she had no intention of calling her friends or her father until she knew he had changed his mind. She had no choice but to seek refuge at the home of a stranger, at least for the time being.

Samantha gave the lady a kind grin. "If you're sure it's not too much trouble, I'd appreciate any help you can give. Where are we going?"

"Home. I was in Los Angeles for a few days to see my sister. The vacation is now over. It's time for me to go back to work. I parked my car a block away. My name is Linda," she remarked as she shook Samantha's hand.

"Hello, my name is... Vanessa. That's right. My name is Vanessa," Samantha murmured, biting her bottom lip. Lying had never come easily to her.

"That's not your name, is it?" Linda asked, her gaze fixated on her.

Samantha was embarrassed. "No, it is not. It's Samantha. You may call me Sam for short."

Linda smiled, nodded, and motioned for her to follow her. Samantha looked back at the town one more time before she climbed into Linda's car. She looked out the window. She did not know where she was heading. All she knew was that she needed to find a safe place for the time being and get as far away from her father and RJ as possible.

CHAPTER SIX

Samantha could feel the stress rising in her chest and was on the verge of crying. She had come to terms with the fact that life was unexpected and harsh. Samantha had lost her mother, but she survived because of her father's love. That was why she had difficulty accepting and comprehending all that had occurred between them.

Her father was a wealthy and attractive man. When her mother died of pancreatic cancer, her father devoted his life to raising her. Submerging himself in his work, Artemus dismissed the women vying for his attention. He didn't take the time to see their admiring expressions or the enhanced sway of their hips as they walked by him. Her father referred to them as distractions.

"Don't worry, Samantha. Things will get better." Linda jolted her out of her thoughts.

When Linda turned into a circular driveway for one of the street's most magnificent houses, there was a minute of stillness before Samantha lifted her head. They passed through a fountain with dazzling water reflecting the moonlight until they arrived at the main house. Linda drove around the rear and parked her car.

"We're here!" Linda stated as she exited the automobile.

Samantha stepped out of the car and looked around at the house. She did not know that Linda worked for an affluent family. It was the most stunning home she'd ever seen. Linda informed her that the owner had built the ranch-style home himself. It featured roughly twelve rooms and a plethora of bathrooms. The property included a magnificent rose garden and a stunning view of Lake Washington. The garage had an excellent collection of classic automobiles.

"The owner is a fervent fan of antique and classic automobiles, especially pricey sports cars," Linda explained.

Samantha's mouth fell open as she walked into the house. Every cornice and molding were planned and handmade. The ceiling was lofty and magnificent, with rafted marble steps leading to the second-floor, and large windows draped in the most exquisite lace curtains. Everything was breathtaking. She got a strange feeling about that house, one she couldn't describe, like if she'd seen it before. It appealed to her as if it were welcoming her—a pleasant place to live.

"Here we are, Samantha. This is where I call home. I am the housekeeper in charge here. I work for a young, handsome, and overworked executive. He is firm yet fair." Linda stated.

Samantha gulped deeply, apprehensive about what she had just heard.

Linda sensed her hesitancy. "Don't be concerned, Samantha. You'll scarcely notice him. He is not usually at home because he travels frequently. We are a team of four. Nancy and I are in charge of the cleaning. It is our responsibility to keep the house clean at all times. Jack is the family driver, while Lucy serves as our chef and Rosalie's part-time babysitter until we find a replacement. A cleaning and pool service come twice a month. Our gardener, Joe, comes twice a week."

Linda peered out the window to check whether there was a car in the driveway. "It doesn't appear like Benjamin has returned home yet. He's probably still at work. Samantha, please come. I'll show you where you're going to sleep. I'll talk to him about getting you a job here as soon as I see him, okay?"

Samantha stiffened up and gasped. "Work? Okay, but I have to tell you something, Linda. I'm not good at working."

"Can you tell me what you used to do?" Linda inquired.

"Shopping, I'm excellent at it."

"Perhaps we'll assign you to go to the market and grocery shop to get our food supplies."

"Well, um..."

"What?"

"It's not exactly the food I shop for."

"What is it?"

"I go shopping for clothing and shoes. I go to the mall and shop till I drop."

"Oh, that type of shopping. I think we have a problem." Linda laughed. "Perhaps you might assist me with cleaning around the house or in the garden. I'll show you how simple it is. There's nothing to it."

Samantha took a deep breath and swallowed. What had she gotten into?

She followed Linda and found herself in a large entry hall with high ceilings, polished beige and white marble floors. Artwork hung on the walls, and big mirrors were elegantly gilded. She also admired the owner's choice of furniture. His mansion was larger and finer than hers.

They made their way down the long corridor to the servant's quarters on the first level. There were four good-sized rooms with a lovely view of the garden. Linda and Nancy shared the biggest room. Lucy was in the other room, and Jack was in the third. Samantha gulped hard at the sight of her sleeping quarters, not to mention the uncomfortable old bed in the corner.

Linda sensed her hesitancy. "Don't worry, Sam. It is clean. I'll be in the next room if you need anything. Just make yourself at home, and I'll see you in the morning."

Samantha nodded. She placed her purse and suitcase on the floor. She glanced around the cramped room and paused for a bit before sitting on the bed. There was a cool draft flowing in through the window. She hated going to bed, because she knew it would be a long night.

SAMANTHA TOSSED AND turned for several hours. Everyone else was sleeping, but she stayed alert and clear. It was her first time sleeping on a firm mattress. Even though it was clean, the blanket smelled funny to her. Her pillow, too, was hard and lumpy. She attempted to fluff it many times to get comfortable, but she kept tossing and turning. She stared at the digital clock. It was nearly midnight.

She closed her eyes, hoping that the combination of nervousness and tiredness would help her fall asleep, but she lost the battle. She was still awake. As she listened to the house's silence, it seemed like the longest night of her life. She got out of bed, headed to the kitchen, opened the refrigerator, and poured herself a glass of milk. She was about to return to her room when she heard a voice from behind her.

"What are you doing here? Who the heck are you?" the guy said aggressively.

Samantha, startled, dropped the glass of milk, which smashed on the floor. She'd forgotten where she was. She yelled at him with all her might.

"Who the heck do you think you are, creeping up on me like that? You scared me half to death!"

The man's jaw fell, and he couldn't disguise his shock at the girl's rudeness. He scowled. "I own this house. I have the right to ask who you are."

Samantha's eyes widened with horror, and she shook her head as if to wake up. Everything became clear to her. She wasn't daydreaming. She wasn't at home anymore, but working as a scullery maid at a stranger's home.

Samantha's cheeks became scarlet. "I'm sorry. I got lost and did not know where I was." She yelled out as she picked up the shattered glass, pricking her fingers on the jagged edge.

The man glanced at her, annoyed, and waited for her response. "I'll ask you again, who the hell are you?"

"I'm, um..." Samantha approached him to introduce herself, but slipped on the edge of the kitchen mat, only for him to catch her, his arm around her waist. Samantha's face flushed with embarrassment. She was mortified at having crashed into him in that manner.

"What the heck happened?" He mumbled. "Are you all right?"

"I'm fine, thank you," she said, struggling to break free from his embrace.

Linda awakened when she heard a noise in the kitchen. She got up to investigate and found Samantha and the man in an awkward position.

"Oh, I see you've met Samantha. She is our new housekeeper."

When the man realized he still had his arms around Samantha's waist, he let go. "New housekeeper?" he inquired. "I didn't realize we needed one."

"Yes, we've needed one for a while. Besides, she needs a place to stay, since she has nowhere else to go."

Samantha was annoyed and frustrated when she overheard their conversation.

I can't believe this is happening. I had to apply for a job in housekeeping. What a pity!

"Excuse me, did you say something?" the man asked.

"No, I said nothing," Samantha said.

The man looked at her, stroking his chin. "Wait a minute. You look to be someone I know. Oh, you're that girl from the coffee shop."

Samantha smiled as she recognized that he was her prince charming. "Oh, my God, it's you!"

To the man's surprise, Samantha did not shake his hand, but went forward to hug him, and he felt lightning leave his body. He briefly lost track of what he and Linda were talking about.

When Linda cleared her throat, she broke their blissful moment. "Do you know each other?" she asked. "Good. In that case, Benjamin, let her stay here for a while, okay?"

"Of course, if that's what you want," he said.

Samantha focused on Benjamin's stunning features. Everything Linda had previously told her about him was wrong. She forgot to mention that he was also a gentleman. Benjamin's behavior toward Linda pleased her.

"Samantha, you are welcome to stay as long as you like. That is not an issue for me." Benjamin's tone was cordial but frigid, with an unhappy glare in his eyes above the flashing grin.

"Thank you," Samantha said. "What should I call you?"

"What? Um, you may call me Benjamin," he said.

"Benjamin sounds elderly. I'll call you Ben, okay?"

"That's fine."

The kitchen was deafeningly quiet. As he stared at her, Benjamin was taken aback and startled. Something inside him softened. He didn't know what it was, but her beauty captivated him.

"All right, then. Welcome to the family, Samantha," he ultimately said before abruptly leaving.

Linda was standing behind them, listening in on their conversation. She was surprised Benjamin had remained calm the entire time. Normally, he would scream wildly.

Something fantastic will happen with these two, she thought to herself, and an amused smile grew across her face.

Linda stated that one requirement for Samantha's employment as a new maid was that she wear the same uniform as they did. Samantha was worried about wearing a dull gray dress with white cuffs and apron, much alone the dreadful gaudy white shoes she never thought she'd wear in her life. She looked at herself in a large wall mirror, embarrassed by her outfit. Her face was etched with dissatisfaction and embarrassment. She leaned her head to the side, staring at herself in the mirror for a long time. Samantha had to admit that when she compared how she looked a few days ago to how she looked now, she was unrecognizable. Samantha had such natural beauty that she appeared beautiful even with her bare face, unattractive, dreary outfit, and hair pulled back in a messy bun.

Perhaps I should give this job a try. There aren't many options here for me.

Satisfied with her look, Samantha entered the kitchen when she met Nancy, a short, overweight lady in her late forties, and Jack, a tall man in his sixties. After they had introduced themselves, Jack gave Samantha a seat.

"Please sit," he said cordially as he brought a chair out for her.

Samantha whispered, "Thank you, Jack," as she slid into the seat.

Lucy, who appeared to be Samantha's age, was not as approachable as Nancy and Jack. She furrowed her brows and transformed into an ice queen when she saw Samantha. She didn't expect her to be stunning. Lucy sat on an empty chair so quickly that it collapsed with her on it and tumbled to the floor with a loud, sharp thump. The room became silent. Lucy clenched her teeth, trying to keep the curse word from escaping. She'd already made a fool of herself in front of everyone. Nancy and Jack seemed unaffected by it, and their conversation continued. But not Samantha. Her mouth made a cute little twist as she tried to hide her grin, but Lucy had seen it and gave her a sly glance. She had just recently met Samantha, but she already knew she loathed her.

SAMANTHA HELPED LINDA in the garden, but even the simplest task, like pulling leaves, was difficult for her. She had several puncture wounds, scratches, and serious cuts. Every time she injured herself, she shouted and wept. Linda shook her head, undecided whether to laugh or scold her.

Samantha persisted, and it didn't take long for her to feel at ease working in the garden. She sang as she raised the flowerpots one by one, clearing away the dead leaves around them when she screamed murder. Linda, who had emerged from the kitchen with a cup of coffee in her hand, was irritated. Samantha, she reasoned, had cut herself again.

Benjamin had just gotten up and was coming out of his room when he heard a scream. He raced down the steps and into the garden, where he observed Samantha scream, hop, and tremble in dread as she pointed to a little garden snail hiding under a flowerpot.

As he looked at her, Benjamin grinned. But when he saw her pale, fearful expression, he felt driven to touch and comfort her for reasons he couldn't fathom.

"Are you all right?" he said, gazing at her.

"I-I'm OK, thank you," she stammered.

"Would you mind taking Samantha inside, Linda? Give her some water to drink. Perhaps that will make her feel better."

Linda nodded and led Samantha into the kitchen. "Sit down and relax while I get you a glass of water." She remarked this as she drew out a chair.

Samantha continued to tremble and shake.

Meanwhile, Benjamin remained in the garden, and when he saw another snail slither out of the pot, he picked it up and tossed it into the trash can.

What if Samantha saw a swarm of snails creeping over the plants and dirt? He chuckled at the thought.

He went back inside and saw Samantha sitting at the kitchen table, examining the wound on her hand. Benjamin cringed as he noticed several cuts on her beautiful hands. "Are you certain you're cut out for gardening, Samantha? Perhaps Linda could assign you some other tasks?"

"No, Ben, I'm OK. Thank you for your concern," she answered.

"Are you sure? If you don't think you can handle gardening, tell Linda and maybe work with Nancy instead."

Samantha took a long breath and swallowed. She was afraid Nancy would assign her a more difficult task, such as cleaning the toilets. That would be the last straw. She needed to get her act together fast, or else. She promised herself she would learn.

Samantha was back in the garden, this time with the goal of honing her talents. It took her many days, and it required a lot of sweat to grasp how much work to keep it up. She spent the entire day tending to a vast greenhouse, where many kinds of plants and flowers thrived at all heights and sizes. Even tiny mishaps like rose thorns, unclean fingernails, a sore back, and other things didn't bother her anymore. She also learned to live with slugs and snails, and they no longer frightened her. Now she understood why her mother enjoyed working in the garden when she was at home or wasn't busy traveling around the world with her father. She was closer to her than she had ever been. It gave her a great sense of accomplishment to see her labor blossom into a beautiful Garden of Eden. It felt good to have achieved something useful.

Samantha wiped her brow with her sleeve. She looked out onto the veranda and noticed Benjamin standing there, drinking his coffee and staring at her. Samantha spotted him looking at her, so she smiled, allowing herself to feel the warmth of her overwhelming attraction for him. Benjamin reciprocated the grin, and from the look on his face, he enjoyed it. He hadn't felt that way about a woman in a long time. He'd only met Samantha a few days ago, but he sensed a powerful attraction between them. His stare remained on her for a split second longer. He thought how nice it would be to kiss her soft lips and wrap his arms around her, never letting her go.

Benjamin shook his head and took a deep breath. What was he thinking? He was losing it. They'd only known each other for a short time, but he was already thinking like a possessive boyfriend, making sure no one else could have her. How ludicrous was that?

Benjamin entered the greenhouse one night and saw the garden in full bloom. Samantha's inventiveness and zeal for the job impressed him. He understood it wasn't her love of the garden that he admired about her. It was more than that. Even he couldn't put his feelings for her into words. These sentiments he experienced for her—the overwhelming desire, the caring...

He knew he wanted her.

CHAPTER SEVEN

It infuriated Artemus as he struggled to understand his daughter's unexpected actions. He felt Samantha was on board with his decision. He didn't know she had a secret plan. It irritated him to see Robert's angry face approaching and yelling, but he didn't care. Artemus was more concerned about what his daughter had done. He couldn't believe she'd defied him after everything he'd told her.

"Didn't you have a conversation with your daughter, Artemus?" Mr. Chandler stated sternly. "I thought you were in control of her. Look at what she did. She made us look stupid in front of our friends and relatives. This is something I will never forgive her for!"

Artemus stuttered and became mute, unable to continue his thoughts. He was furious, gritting his teeth and flailing his arms at Mr. Chandler.

"Would you mind?" he said. "You're annoying me, Robert. Before I say anything further, I think you should get the hell away from me."

Mr. Chandler's wrath surged through him as his hands clenched. He sighed and came to a halt, striving to calm himself. "Okay, alright. We have no reason to fight right now. Let's think this through."

Artemus was speaking calmly now. "I'm not sure what got into Samantha. I thought she got it." He stopped before continuing. "I'm going home to deal with this. I need to talk to my daughter. If you'd like, you're welcome to join me."

"Fine," Mr. Chandler said. "Let's see if we can still fix this."

Mr. Chandler joined Artemus as he got into his automobile. Artemus hurried away. When a car drove in front of him, causing him to swerve and hit the brakes, Artemus sounded his horn and called the driver every obscene term he could think of. Artemus hit the accelerator again and sped away. His car screeched as he reached their driveway. He stormed to the door and called for his daughter.

"Samantha, where are you? What did you do? I thought I warned you there would be repercussions if you disobeyed me. Do you get what I'm saying? Samantha, where are you?"

His arrival startled their housekeeper.

"Samantha was in the limousine when it left earlier, sir. Is she not at church?"

Artemus disregarded her and shouted even louder for his daughter. He ran upstairs, searched her room and the rest of the house for her, but she was nowhere to be found. He eventually realized his daughter was not in the house.

"Robert, hurry. Let's talk to her friends about it. Where else could she possibly go? I'm convinced she's hiding with one of them, and we'll find her even if I have to search their homes individually."

Mr. Chandler was outraged that they hadn't located Samantha at her residence, but he knew it wasn't the time to show his anger. He climbed into Artemus' car and went to the Grandevilles' house.

Artemus knocked on the door of the Grandeville home. "Open the door," he yelled.

"Mr. Grandeville is not at home, sir. They're at the wedding," Carmen, the cook, announced over the intercom.

"Just open the door! This is Artemus St. James from across the street. Samantha, my daughter, has gone missing. I'm sure she's in there."

"No, sir, she's not here," Carmen responded nervously.

"Open the dang door!" he yelled again.

"Sir Artemus, certainly. Please give me a minute."

When the door finally opened, Artemus stormed in.

"Where is my daughter?"

"Miss Samantha is not here, sir."

Artemus paid no attention to her. "Samantha! Where are you?" he shouted.

"Sir, I told you. She isn't here. Only the family driver and I are present."

Artemus would not believe her. He and Mr. Chandler searched the house, but couldn't find Samantha. Artemus left as fast as he came in, his lips stiff and his brow severely furrowed. He and Mr. Chandler both stormed out in a rage. They then went to Jennifer's house, where they found her drinking with her friends Rachel, Stephanie, and Alexandra. Artemus wondered why he hadn't seen them at the church. The expressions on the girls' faces struck him the most. They looked to be having a good time.

"Have you heard anything about Samantha?" Artemus begged the girls to tell him. He continued, "I don't understand why she would flee when she committed to the wedding."

No matter how hard Artemus pleaded, no one could tell him where she was—the girls preferred to remain silent.

When Artemus demanded to see his daughter, Jennifer let them check the house. Samantha was nowhere to be found. Artemus and Mr. Chandler were even more enraged. As soon as they departed, the girls began their celebrations, praising each other for a job well done. They couldn't believe their plan had worked.

RJ was at the reception area of Grandeville's resort when his father called to say they couldn't find Samantha. He frowned and did what he normally did when he was having a tantrum. He threw anything and everything he could get his hands on. RJ yelled as he remembered Samantha and the embarrassment she had given him, and foul words flowed out of his mouth. A few guests who had arrived at the reception and had just learned about Samantha storming out of the church shuddered as they left.

RJ saw that Artemus had returned and raced to meet him, telling him that if he couldn't produce Samantha soon, he'd regret crossing his family.

"You know what would happen to you, Artemus, if Samantha didn't return," he forewarned.

Artemus tightened his teeth and snapped at him. "Are you forgetting to whom you're speaking, RJ? Don't even think of threatening me! You and your father may be privy to my darkest secrets, but you soon realize that I wield more power and authority than you and your father together."

"Humph!" RJ rebelled.

He took the keys from his father's hand and quickly hopped into his dad's car, driving off. His head was spinning as he shifted into gear, accelerated down the street, and drove to Jennifer's house. He jumped out of his car after parking it in the driveway. He knocked on the door until the housekeeper opened it, stormed in, and found Samantha's friends still drinking.

"Are you celebrating something?" he asked irritably.

"By all means, come join us," Jennifer hissed. "Do you want something to drink? Perhaps rat poison?"

The girls laughed.

"Never mind about the insensitive remarks. Just give me something stronger," RJ stated.

Jennifer looked at her friends, who shook their heads in reaction to RJ's rudeness. She poured whiskey into a glass and slammed it on the table in front of him, spilling it. RJ looked at her angrily, but she smirked and walked away.

RJ asked the girls to locate Samantha for him. He told them he loved her and all the things he planned to do with her after the wedding. He sometimes looked at them to see how they reacted, but they stayed silent. The girls weren't sure if they believed the story he told, but RJ's presence and strong demeanor made them want to leave the room.

RJ downed his drink in one gulp, recognizing he had failed to impress anybody.

"I know you're all plotting against me," he snarled as he hurled the glass against the wall. "You can all go to hell!" he said as he dashed out the door.

The girls laughed at his childish behavior.

Samantha's abandonment of RJ at the altar made headlines the next day. It infuriated RJ even more. The shame was unbearable, and he was convinced he would be the town's laughingstock. He couldn't bear the thought of Samantha putting him in that situation. How could he have missed her plan to flee?

Mr. and Mrs. Chandler were not spared from embarrassment, either. Their family was the subject of considerable discussion and criticism at the country club. Mrs. Chandler was in a meeting with her secretary when she noticed people whispering and chatting behind their backs. They left, fearful that the day would only get worse. Mr. Chandler was enraged when his wife told him about it, and he vowed to track Samantha down and make her pay for what she had done.

"RJ, we have to find her. The local gossip and tabloids are having a field day humiliating us. I will not allow that girl to mock our family. You must locate and marry her. After you've married, there will be no mercy. We'll steal all their money and leave them penniless. We'll have the last laugh," Mr. Chandler added.

"Yes, Dad. I've already assembled a group to track her down. We'll find her soon," RJ said, his face flushed with rage.

It was, however, easier said than done. After a few days, RJ's patience was wearing thin. His men could not supply him with any information on Samantha, as if she had vanished. He was growing increasingly furious by the minute. RJ, still baffled about what to do next, hired a bunch of private investigators to track down Samantha, but even that failed to provide results. RJ was becoming more aggressive. He hired extra security to monitor Samantha's family and friends. He also directed that all their assets be checked. This created an issue, since Artemus alone had multiple residences and businesses across the country and around the world. Samantha's acquaintances, notably the

Grandevilles, owned various commercial and residential properties.

It did not discourage RJ from continuing his search for Samantha. He sent the detectives to travel to each of their foreign properties and stake them out, but when his father discovered what he was doing, he instantly stopped them.

"I got a copy of the investigation report from the private investigators you hired, RJ," his father remarked.

"You already have a copy?" he said, his voice shaking.

"If I understand properly, you allowed more crew to check not just Artemus' properties, but also Samantha's wealthy friends?"

RJ glanced over at the report quickly. "Yes, it's true, Dad. I believed hiring additional people would help us locate Samantha faster. I know they're keeping her hidden."

"I get that, but do you know how many properties Artemus owns? And how about the Grandevilles? It would be impossible to check them all, let alone be costly to have each one investigated. Look at our financial situation, RJ. We can't let anyone know we're bankrupt. Do you follow me? This is the reason we came up with this scheme against Artemus. We have to play our cards right."

"Don't you think you're a little exaggerated, Dad? When we find Samantha, everything will be back to normal. The faster we marry, the sooner we will seize control of their assets. We will regain our wealth."

Mr. Chandler groaned and shook his head in exasperation. "We should have thought about it sooner. We should have suspected she was up to no good. Samantha is from a wealthy family. I'm sure she has access to resources her father isn't aware of.

She's a bright young lady, but we have to outsmart her. Inform your private investigators that their job is complete. Artemus is still with us, and I have him wrapped around my tiny finger. He knows what is at stake. He understands what he needs to do."

"But..." RJ objected before his father cut him off with a finger wag in the air.

"Do as I say, RJ," his father said.

RJ couldn't do or say anything except follow his father's orders.

"ARTEMUS, THIS IS ABSURD. You promised to find your daughter by now, but it's been over three weeks. What happened to her?" RJ yelled. "By hook or by crook, she'll marry me."

"I understand your frustration, RJ, but my daughter is like her mother, God rest her soul. Samantha is stubborn, and she always gets her way. It's difficult for her to comprehend that I'm pushing her to do something she doesn't want to do after all these years. The strain I put on her, the last-minute wedding plans, and your desire to have the wedding sooner may have been too much for her."

"She is your daughter. Make her listen to you. If we don't find her within the next two weeks, I'm praying my father won't do something reckless in response to your troubles at the casino. Just remember that if you don't find her, I'll make sure someone does."

"Exactly what do you mean by that?"

"Forget about it, you should not be concerned."

"But..."

"There are no ifs or buts. Just help me find Samantha."

"RJ, you're going to make things worse," Artemus said. "I've already hired people to find my daughter. I'll notify you as soon as I get any fresh information."

"Well, the more the merrier then," RJ said. "Let me remind you, Artemus, how much you owe my father and me. You did something dumb, and my father and I took care of it. It's now time for retaliation. And don't forget about it. You agreed to the terms of the deal, which included your daughter's hand in marriage."

RJ had already departed, but Artemus was still standing there, apprehensive. He knew the kind of people RJ was referring to. He was afraid he wouldn't protect Samantha. His eyes were stinging from his rage. Not for Samantha, but for himself.

"It's all my fault," he sobbed, burying his face in his hands. "If I had called the police right away, my daughter would not be in this situation. I love her, but there was no getting away from this mess. If I disagree with Robert, he will ruin me and I may spend the rest of my life in prison."

Artemus stepped into Samantha's room and sat quietly on the bed. Nanny Lorraine stood by the dressing table, holding a folded letter. She turned around and looked at him.

"I found this under the music box," she said, handing him the note.

Artemus snatched it from her grasp and opened it.

I'm sorry to have to leave you, Dad. I realize you're in trouble, but what will happen to me if I do what you want? I need to figure out what my destiny is. Please don't look for me, since it will just add to our misery. When the time comes, I'll return home. Take good care of yourself. Love, Sam.

Artemus tucked the note into his pocket. He got up and walked around the room. "She irritates me beyond belief. Does she think leaving will solve the problem?"

"Can you blame her? You didn't give her much of a choice," Nanny Lorraine made a point of mentioning it.

Artemus knew he was wrong. He shouldn't have involved his daughter in his problems. As he stared out the window, he struggled to regain his composure.

"We have to find Sam."

Nanny Lorraine sighed.

"What will you do when we locate her? Will you force her to marry RJ again?"

"Lorraine, I don't know. Right now, all I care about is finding her."

Nanny Lorraine smiled at him. "Artemus, you hurt Sam. She will not readily return. You know how you brought her up, and she's not afraid to say what she thinks. No matter how hard we try, I believe we will have difficulty finding her. We should give her the space she needs. Allow her to go for a while and respect her wishes. Perhaps you, too, require some alone time to reflect."

For the first time in his life, Artemus was uninterested in anything else. He only wanted to see his daughter return safely.

"You could be right, Lorraine," Artemus said. "For the time being, this could be the best option. Okay, I'll step back and allow Samantha some breathing room. I'm hoping she'll at least let us know where she is and that she's safe."

"Don't worry, Samantha will be fine. She is self-sufficient."

Artemus stood up and stepped out the door. Nanny Lorraine trailed behind him.

RJ WAS AT HOME, DRINKING himself to death. Samantha had been missing for over a month, with no clue as to her whereabouts. He was enraged at his wedding debacle, and it took a long time for his fury to die down. RJ had personally taken his humiliation personally, and he was not about to take it anymore. Samantha made him the laughingstock of his family, friends, and colleagues. RJ drank another glass of vodka. He twirled about with this one, messing with it rather than drinking it. RJ seemed calm, but his lips were set, and dark wrath filled his gaze. He, Robert Chandler Jr., the most attractive and desirable bachelor ladies flocked to, couldn't believe Samantha had degraded him. RJ couldn't let that happen, but he admitted he still wanted her, as he'd never wanted another woman before. He'd understand and forgive her as long as she returned and the wedding went on. He'd then make her pay for his humiliation. RJ became upset and grabbed a shot glass and tossed it at the fireplace. His father did not approve of hiring more investigators, so it was up to him to find Samantha.

"Get the word out on the street," he instructed his bodyguard. "Whoever finds Samantha and delivers her to me gets a million dollars."

"Are you willing to pay that much for her return? What if she refuses? She didn't love or care about you. She wouldn't have left in the first place if she wanted to marry you." His bodyguard noted, perplexed, why Samantha fled or what the father and son had against the wealthy Artemus St. James.

His bodyguard's comments angered RJ. He tensed and grimaced.

"I knew she was crazy for standing me up at the altar, but she was the only one who had the courage to come up to me and insult me. She has the sparks I look for in a woman. There will be no church wedding next time. We'll get married here at the house, surrounded by bodyguards, with all the windows and doors shut. She will never run away from me again. It's now my turn to retaliate against her for humiliating me."

"I don't think she realizes who she's dealing with," the bodyguard chuckled.

"You're absolutely correct. Samantha can't mess with me, or my name isn't Robert Chandler Jr."

"What if Mr. St. James finds out about your plan?"

"He won't find out. Unless you tell him to. Believe me when I say that doing so would be a tremendous mistake on your part. Nobody likes a snitch, especially me."

CHAPTER EIGHT

Linda recognized that the more she got to know Samantha, the more she appreciated her company. She did not know that someone new would come along and excite everyone, especially a bored Benjamin McClain, who became livelier and more enjoyable to be around after many years of gloom and despair. Samantha provided happiness and laughter to their household. Unfortunately, not everyone felt the same way.

Samantha had become a direct threat to Lucy, and nothing was worse than a woman scorned. Lucy was a crafty and malicious little witch. She was envious of Samantha's attention from everyone at home, especially Benjamin. She had a feeling he was giving Samantha more than just closeness, and she couldn't have that. Lucy had been in love with Benjamin for a long time. She'd had a romantic dream about Benjamin. Maybe it was the way he looked at her or the way he uttered her name, or maybe she simply liked everything about him. He emanated sex appeal. Then Samantha entered the picture. Lucy was enraged at the notion of taking away all she had worked so hard for. Being ignored by a man she cared about hurt her. She vowed to make Samantha's life miserable, even if it meant destroying her reputation, to get rid of her once and for all. But how would she go about it?

Lucy finally got the break she had been praying for. Benjamin had asked her to go to the market that morning to get seafood for a dinner party he had planned for a visiting friend from New York.

"Take Nancy with you to help you carry those groceries," Benjamin said as he hurried out of the house for an early meeting at the office.

Lucy nodded. Her lips twisted into a devilish smile. She would not take Nancy with her. She would take Samantha instead. Lucy had a scheming plan to fool Samantha, revealing who she was to everyone. And everyone at home would know she was a fraud, Lucy reasoned. Her evil grin reappeared.

"Come on, already!" Lucy yelled. "The sun is sinking. We'll be late."

Samantha couldn't believe she'd let Lucy persuade her to go. She had tried every excuse she could think of. Samantha didn't want to go to town or anywhere. It worried her that someone may recognize her in the market, but Lucy wouldn't budge and insisted on accompanying her. With three layers of clothing, Samantha unwillingly went.

THE SEAFOOD MARKETPLACE in downtown Seattle was buzzing, with local fishermen displaying their fresh catch of the day as customers browsed the tables of freshly caught seafood on ice, including fish, lobster, crab, clams, and shrimp. Some shoppers were roaming about, soaking in the sights. Locals flocked to the market's fruits and vegetables section, which featured the best prices. Some were chanting enticements, attempting to encourage more customers to buy their wares.

Samantha wrinkled her nose as she walked by the fish vendors. "Ew."

"What do you mean, ew?" Lucy made an ugly expression. "Do you think you're such a princess that the mere scent of a fish repulses you?"

Samantha glanced at her and remained silent, hoping to have as little interaction with Lucy as possible.

"Okay, Samantha. We're looking to buy some good fresh fish. Perhaps lobster, rock crab, and shrimp as well. That is Sir Benjamin's request for today."

Samantha nodded, saying nothing.

"How much is a catfish?" Lucy asked the fish vendor.

He remarked, "Twenty dollars for a five-pound catfish."

Lucy turned to Samantha and told her to choose one and have it cleaned.

It infuriated Samantha, and she couldn't keep her mouth shut anymore. "There's no way I'm touching the fish," she screamed. "You pick it up!"

"Hello? Who do you think you are? I have seniority over you. Do you get what I'm saying?" Lucy spoke up.

"Like hell you are!" Samantha scoffed.

"Samantha, may I remind you that you are the new maid? If you don't do as I say, I'll make your life at home miserable. Is that clear? Pick it up now!"

"Humph." Samantha scowled again. The last thing she wanted to do was cause a commotion in the market. She bit her bottom lip to not say anything. Samantha hesitantly picked up the fish, wrinkled her nose, and said, "I smell something horrible." She had never felt so disgusted in her life. Samantha pulled a folded paper towel from her pocket and wiped her fingers on it.

"Oh, for Christ's sake. You're full of nonsense. You have a flair for the dramatic. Enough of acting like a diva. Remember, you're just a maid! Do you follow what I'm saying?" Lucy yelled, as though she wanted everyone to know Samantha was a servant.

I am not a maid. You are! Samantha was inclined to say.

"Did you say something?" Lucy asked, her brows raised.

Samantha shook her head.

"I will train you to be a terrific servant, which will take some time, given your disposition. But don't worry, I will be there for you every step of the way."

The hell you will, Samantha whispered.

"Will you hurry up? We don't have all day." Lucy hissed.

Samantha was still apprehensive, staring at the fish for a long time. She made such a comical look that the fish vendor couldn't help but laugh. He was about to choose a fish for her when Lucy stopped him and shook her head.

"Let her do it," she said.

"OK," the seller answered, frowning.

Samantha's jaw clinched in disgust as she attempted to pick up the fish again. It was slimy and slippery, and it dropped to the ground. She watched as the fish wriggled and flipped many times. Samantha sprang to her feet and screamed when the fish soared high in the air. Lucy laughed at her.

Samuel, a handsome fisherman, was strolling by when he observed a large crowd of people laughing. Curiosity got the best of him, and he pushed himself to the front. He stood there, staring at her. Samantha was a sight to behold. He had never seen a more beautiful face than the one he saw in front of him.

"The show is over, folks. You may return to whatever you were doing." Samuel addressed the crowd.

Samuel picked up the squirming fish from the ground and returned it to the water. He reappeared moments later, carrying a box containing a few freshly caught catfish from his table, as well as rock crab, lobster, and giant shrimp.

Samantha smiled as he made a quick move.

"How much do they cost?" she asked.

"It's free," Samuel remarked.

Samantha thanked him and shook his hand, while Lucy tried to give him the goo-goo looks. Samuel even helped them carry the box to their vehicle. Unfortunately, Lucy's car had a flat tire, and the spare tire was extremely low. Samuel offered to drive them home.

"Who will monitor your stall and sell the fish?" Samantha asked. "We don't want to impose. You've given us so much already."

"Don't worry, my brother will take care of it," he stated.

Samuel placed the box in the rear seat of his truck and opened the front passenger door for Samantha to enter. Lucy pushed her aside and got into the front seat with a whispered "sorry." Samuel shook his head at Samantha.

"It's OK," Samantha said.

They were in the truck and on their way home in a matter of minutes. Lucy stroked her fingertips across her lips as she applied lip gloss. Samuel paid little attention to her. He kept his gaze fixed on the road while driving. Lucy then twisted her hair to attract his attention, but he didn't even look at her. When it didn't work, Lucy reached out and touched his shoulder, caressing it with her muscled arm, as she thanked him for driving them home. Samuel disregarded Lucy's advances. Instead, he combed his fingers through his hair, peered in the rear-view mirror, and craned his neck to gaze at Samantha's lovely face.

It was only a ten-minute drive to McClain's estate. As they approached the circular driveway and saw the massive house in front of them, Samuel's eyes widened and his jaw dropped open. He jumped out of the truck and pushed open the door for Samantha. Lucy waited for Samuel to walk around the truck and open the door for her, but he remained still. This angered Lucy.

"I did not know you worked for Mr. McClain," Samuel remarked.

"Yeah, I've been working with the McClain family for five years since I was seventeen," Lucy said as she exited the truck. "By the way, my name is Lucy. I'm the cook here."

Samuel shook her hand, but returned his attention to Samantha. "What about you, beautiful? What is your name?"

"Ignore her. She's only a maid," Lucy elaborated.

"You mean like you," Samuel commented, winking at Samantha.

Lucy frowned, unsure of his words, while Samantha giggled, her lips pursed.

"If you don't mind, I'd still like to know your name." Samuel made the request.

Samantha smiled at him. "My name is Samantha. Sam, for short. Thank you again for the free fish and the ride home."

"How about that? My name is Samuel. Sam, for short. I'm glad to meet you, Sam. I hope you don't mind if I call you at some point?"

Lucy frowned. Samantha also piqued Samuel's interest. She was envious again.

"They don't allow her to take calls," she stated. "But you may call me whenever you want, handsome."

Benjamin was standing at the front door, unnoticed by the three, and he heard all they said. He'd returned home after realizing he'd forgotten his briefcase. He didn't know why, but he slammed the door behind him with such force that the surrounding walls rocked.

"What was that?" Samuel asked.

"It must be the wind. Thank you again, Samuel, for the seafood and for driving us home."

"It was my pleasure," Samuel said as he retrieved the box from the truck and handed it to Lucy. Lucy put the box down and gave Samuel a nasty look.

Samuel smiled and waved as he drove away. Lucy waved back, and as soon as he was out of sight, she turned to Samantha, chastising her for flirting with Samuel.

"I did not do such a thing," Samantha responded.

"That's not what I saw," Lucy mocked.

They were still bickering as they entered the house, but they came to a halt when they noticed Benjamin standing in the foyer with a furious expression on his face.

"Follow me to the study room," he said to Samantha. He turned around and walked away. Although he was late for his meeting, he made the time to speak to Samantha as if she were more important to him than anything else.

"Uh, uh," Lucy cautioned. "I recognize that tone. He's going to yell at you."

Samantha frowned. "What did I do?"

She walked into the study and saw Benjamin looking out the window, his hands tucked in his pockets. He turned around and stared at Samantha with an expression she had never seen before.

"I know you're new here, Samantha, but there are some ground rules you must follow," Benjamin said.

"Such as?" Samantha asked, her worry mounting by the minute. It was as if they summoned her to the principal's office.

"I expect nothing special from you, but I want to warn you about entertaining suitors. There will be no hanky-panky while you work here. Your duty is to work, and I expect you to do a good job."

"Suitors? Hanky-panky? What exactly do you mean?" Samantha asked.

"Who was the guy who helped you bring groceries here and called you beautiful?"

"Are you referring to Samuel? We met him at the market. We had a flat tire, and he was gracious enough to drive us home."

Benjamin scowled. "What were you doing at the market? I forbid you from leaving the house without my permission." Benjamin realized his error. He sounded like a jealous boyfriend. "I meant your job was gardening, not going to the market," he clarified.

"Why don't you talk to Lucy about it? She woke me up early this morning and requested I accompany her to the market," she stated.

"Is that right? I'll make it clear to Lucy then. I'm expecting you to stay at the house from now on. You must tell me if you want to go out so that I can accompany you. I mean, Jack will drive you." Benjamin muttered as he continued to embarrass himself. "Aside from gardening, I'm assigning you to look after Rosalie, with a pay raise, of course. She'll be returning from summer camp and will require the services of a nanny."

"Yes, sir!" Samantha said this as she saluted him. She was pleased with herself for being able to laugh, instead of becoming irritated with him for criticizing her.

"Don't be a smart aleck."

Samantha detected a smile in Benjamin's voice. She thought she saw a grin curving on his lips. Before he could say anything, Samantha stepped out of the room, chuckling. Benjamin grinned unknowingly.

Who is Rosalie? Samantha reflected on this as she exited the room.

Lucy gave Samantha a sour look when she returned to the kitchen a few moments later. Lucy said nothing to her, not even a smile or an insult. There could only be one explanation for her unusual behavior. Benjamin had talked with her and may have punished her. Samantha smiled as she considered the idea.

Good! Perhaps she'll leave me alone from now on!

SAMANTHA WAS WATERING the plants in the yard when she noticed Linda strolling with a cute nine-year-old girl. She saw Benjamin's eyes light up as he spotted the girl.

She must be Rosalie.

Samantha felt a small tightness in her heart, and an overwhelming sense of sorrow washed over her. It never occurred to her that Benjamin was married and had a child. Samantha didn't understand why she felt her world crumble at the revelation. She admitted it was infatuation, but she knew her position now. She would never date a married man. Samantha understood she shouldn't explore any feelings she had for Benjamin. She would not have it. Samantha had no option except to distance herself from him, no matter how bad it would break her young heart. She needed a place to hide for the time being, and Benjamin McClain's house was perfect. She should ignore her feelings for him. That was the right thing to do.

Benjamin arrived home one night with bags from Seafood to Go takeout for everyone. Linda, Lucy, Nancy, and Jack were all taken aback by Benjamin's quick change in attitude. He became friendlier and more attentive, not to mention that he was arriving home earlier.

"What's the deal with him?" Nancy asked.

"Oh, you noticed that, too?" Jack replied. "When was the last time he did something like that for us? I'd say never. He looks more at ease and comfortable these days."

Everyone grinned as they exchanged glances. They agreed they liked the new Benjamin.

Linda and Nancy prepared their dinner on the patio and covered the table with old newspapers to preserve it and keep it clean. Lucy laid the table for Benjamin and Rosalie in the dining room.

Rosalie studied the food on the table. "Wow! French fries and catfish, my favorites!" she exclaimed.

Samantha was about to leave to join Linda and the others on the patio when she heard Benjamin call her.

"Yes?" she asked.

"Why don't you sit down and join us for dinner?"

"Excuse me?"

"Why do I always have to ask you twice, Samantha? I'm sure you're not deaf." Benjamin lowered his voice and pleaded with his eyes. "Please, just sit."

Samantha frowned and paused for a while, undeciding whether to stay or go. She pondered for a moment before accepting. Samantha was washing her hands in the kitchen when she heard Linda, Nancy, Jack, and Lucy laughing and eating on the patio. She stuck her head out and said hello. Linda invited her to join them, but she stated Benjamin had requested her to join him and Rosalie at the dinner table.

Lucy's face flushed with rage. "You've got to be kidding. Sir Benjamin had invited none of us to join them at the dinner table."

"I think he wants to make sure Rosalie doesn't choke on shellfish," Samantha remarked.

Lucy was taken aback, and Jack mocked her by saying Benjamin had never asked her to join them for dinner, even while she babysitting Rosalie.

Lucy threw him a snide glance. "Oh, shut up, Jack!" she screamed.

Samantha entered the dining room and took a plate from the cupboard. She sat down to join Benjamin and Rosalie, who were already eating. She simply selected a salad from the assortment of foods on the table.

Benjamin scowled. "You don't like seafood?" he said as he peeled shrimp for Rosalie.

"I'm not a great lover of shellfish," she said.

Benjamin knew that no one would refuse seafood. Samantha was a picky eater, which was unusual for a housemaid. But Benjamin had a feeling Samantha was one-of-a-kind.

Samantha was cleaning the table after supper when Benjamin stopped her and told her Lucy would do it.

"Just get Rosalie ready for bed," he said.

"All right," Samantha answered with a smile.

Lucy was in the kitchen, covering the leftover food with plastic wrap. Linda came into the kitchen and told Lucy that Benjamin and Rosalie had finished eating and should begin tidying up. It infuriated Lucy when she entered the dining room and saw no Samantha present to help her.

"Where did she go?"

She was about to look for her when Linda walked in and told her Samantha was taking care of Rosalie.

In a fit of anger, Lucy slammed the dishes on the table. Linda scowled as Lucy apologized.

SAMANTHA WATCHED ROSALIE brush her teeth and gargle with mouthwash. Rosalie complemented her delicate hands as she brushed and dried her hair.

"I like you, Sam. I hope you'll stay with me forever," Rosalie said.

"What made you say that?" Samantha asked.

"There's something about you, Sam. I have a feeling I am getting close to you. Do you have a mother and father?"

Samantha's eyes welled up with tears as she remembered her mother.

"Sam, are you all right? Is it something I said? Please don't cry. I'm sorry."

"Rosalie, you did nothing wrong. It's just that I miss my mother. She died many years ago."

"What about your father? Is he also dead?"

"No, he is not dead, but I miss him too. If you don't mind, I want to stop talking about him."

"OK."

"Rosalie, do you mind if I ask you a question?"

"Sure," Rosalie murmured as she stroked her doll's hair.

"Where is your mother?"

"My mother is beautiful and a model. She is in France. That's what my dad told me. She'll be home soon."

Rosalie pulled a little box from the drawer containing her mother's stuff. She opened the picture album and flipped through the pages, looking for a photograph of her mother.

"Here's a picture of my mom and me at the zoo," Rosalie said.

Samantha snatched Rosalie's album. Her mother was the embodiment of perfection. She was much more stunning than she had imagined. Samantha groaned and gave the photographs back to Rosalie. She felt a pang of jealousy.

"Get ready for bed," Samantha told Rosalie.

Rosalie asked, "Will Daddy tuck me in?"

"Don't worry, he should be here soon," Samantha stated.

Benjamin entered Rosalie's room a few moments later. He sat on the edge of the bed and kissed Rosalie on the cheek. Samantha felt a pang in her heart as she observed the father and daughter's sweet moment. She pondered what it would be like to have a man like Benjamin McClain in her life. Rosalie's mother was lucky—very fortunate, in fact—to marry the tall, dark, and dangerously handsome Benjamin McClain, and she envied her life and her perfect family.

CHAPTER NINE

Temperatures in western Washington hit triple digits, making it the warmest day in Seattle history. As the day progressed, the blistering breeze made it excruciatingly hot to walk. People went to the beach to relax, while their children screamed in delight as they frolicked in the ocean. A few people went to the mall's air-conditioned comfort to escape the heat with their families.

Benjamin beat the heat by swimming in the pool with Rosalie. She had finished her swimming program at King County Swim School, and wanted to impress him with her swimming ability.

"Is it lunchtime, Daddy?" Rosalie inquired.

"Speaking of lunch," Benjamin asked Rosalie, "what would you want to eat?"

"Hot dogs and some marshmallows!" Rosalie stated.

"What a brilliant idea!" said Benjamin, chuckling.

He asked Lucy to fire up the grill and marinate the steaks. He recommended hot dogs and marshmallows. Lunch would be a BBQ on the patio.

Benjamin frowned when he didn't see Samantha. "Have you seen Samantha?" he asked Lucy.

Lucy shook her head and gave him a furious look. Fortunately for her, Benjamin did not notice.

"Lucy, tell everyone we'll be eating lunch together," Benjamin said, rotating his head from side to side, looking for Samantha.

"Yes, sir," Lucy answered, surprised.

Benjamin's heart started beating as soon as he saw Samantha approaching. It remained a mystery how she had so casually captured his heart and thoughts. All he knew was that without Samantha, his day would be incomplete. He waved and smiled at her.

"Where have you been?" he asked, smiling.

"Where else except in the garden?" she replied, smiling back.

They both laughed, which helped break up their awkward moment.

Lucy made their lunch as requested, including corn on the cob, Caesar's salad, and potato salad to round off the meal, while Jack helped with the grill. Linda and Nancy set the tables up.

"I never imagined the day would come when Sir Benjamin would invite us to eat together. He's changed a lot. You know, since Samantha started working here, he's always been in a good mood," Nancy said.

"You're absolutely right, Nancy," Jack said. "He's much more relaxed now. When was the last time he went on a trip? Sir Benjamin must have a crush on Samantha," Jack said, and everyone agreed except Lucy. She didn't like it one bit.

"She's a crafty little witch, if you ask me," she said.

"What makes you say that?" Nancy asked.

"I don't believe she is who she appears to be. I know she's hiding something from us. And I'll find out what it is."

Linda was concerned after hearing what Lucy had stated. She knew Samantha hadn't been completely honest with her about her actual situation, but she realized she needed help. Lucy was causing problems, and she needed to stop it. Samantha was the best thing that ever happened to Benjamin, and she wanted nothing or anyone to ruin that.

"Stop this nonsense right now, Lucy. You don't know what you're talking about," she said. "If you press this further, I'll have to tell Benjamin."

Lucy was taken aback. Linda had yelled and threatened her for the first time, and it was all because of Samantha. She clinched her teeth, but all she could do was keep her mouth shut for the time being.

SAMANTHA SPENT A LONG, sleepless night. Although her room was air-conditioned, warm air seeped in. She walked outside to chill in the night's stillness, and the swimming pool looked inviting. She suddenly remembered her SBP friends and their several beach trips. Oh, how she missed them. Samantha reasoned that, because everyone else was asleep, she should take advantage of the chance to swim. She scanned her surroundings by rotating her head from side to side. It was really quiet. There wasn't a single sound to be heard. She stripped down and dove into the pool, leaving only her underwear on. It felt amazing as she splashed and paddled around, feeling the water, which was chilly at first, but quickly warmed up.

What she didn't realize was that Benjamin wasn't sleeping, and he watched her from his second-floor bedroom window.

He'd brought his work home, so when he heard a splash of water from the pool, he peered out the window to see what it was. And that was a sight to behold. He saw Samantha swimming. She was a goddess. Her flawless beauty captivated him. She was stunning in every aspect, and he couldn't take his gaze away from her even if he tried.

Samantha got out of the water, but she stepped on Angel, Rosalie's cat. She stumbled and fell into the pool after striking her head on the railing. When Benjamin saw what had happened, he immediately raced to her rescue.

He found an unconscious Samantha, pulled her from the water, and performed mouth-to-mouth resuscitation on her. Samantha gagged and spat water out of her mouth after a few minutes. When she looked up, she saw Benjamin looking at her. She then passed out.

Benjamin was at a loss for what to do. He snatched her garments off the chair and then picked up Samantha. Benjamin brought her into the house and carefully placed her on the couch. He checked her pulse, relieved to see that her breathing was normal and her color was returning. He took a towel from the linen closet and wiped her wet body and hair. Benjamin dressed her and covered her in a throw blanket. He took a seat beside the sofa and remained by her side. Benjamin stared at Samantha, who was lying on the couch for a long time. He wanted to kiss her, those lovely lips he had desired to feel and touch, but something stopped him. He took a step back, exerting his self-control. As he watched Samantha, who was still sleeping, he returned his eyes to her lovely face.

She has long, black, straight hair and gorgeous eyelashes, comparable to Catherine Zeta-Jones. Her long legs remind me of...

"Have I been a burden?"

Samantha's voice startled him back to the present. Benjamin noticed her with an eager smile on her face.

"Huh, w-what?" he stammered.

"I'm sorry for giving you so much trouble."

Benjamin shook off the short drowsiness caused by his wandering thoughts.

"Not at all," he said. "I'm glad you're safe. Are you OK? Do I have to take you to the hospital?"

"No, I'm fine, Ben," she responded.

Samantha slipped off the sofa and realized she was wearing the same clothes she had worn before diving into the pool.

How did I get into my nightgown? Whoa! Did he dress me while I was unconscious?

She became crimson. Samantha didn't understand why she was embarrassed that Benjamin saw her in only her underpants. It had never troubled her before, especially when she and her SBP friends loved to flaunt their envious curves at the beach in tiny bikinis.

"Did you change my clothes?" she asked, although she already knew the answer.

Benjamin scratched his head. "I'm sorry, Samantha," he said, his face flushed. "I had to change your clothes. You were wet and..."

Samantha reddened and felt silly. She couldn't look him in the eyes, making it difficult for her to talk.

"Don't worry, it was my fault. I shouldn't have taken a swim. But I'm delighted you came to the pool area and found me when you did. Thank you, Ben," she stammered.

"Are you sure you are OK?"

"I'm fine, don't worry."

Samantha stopped for a moment before returning her gaze. "I'd want to thank you again, Ben, for rescuing me. I'm going to bed now."

"It was my pleasure," he remarked, beaming at her.

Samantha waited a minute before bracing her hand against the chair and attempting to stand. She stood up, swayed a little, regained her balance, and resumed walking. Benjamin rushed over from behind to help her. He offered to accompany her to her room.

But she rejected it, saying, "No, thank you, I can manage," as she walked towards her room. Her legs shook beneath her, as if they were ready to give way at any moment. Samantha believed Benjamin was watching her, because she felt the walls were full of eyes waiting for her to collapse.

She turned around, and she was correct. Benjamin stood in the middle of the room, hands buried in his pockets, watching her. After a few seconds, she became uneasy with the gaze, and her color changed. Samantha returned the steady gaze that had invaded her soul. She grimaced as she walked, felt the room spin, and placed her hands on the table to hold herself.

"I've got you," Benjamin said.

He picked her up in his muscular arms, but their proximity made her nervous. She blushed and drew back, wanting to free herself from his grip. Her thoughts were racing, and her pulse was pumping.

"Do I make you feel uneasy?" Benjamin teased.

"Of course not. Don't be silly." Samantha responded, although the situation was putting her out of her comfort zone. A powerful attraction formed within her, and the tension was unbearable.

Benjamin took her to her room and placed her on the bed without saying anything. He placed a blanket over her, kissed her on the cheek, and went away. Samantha blinked in disbelief, perplexed why Benjamin had done such a thing. He acted as if he didn't have a wife and child, as she could hear him whistling as he walked away and shut the door behind him. Samantha didn't know why, but she had a smile on her face and caressing her cheek as if she was still feeling him. She got up, dried her hair with a hairdryer, and changed into dry, clean clothes.

That night, Benjamin lay in bed, looking up at the ceiling, thinking. Was it a coincidence that Samantha ended up living in his house after he helped her at the coffee shop? Whether it was a fluke or not, Benjamin knew Samantha was always in his heart and mind. He wasn't looking for love, and he wasn't ready for a relationship, but the urge was strong and clear. Benjamin was smitten. He'd never felt this passionate about a woman before. Benjamin couldn't deny he felt something for her... something more than desire... something profound. That last sentence might be correct. The first time they met in the kitchen, he realized he had feelings for her. Benjamin struggled to ignore it, but he couldn't get rid of it. He wanted to hold her, kiss her, and make love to her. Samantha's beauty was a sight to behold.

Meanwhile, Samantha's mind was captured by Benjamin's gorgeous face and teasing smile. The strange feelings she had throughout her body puzzled her. Samantha had felt nothing like it before. She attempted to disregard the notion. She understood she couldn't have him. He was already married and had a child. So why was she still pining for a romance? She could surely disregard whatever feelings had creeped up on her. She had to do it for her sake.

Samantha avoided Benjamin until he caught up with her in the kitchen the next day, causing great tension between them. He tried many times to engage her in conversation, but she kept her eyes diverted and continued moving about until it became too difficult to ignore him as he sidestepped to block her path. Samantha was nervous as Benjamin took hold of her hand and struggled to free it from his death grasp.

"Please, Sam, talk to me. Are you upset? Is it about what happened last night? I promise I didn't look when I changed your clothes. I swear."

Samantha came to a halt and looked at him. "Don't be foolish, Ben. As I told you last night, I was grateful for your help. I appreciate it."

"Then why are you so cold, and it's clear you're avoiding me?"

Samantha couldn't look Benjamin in the eyes. How could she tell him she wanted more than friendship? She didn't want to tear up his family. She didn't want Rosalie to grow up in a broken household. Samantha didn't answer his comment.

"Truce?" he said, extending his outstretched palm.

"You did nothing wrong, but all right, ceasefire," she said, smiling and shaking Benjamin's hand.

But that was easier said than done. Samantha was still disturbed by what happened between them. His kiss on her cheeks affected her, no matter how hard she tried to forget. Samantha took her time in the garden, hoping to avoid Benjamin in any way she could. She realized she was merely postponing the inevitable. Samantha was still nervous around Benjamin. She noticed she'd over-watered the plants and knew she'd procrastinate as long as she could.

Stop putting it off, she told herself.

Samantha entered through the back entrance and checked to see if everything was OK. Fortunately, no one was around. She ducked out of sight when she thought she heard someone coming. She slipped as quietly as she could past Linda's room and into her own. When she unlocked the door, she discovered her bed, as well as her luggage, had disappeared. She was surprised when she heard a voice behind her.

"Sam, tell me the truth. You've never slept on a firm mattress before, have you?"

Samantha turned around to see Benjamin standing behind her. He was too close to her, and it made her weak.

"Ben," she muttered, her cheeks flushed. "W-what makes you say that?" she asked.

"The five comforters on your bed tell me you haven't."

"Okay, I admit it. I've never slept on a hard mattress before, but it doesn't mean you can take away my bed for using the comforters and force me to sleep on the floor."

Benjamin couldn't hold back his laughter and came out laughing. "Sam, your innocence is driving me insane. For your information, I had that filthy-looking bed thrown away. We will use this space for storage."

"And where do I sleep? In your room?" she asked.

"If you want to," he teased.

"Come on, Ben. No more jokes, OK?"

"I moved your belongings to your new room."

"My new room? Are you serious? Ben, you can't make a joke about something like that."

"Who says I'm joking? Come on, I'll take you there."

Samantha's heart rate increased as he brought her upstairs. She looked at him, her eyes wide with confusion. Before entering the room, Benjamin walked behind her and covered her eyes with his hands.

"I can't see, Ben." Samantha tried to shift his hands, but she couldn't keep her thrilled smile from her face.

"Shh, Sam, you're being impatient."

Samantha heard the door open, and the brisk air hit her as they entered.

"May I now open my eyes?" Samantha asked, her tone a little higher than usual because of her excitement.

"Sam, you're becoming impatient again. Are you ready?"

"Oh, absolutely! The suspense is killing me," she said.

"Okay, check out your new room," Benjamin said as he removed his hands from her eyes. "I hope you like it. Linda and Nancy rearranged the furniture for you, and have already changed the linen and draperies."

Samantha opened her eyes and felt them widen at the most beautiful sight she had ever seen in a long time. Her face brightened with a smile. The room was far larger than she expected. They furnished it with peach and burgundy draperies and bed linens. There was a shower cubicle and a separate, large tub in the bathroom. This bedroom was larger than the one at home.

Samantha opened the window, allowing fresh, cool air to enter the room. She looked out the window and noticed the trees and plants that surrounded the pool and yard.

"Do you like it?" Ben asked as he leaned against the bedroom door.

Samantha smiled at him. "I'm happy, Ben," she said as she whirled around the room. She walked over to him and hugged him. He reciprocated her hug.

Samantha gaped at him. "I... I... thank you, Ben. This means a lot to me."

Ben ran his fingers through his hair. "Sam..." he whispered quietly.

"Yes?"

"I-I..." he stammered.

Samantha and Benjamin exchanged silent glances before laughing. It was their first honest and meaningful moment together since Samantha moved in.

CHAPTER TEN

It had been another humid night. In fact, it was one of the warmest July evenings on record in Seattle. Samantha could not sleep because of the extreme heat. She kicked off the covers because they were too hot around her. She looked at the digital clock on the nightstand. It was 12 a.m. Samantha struggled to place the pillow over her head, which proved more difficult than she expected. She shifted her weight on her back to get a more comfortable position, before exhaling a long sigh. Samantha still couldn't sleep.

She was still awake an hour later, tossing and turning and breaking out in a cold sweat. Samantha sprang up and sat on the edge of the bed. She wondered if Southern California was experiencing the same situation. Samantha was lonely.

I hope Dad is doing well. Oh, how I miss him. I'd rather be at home, sleeping in my bed, than in someone else's.

She stood up and opened the windows to allow in some fresh air. She had an excellent view of the swimming pool. It looked refreshing. The pleasant aroma of flowers from the garden wafted through the air, but she immediately felt the pain in her heart for her mother. The emptiness mirrored the sadness in her eyes. She remembered spending many mornings in the greenhouse with her. Her mother would take a pair of clippers from her apron and cut a rose for her to smell. She longed for her mother.

She stared at the pool, and it seemed inviting—borders of lush tropical greenery surrounded the bright blue water, and those magnificent flowers were everywhere. Samantha needed to go swimming to relax. Ignoring her prior incident at the pool, she dashed into her robe and yanked open her bedroom door. Samantha stood outside Benjamin's room, listening for any movement to ensure he was sound asleep. She didn't want him wandering about the house again, as he had before. Samantha heard nothing. She went downstairs on tiptoe.

Except for the cast of silver moonlight, it was dark and quiet. Rosalie's cat, Angel, was nowhere to be seen. Samantha grinned as she glanced at the tempting, cool water—exactly what she needed. She took off her robe, placed it on the back of a lounge chair, and undressed down to her bikini.

She jumped into the pool without first testing the water. She was right. The water felt nice. It felt great on her skin, as if she was washing her problems away. Samantha swam a few laps from one end of the pool to the other while her body warmed up to the temperature. She swam in the open water like a mermaid, gracefully and joyfully. Samantha came to a halt when she heard a splash and let out a loud scream as Benjamin appeared from the surface of the water and was by her side in seconds. He grinned.

"Relax, you'll rouse everyone in the house," he issued a warning.

"What are you doing here?" Samantha inquired.

"Well, I, too, want to cool off."

"I'm sorry for going for a swim. I didn't think anyone was awake. What are you doing here at this hour? I thought you were sleeping."

"Do you remember I lived in this house? I don't have a curfew," Benjamin chuckled. "I enjoy swimming at all hours of the day. Am I making you uncomfortable, Sam?"

"N-not at all," she stuttered.

Benjamin smiled and gave her a thoughtful look.

If only he knew. Samantha feared what her weak heart would do. Even though she knew he was married, the sight of Benjamin next to her almost made her pulse race. She couldn't deny how much she enjoyed being with him. She liked him a lot, but it couldn't happen.

"Could you turn your back, please? I need to get out of the water," she said, her eyes begging. Samantha couldn't figure out why she was uneasy to show Benjamin her body. She spent a lot of time at the beach and was always seen in a bikini. In fact, she loved flaunting her enviable curves. Why was she acting stupid now?

Benjamin locked his attention on her for a long time. "Don't go yet, Sam. Please stay," he implored.

"It's OK, Ben. I'm good."

Benjamin came out of the pool. "Please stay, Sam. I want you to stay."

"I'm done swimming and I'm already tired," she said, shaking her head and blinking wetly.

For a long time, Benjamin remained immobile and silent. Samantha felt as if she was melting beneath his gaze. She grew dizzy when Benjamin's hands were tight around her. His hands caressed her waist and hips as they probed her body. Samantha's heart skipped a beat. She held her breath. He'd kiss her. She wanted him to kiss her. She closed her eyes and waited for Benjamin. And then he released her, much to her disappointment.

She opened her eyes and glanced at him, perplexed, knowing that it should have relieved her that he didn't kiss her, hug her, or make love to her.

Samantha could hear Benjamin moan in exasperation. She stood dripping wet, arms folded around her chest, trembling from the cold air.

Benjamin grabbed the large towel off the chair. "You're trembling," he said as he wrapped the towel around her, bringing her close to him, their hips touching. He kissed her lips softly. Samantha let out a soft moan. It felt amazing.

"You make me lose my mind, Sam," he murmured. "You set me on fire just by being near you."

Benjamin reached out and brought her into his arms, his lips again seeking hers. He kissed her with such passion and desire. Samantha couldn't help but kiss him back with the same intensity. She gasped as his lips brushed over her neck, sending a thrill through her body. Samantha clasped Benjamin's arm as he carried her into his arms. For the time being, she appreciated the warmth of his kiss and the pleasant sense of security she felt in his arms. She was caught in the amazing sensation of his hands on her, wandering... wanting... probing.

"Sam," he whispered, an undertone in his voice forcing her to hold her breath. He ran his hands through her hair, grasped the back of her head, and kissed her passionately.

Samantha held her breath again, waiting in complete silence. She closed her eyes as a shiver ran through her, submitting to the heat of his kiss again, wanting to feel all of him at once. Samantha allowed herself to imagine having a wonderful life with him. But it only lasted as long as he had her in his arms. Reality flooded back, and she drew away in an instant.

She blinked open her eyes. Samantha regained her composure as she remembered Rosalie and her mother in France. She let go of him.

"I believe it is time for me to go."

"Sam," Benjamin muttered as he kissed her on the lips.

"Good night, Ben," she mumbled, trying to pull away from him, but his grasp was too strong.

"Ben?" Samantha pleaded pitifully.

"Please stay with me a little longer?"

"I'm afraid I can't."

Benjamin held his gaze on her for a long time, before releasing his grasp and turning away. Samantha gathered her things and left quickly. Benjamin remained there, looking at her, not moving until she was out of sight.

Samantha entered her room, took a quick shower, blow-dried her hair, dressed, and staggered into bed. Samantha couldn't stop thinking about what had happened between them in the pool. How could she explain that she could still feel Benjamin's hands all over her body? Samantha had told herself several times that she would forget everything that had happened, but despite her best efforts, she couldn't bring herself to do so. She touched her lips, where she could still feel his imprint. She detested him for kissing her, but she despised herself even more for allowing it to happen. Her thoughts were as chaotic as the waves, one after the other, crashing in on the next. Their kiss had been unforgettable—almost divine. She made a shaky motion with her head.

No, it is not right. Ben is a married man. The kiss has no meaning.

Samantha tried to convince herself that it was only a kiss. She dwelt on her displeasure and bewilderment as she lay in bed, listening to every sound that came in and out of the house. Samantha heard a slight shuffle outside her door. She listened, but she heard nothing for the next minute. She was about to fall asleep when she heard footsteps outside her door again. Someone was making their way down the corridor toward her room. Her anxiety grew. The sound became louder as the steps moved closer. Samantha pulled up the blanket and crawled beneath it, listening. Sweat beads formed on her forehead, which she wiped away with the back of her palm.

The door slid open when someone turned the doorknob. Samantha's heart stopped beating. She curled herself in the blanket and feigned sleep, but she opened her eyes to the darkness. She heard the odd and uneven breathing sound of one steady inhalation. Her eyes were accustomed to the darkness, but she couldn't see the person's face. She tried to figure out who it was, but the room was too dark to see the shadowy form.

"Sam?" In the faint light, Benjamin murmured.

He assumed Samantha had fallen asleep when she didn't respond. Benjamin debated waiting until daylight, but he couldn't let another minute go by without speaking to Samantha and apologizing for kissing her. He knew he had broken her trust and that the damage may have been irreparable.

"Are you awake, Sam?"

"No," she said calmly, relieved to know it was just Benjamin cowering in the shadows.

"So, why did you answer?" he laughed.

"What is it?" she said, rising to a sitting position. Samantha scrambled for the light shade button, found it, and pressed it. The room lit up.

"Did I wake you?"

"No, Ben, I'm OK. Don't worry."

"I want to make sure you're not upset with me. You know, about what happened between us? I don't want you to think I just kissed any woman." His tone of voice made it clear that he was serious.

"Don't worry, Ben. I'm OK." Samantha tried to remain composed. She couldn't tell him how much she loved having his arms around her, as much as their first kiss.

Benjamin was lost in thought as he stared at her. How could he tell her he couldn't forget the kiss they'd just shared, and that he didn't want to stop now? He wanted to kiss her for the rest of his life, but he didn't want to frighten or rush her.

He turned to leave her room, then returned and kissed her on the lips. Samantha said nothing as he pressed his hands on her, one at the back of her neck and the other grasping her. Benjamin moaned and extended his kiss. He hoped he could kiss her all night. He wanted her to depend on him as much as he was on her.

Samantha felt as if she was still in his embrace, floating inches above the ground as his lips left hers. Benjamin cradled her in his arms as her face reddened.

"I suppose I should leave now before you insist on my stay," he joked.

"I suppose you are correct," she whispered.

Thanks to her laughter, Benjamin's ears were filled with the best tune he'd ever heard. In his wildest dreams, he never imagined he'd find such happiness with a woman he hardly knew and had only known for a short time.

"Good night, Sam. We'll speak about it tomorrow." He muttered as he exited the room, stroking the tip of her nose.

Samantha's pulse skipped a beat, an electric current rushing through her veins. Benjamin's actions had taken her surprise. Her heart was racing, and all she could think about was that passionate kiss she'd shared with Benjamin. She trembled at the memories of the night, replaying that moment repeatedly in her head.

Samantha slept well for the first time in weeks. It was the most incredible night of her life!

CHAPTER ELEVEN

S amantha was waiting for Benjamin at the kitchen table with a cup of coffee in her hand. She waited a long time for him, and she was so nervous she was getting nauseous. An image of Benjamin from last night formed in her mind. She caressed her lips, as if she were still sensing Benjamin's kiss. The sensation of his lips against hers jumbled her thoughts. It complicated their relationship. Samantha was aware of her feelings for him, but was unsure if they were those of love or infatuation. She knew she should leave well enough alone and not ask herself too many questions, but her mind had other ideas. Samantha had no intention of falling for a married man, but she couldn't ignore their powerful attraction. She was surprised when she heard a voice from behind her.

"Good morning, beautiful," Benjamin smiled as he kissed her on the lips.

Samantha became nervous. Seeing him in this state, knowing he desired her, had her heart racing.

"H-hi," she murmured, her voice trembling as she attempted to conceal her uneasiness.

"How did you sleep?" he asked, bemused.

She waved off his question, avoiding an obvious lie. She couldn't tell him she'd been dreaming about him and their kisses.

"Sam?"

"Ben, I'd want to... I'd like to..." Samantha was overwhelmed and at a loss for words. She paused for a bit to reclaim her voice. "I suppose I slept well. Why'd you ask?" she stuttered.

"I was afraid you wouldn't sleep a wink after what transpired between us last night."

"No, I have no recollection. Should I?" She made a false statement.

He frowned. "You don't recall what occurred to us last night? Permit me to jog your memory."

Benjamin stroked her cheeks and tilted her head back. She closed her eyes and surrendered to his embrace. Her heart raced as he locked his gaze on her. Her fingers shook as she allowed him to take her mouth and place it in his. His kiss was slow and sensual, almost whisper-like in its intensity. In a long, lingering kiss, his lips devoured hers. He moved her closer and kissed her again, this time softly, not carelessly.

Samantha had never had a kiss like that before, and she enjoyed it. Benjamin cradled her in his arms and kissed her again, deeply and slowly this time. He was now feverishly kissing her, as if he couldn't get enough of her lips' sweetness. Samantha lost herself in passion for a moment, and she unconsciously kissed him back, mesmerized by him. She'd felt nothing like this before, and she wanted him to continue. Samantha was powerless to reject their physical desire. Their kisses intensified until Benjamin knocked Samantha's cup of coffee over, soaking the countertop.

Samantha froze in fear when the cup shattered and fell to the floor. Neither of them spoke a single word. She held her breath and waited to see if anybody else had heard the crash in the house. She heard nothing.

Benjamin grabbed her by the waist as she laughed at his clumsiness. He kissed her again, and Samantha kissed him back, but they moved away when they heard approaching footsteps.

"What happened here? Are you okay?" Linda asked, her attention drawn to the fragments of glass on the floor.

The room became silent. The tension became intense. Samantha stuttered for words as her cheeks turned crimson.

"I-I was making coffee and knocked over the cup," Samantha mumbled, trying not to make eye contact with Linda.

Benjamin grinned at Samantha's dishonesty.

Linda scowled, curiously staring at them. "Did I disrupt something?"

"Don't be silly, Linda. Of course not. What made you think that?" Samantha asked, her voice shaking.

"No specific reason," Linda remarked before leaving the room with a doubtful frown on her face.

Samantha watched as she walked away. That suspicious look on Linda's face immediately caught her eye. She knew that look. How could she have done this? How could she have been so naive?

Samantha realized she'd made a terrible mistake. She couldn't have a relationship with a married man. That would add to the problems she was already dealing with. Samantha assumed a romantic relationship with Benjamin that didn't exist or could never happen. She couldn't put her heart at risk in that way. Samantha had no future with him. She couldn't be a mistress. She would not let that happen. Samantha had to focus on her major problem. She was still at war with her father, RJ, and his family.

Samantha left the kitchen in a hurry, leaving Benjamin confused. He followed her to her room. Benjamin knocked, but received no response.

"What's the problem, Sam? Please let me in," he implored. There was no reply.

"Please, Sam, talk to me. Did I do something wrong? If it's Linda, don't worry. I'll talk to her."

Benjamin listened through the door, but there was still no response. He tried the door, but Samantha had locked it.

"Okay, Sam. I understand. I'll leave you alone. If you need me, I'll be downstairs."

Samantha heard shuffling footsteps coming down the stairs. She was weeping on her bed, staring at the ceiling. She was heartbroken. Samantha had finally admitted to herself that she was in love with Benjamin, but couldn't act on her feelings. She didn't want to break Rosalie's little heart. Living under the same roof with Benjamin made things more complex than she had hoped. She had to set her feelings aside. She had to let go of Benjamin, whom she loved. But how could she do the impossible when her heart was yearning for him? Samantha needed to weigh her options.

The next day was hard for her, as she kept her distance from Benjamin. Samantha couldn't risk getting too close to him. She needed to let go of whatever feelings she had for him, and the sooner she did, the easier it would be to get over him. Samantha didn't want to ruin a happy family. Fortunately, she didn't have to exert too much effort. Benjamin worked long hours and returned home late most evenings, which was just as well.

"WHERE HAVE YOU BEEN?" Benjamin asked when he eventually caught up with her in Rosalie's room, after she had put her to bed.

"I've been around. You know, here and there."

"If I hadn't known better, I'd have thought you were avoiding me," he said. His eyes are sadder than any she'd ever seen.

"What?" Samantha faked a grin at him. "Where did you get such a crazy idea? It's just that we were both busy."

"Is everything all right, Sam? Is there anything you'd want to tell me?"

"No. What is there to say?"

Benjamin stood there, watching as she exited the room and shut the door behind her. He followed her. He stepped behind her and encircled her waist with his arms. She twisted out of his hold, trying to break free.

"What's the problem? Are you upset with me?" Benjamin asked.

"Of course not," Samantha said uncomfortably. "It's just that I don't want Rosalie to walk on us like this!"

"Don't you know I would never hurt you, Sam? I'm concerned about..."

"Excuse me, Samantha," Linda interrupted their serious moment. "There's a young man downstairs looking for you."

Benjamin smirked.

A man looking for Samantha?

It worried him, and he had no intention of concealing his curiosity. Meanwhile, Samantha's heart was hammering, and she was afraid it would spring out of her chest, bracing herself for the prospect that RJ had found her.

"Who is it?" Benjamin asked, his voice becoming agitated.

Linda remarked, "He said his name was Samuel."

Samantha exhaled a breath of relief. "I'll be down in a minute," she said to Linda.

Linda nodded as she made her way downstairs.

For a moment, Benjamin mistook Samantha's warm grin. It irritated him.

"I see why you were avoiding me now." Benjamin despised himself for being so straightforward. He didn't mean to phrase it that way, but his jealousy got the best of him.

"What are you talking about, Ben? Samuel is not an admirer. He is a friend."

"That's what you think," he said.

Samantha locked her gaze on him. "Stop, Ben! I just met Samuel at the market that day, and I haven't spoken to or seen him since. Please don't make a fuss about nothing," Samantha said. She was perplexed why Benjamin was behaving like a jealous boyfriend. He wasn't even bothered that Linda had seen them embracing.

Benjamin was deafeningly silent and refused to look at her. His anger blended with his jealousy, and for a moment, he clenched his fist as if he wanted to shatter things or punch someone in the face—like Samuel. He loathed violence, yet he was about to engage in it himself. He was jealous.

Samantha had not expected it. She had to admit that the attention delighted and impressed her, especially because Benjamin was acting like a possessive boyfriend. Samantha's heart leaped at his jealousy, but she pushed her thoughts aside. Sure, they kissed a few times, and she hadn't regretted it one bit. She would kiss Benjamin every minute of the day if she could, but she wasn't sure whether this relationship would work out. They never talked about it, and if they did, was she ready to go the extra mile and become a mistress?

Samantha remained silent in response to the self-directed query. She had to admit that her current predicament was becoming a little complex. She sighed deeply and excused herself to go downstairs. Benjamin merely looked at her. Samantha paused for a bit, trying to figure out what was wrong with Benjamin's weird behavior. But she couldn't handle him just now. She shrugged and made her way downstairs.

Although she had only just arrived, Lucy was amusing Samuel with a warm smile. She had just returned from a week-long vacation with her mother in Santa Barbara. She was all over Samuel, making him feel welcome, charming, and flirtatious.

"Hello, Samuel," Samantha said. "To what do I owe the pleasure of your visit?"

Samuel rose to his feet. "Sam, good evening. Please accept my apologies for disturbing you at this hour. I'd want to speak with you privately about something if you don't mind."

"Of course," she said.

They fixed their gaze on Lucy, who was listening in on their conversation and had no intention of leaving them alone.

"Why don't we sit on the terrace, Samuel? It's pleasant and warm outside. I'll be right out with some refreshments for us."

Samuel nodded as he stepped outside. Samantha went into the kitchen and began making snacks for them. Lucy trailed behind.

"I've only been gone a week, yet a lot has happened. You've had the nerve to entertain your friend at Sir Benjamin's house! He'd be enraged. He let none of us have guests in the house."

"Is that right? For the record, he was upstairs when Linda called me. He didn't seem to mind at all."

"Do you know how much of a flirt you are?" Lucy said.

"I'm not even going to dignify it with a comment," Samantha answered, trying to keep her anger under control. Lucy was a troublemaker, and she wouldn't let her get to her.

"Just don't forget, Samantha. You work as a servant in this house. Don't take advantage of Sir Benjamin's generosity and kindness."

Samantha shook her head and ignored her warning. She didn't believe she'd done anything wrong. Samuel was a friend, and he was here visiting her. That's all.

Samantha noticed Samuel walking back and forth across the stone floor as she neared the patio. She placed the tray on the table and poured him a glass of orange juice, which he carefully sipped.

"So, what do you want to talk about?" Samantha started the conversation.

Samuel took a deep breath before speaking. "Samantha, I've been thinking about you since the day we met, but coming here terrified me. I continued driving by this house, expecting to get a glimpse of you, but I didn't see you. That is why I took a chance and came here."

Unbeknownst to them, Benjamin was hiding on the balcony above, listening in on their conversation. Fear gripped him as he realized Samuel was trying to woo Samantha. Would she let him? Samuel was tall, dark, and handsome. Even if he tried, he couldn't deny it.

"Samantha, I've never felt anything like this before. You're always on my mind, and I'm constantly thinking of you. I'd want to court you." Samuel gave her a serious expression.

Benjamin heard it clearly and held his breath as he waited for Samantha's response. He'd never been so worried in his life.

Samantha was at a loss for words.

"Do you mind if I court you, Sam?" Samuel asked again when Samantha did not answer.

Samantha felt her heart belonged to Benjamin, even though she knew she couldn't have him. She wasn't sure where her feelings would take her, but she couldn't deny that only Benjamin could fill her heart with endless happiness. She was confused. Whatever it was, she couldn't keep Samuel waiting.

For a moment, Benjamin's heartbeat stopped. His chest tensed. All his thoughts, sensations, and emotions collided as he waited for Samantha's response.

"Sam?" Samuel whispered. His palms were sweating, and his mouth was dry. He hadn't been this nervous in years, if ever. The silence was practically unbearable, and it seemed to last forever. His heartbeat slowed as he waited for her response.

Samantha lifted her head to meet his gaze. "Samuel, I am flattered that you would consider dating me, but my heart already belongs to someone else. If you had asked me sooner, I would have likely said yes."

Benjamin heaved a sigh of relief as he heard Samantha's words. He smiled. Benjamin realized at that moment that Samantha's heart belonged to him. Hearing what she said felt like heaven to him. He couldn't put into words the feelings that overwhelmed him. All he knew was that he was falling for her. Should he move, walk downstairs, and passionately kiss Samantha, or stay put?

"I know you're a good man, and an attractive one at that. You will have no trouble finding your match. All you have to do is look for her. Don't put it off for too long. Ask the girl straight away. Otherwise, you may find yourself in the same situation as you are now."

Samuel was heartbroken. Samantha had turned him down, but he appreciated her honesty and the fact that she wasn't playing games with him.

"Samantha, I appreciate your candor. It was all my fault. If I hadn't been so afraid to ask you sooner, perhaps we might have had a future together."

Samantha escorted him out as Samuel dragged his feet to the front door, his head lowered and a mournful expression on his face.

"You're such a jerk, Samantha," Lucy said in a rage. "What did you do to Samuel?"

Samantha gave her a blank stare. She walked into the kitchen and washed the dishes. Samantha went to her room and collapsed on her bed, exhausted. She contemplated Samuel's proposal, and if it had been Benjamin and he was unmarried, she might have felt differently.

Meanwhile, Lucy followed Samantha into her room to give her a piece of her mind, but she found empty baskets and boxes piled on the shelves.

"Where does Samantha sleep now?" she pondered.

"She sleeps upstairs, next to Rosalie's room," Linda explained.

Lucy was on the verge of passing out. "Do you think it's strange that Sir Benjamin let Samantha move into the guest room? She is a flirt. She is skilled at capturing people's attention." Lucy expressed her thoughts.

"Lucy, put an end to this insanity right now! What they do is unimportant to us. They are both adults."

"Doesn't it bother you, Linda? Do you think I'm unaware of Samantha's proclivity for flirting with Sir Benjamin?"

"Lucy, it's none of our business."

"But this is crazy."

"Don't think I'm unaware of your flirtation with Benjamin, Lucy."

Lucy laughed mockingly. "I'm not sure what you mean, Linda."

"You may deny it all you want, but Benjamin isn't interested in you. It doesn't get much clearer than that," Linda added. "I'm telling you this as a friend. Benjamin has a crush on Samantha. The best thing you can do is let go of the idea that he will fall in love with you. Walk away with dignity, Lucy. That's the only thing you could do for yourself."

Lucy knew Linda was right, but she couldn't figure out how this could happen.

"What did he see in her that I don't have? Why does Samantha seem to attract so many men?" Lucy asked, swirling around in front of the enormous mirror, looking at herself.

Linda walked away, rolling her eyes, leaving Lucy confused and depressed.

CHAPTER TWELVE

S amantha was awakened by the sound of two loud voices speaking outside her door in the corridor. She blinked her eyes open and looked at the digital clock. It was two o'clock in the morning.

Who in their right mind would be up at this hour of the night?

Samantha stood up and put on her Mickey Mouse slippers. She walked to the bathroom to wash her face. She opened the door just as the conversation ended.

"Benjamin, I grabbed your suitcase and Rosalie's from the closet. When are you leaving?" Linda asked a question.

"Within an hour," Benjamin said.

Linda nodded and proceeded downstairs to make some coffee.

"Are you planning a trip, Ben?" Samantha, rubbing her eyes, asked.

Benjamin turned around and saw Samantha staring at him. He moved in closer and lightly kissed her on the lips. Benjamin had never seen her more beautiful, now that he knew she had feelings for him. Much to Samantha's surprise, he lifted her off the ground and swung her around several times.

"It must have been some night, Ben? You look much more rested and upbeat this morning."

"I'm not sure what you're talking about, Sam," Benjamin said with a smile.

Samantha made a clicking gesture with her tongue.

"Ben, you made faces at me last night."

"No, I didn't," he laughed. "There must have been something in my eye."

"Ben!" Samantha yelled.

Benjamin fought to hold back his laughter as he chuckled at her teasing tone. "It's my grandfather's 80th birthday, as well as our annual family reunion. We're spending the weekend in our Santa Barbara family home. I expected us to enjoy wine tasting too."

Samantha saw this as an excellent time to assess her options. While Benjamin was away, she had time to call her SBP friends and ask for advice on what she should do. She wondered whether they heard anything about her father and RJ.

"What a brilliant idea," Samantha remarked. "You must relax and spend time with your family. Everyone will be happy to see you and Rosalie. While you're gone, I'll take care of the gardening. Linda bought some seedlings and wants to show me how to prepare the soil for planting."

"And who says you have to stay here? I will not let you out of my sight. I don't want another suitor to come knocking while I'm away. Get your things ready. We'll be on our way soon."

Samantha broke out laughing, as if she were a schoolgirl. An incredible pleasure arose within her because of Benjamin's extra attention.

Maybe I'll figure things out later.

She was attempting to convince herself that she deserved some rest and relaxation, and that Santa Barbara was the ideal place to do it.

Samantha quickly showered, dressed, and packed her belongings before leaving. It turned out that she, Rosalie, Benjamin, and Jack were the only ones going. Lucy was furious.

Why has Samantha received so much attention? Her anger grew with each passing second. *Samantha, your day will come.* Lucy made a promise to herself as she watched the car pull out of the driveway.

AFTER DRIVING FOR EIGHTEEN hours, they arrived in Santa Barbara at half-past nine p.m. Samantha's first night at the McClain Ranch was agonizing. The dogs had barked non-stop all night, and the crickets had blended in with the noises. She pulled the covers over her head, grabbed one of her pillows, and hugged it. She couldn't fathom how people could live in such a manner.

The alarm clock beeped in Samantha's ear early in the morning. She leaned over and hit the snooze button for a few more minutes. She looked at the clock on the nightstand. Not only had she slept, but she had also overslept. It was ten o'clock. She pulled herself out of bed and into the shower.

Samantha shook her head as she headed downstairs in her maid's uniform. Despite Benjamin's request that she dress casually, she thought she should dress appropriately because she was the nanny. She admitted she missed wearing colorful designer clothes from Paris, but also enjoyed wearing her uniform.

Samantha liked her new look. She didn't have to spend hours getting ready. All she had to do now was shower, apply lotion, and put on her uniform.

Samantha wandered around the house and made her way through the kitchen. She made herself a cup of coffee, sat at the dining table, and wondered why it was so quiet.

Where is everyone?

A loud noise erupted from outside a few moments later. Samantha peeked out the window. She noticed that the Mc-Clain family had begun the day's activities. Her eyes widened as she observed countless lines of colorful buntings and banners hanging from post to post. Balloons, cotton candy machines, and many other games for children and adults have been set up. Teenagers danced to the beat of a car's sound system. Samantha smiled as she watched Benjamin and his three brothers, whom she had met the night before, playing football. Everyone else was asleep when they arrived. She looked around the living room. Several sports trophies and medals adorned the bookcases. She was completely unaware that Benjamin was standing next to her as she admired the exquisite decorations and paintings on the walls by famous painters.

"Sam, meet my father," he said.

"You must be Samantha. My name is Julius McClain, and I am your host," the man said, smiling and offering his hand to her.

Samantha smiled back and shook his hand. "Good day, sir. My name is Samantha St. James, or Sam for short. I'm delighted to meet you," she stated.

"St. James? That name sounds familiar. I suppose I know a St. James in Beverly Hills," he remarked, stroking his chin. "Oh, yes, I remember. Do you know Artemus?"

Samantha choked on her saliva. Thank God for Benjamin, who rescued her from his father.

"And this gorgeous lady here is my beautiful mother," Benjamin bragged as he kissed her on the cheek.

"Samantha, welcome to the ranch. It's a pleasure to meet you. We've heard a lot about you. Benjamin got it right." Mrs. McClain glanced at her and said, "You're beautiful."

Samantha blushed at the remark, but wondered why Benjamin would mention her to his mother. What would his wife think about that?

"Nice to meet you, Mrs. McClain," she said as she greeted her and had a lengthy conversation with her.

"Would you like to join us later, Samantha? We could use your help in making the table centerpieces."

Samantha, of course, had to say yes, and minutes later, she joined a group of youngsters busily crafting centerpieces for the tables, bursting with colorful fresh flowers. She struggled to keep up with them, but had to admit she enjoyed it.

Samantha was an all-natural beauty who stood out among the crowd. A few socialites who were sitting around watching everyone work noticed her right away.

"Who is she?" Cassandra, a tall, attractive blonde who had been attempting to catch Benjamin's attention for years, inquired.

"I heard her name was Samantha," one of her pals stated. "She's the nanny."

Cassandra smirked. "It's no wonder she looked so terrible in her outfit."

Samantha heard them repeat her name several times, but she couldn't hear what they were saying. She ignored them and went about her business. Meanwhile, Benjamin was sitting behind a large oak tree when he spotted Cassandra and her friends giggling behind Samantha's back. He rose to his feet and proceeded towards them. As he got closer, Benjamin heard them laughing and whispering about Samantha. He shook his head as he passed them, then walked over to Samantha, squeezed her shoulder, and smiled at her.

"How's it going?" he asked.

"I'm afraid I'm not good at this," she said, rummaging through the flower basket.

"What matters is that you tried," Benjamin said.

Samantha smiled as she looked up at him.

Cassandra smirked when she saw Benjamin talking to Samantha. They looked happy. She didn't know he was close to the nanny.

"What the hell is going on here?"

Cassandra's brow furrowed, and her eyes narrowed. She needed to interrupt their tender moments. As she approached Benjamin and Samantha, Cassandra was visibly annoyed.

"You must be the nanny. I've heard so much about you. Benjamin, where are your manners? Aren't you going to introduce me to your nanny?" Cassandra said, wrapping her arms around him and grinning deviously at Samantha.

"Sam, this is Cassie. She's a family friend."

Samantha looked up, and when she noticed Cassandra's suspicious expression, she wasn't sure whether to smile or not.

She said, "Hello, Cassie," without offering her hand, having already concluded she didn't like this woman.

Cassandra fixed her focus on her and feigned a smile. "I'd love to stay and help, but my friends and I are due for a horseback ride," she said as her pals raced over.

Samantha diverted her sight from the mocking glint in their eyes. She could hear them laughing as they went away. She had the distinct impression that they were talking about her. It didn't escape Benjamin's notice. He was not blind to the girl's unpleasant attitude. He planned to have fun with them.

"Why don't you accompany me, Sam? I'll show you around the property and to my favorite spot. The view of the lake is spectacular."

"But I haven't finished my centerpiece yet."

"Don't worry about it, we can finish it later."

Samantha's heart was beating as Benjamin took her hand in his and put his arms around her. He showed her around the ranch and his secret hideaway, where he used to hide from his father as a child. Samantha closed her eyes and breathed in the fresh air as Benjamin kissed her on the lips.

Cassandra was in the stable, rubbing the horse's shaggy mane, when she saw Samantha and Benjamin walking hand in hand, laughing. She felt her eyes grow blazing red with rage when she watched them kiss.

Still agitated, she asked, "What the devil is going on here?"

"He's playing her, Cassie. She's not Benjamin's kind of girl. There is nothing to worry about. She's just the nanny," said her pal.

Cassandra remained skeptical. "That witch is stealing my boyfriend, but I will do everything it takes to get him back," she promised. "I will end her social climb and return her to her appropriate place—a lowly servant!"

BARRELS OF BEER, WINE, and other alcoholic drinks had been delivered. Samantha helped place the tablecloths and decorations. They set up a giant buffet table in the style of a luau under a large blue canopy. It had been a long day for everyone, even the youngsters. They finished the setup and decorations by three o'clock.

"Ben, do you think I can shower and change for the party?" Samantha asked as she noticed everyone had left to get ready.

"Of course. There is nothing else to do. Do you want me to join you in the shower?" He teased with a chuckle.

"W-what? I, um..." she stuttered. Her cheeks had turned red.

"Sam, take a deep breath. I was kidding, of course." Benjamin burst out laughing.

"Oh, right," Samantha laughed.

Samantha pondered what to wear after taking a shower. She didn't want the socialite girls to outdo her, but she didn't want to go crazy either. She was glad she had heeded Benjamin's advice and brought extra garments. Samantha changed a few times, finding something wrong with each dress she tried on. Samantha chose skinny jeans that complemented her slim and beautiful proportions, as well as a figure-hugging white shirt with a flattering low-cut neckline that showed off a hint of her cleavage. She paired it with a pair of black high heels. Samantha began styling her long, black hair, which she tossed carelessly over her shoulder for the occasion. Her makeup was simple, but elegant. She resembled the old Samantha, the Beverly Hills socialite. She looked in the mirror one more time, appreciating what she saw.

What would Benjamin think of my new look now?

The music played, and the party got started. Everyone was looking forward to having an enjoyable time. Benjamin looked sharp in Levi's jeans, a white polo shirt, cowboy boots, and black sunglasses. He was drinking a beer with his younger brother, Tim, when everyone watched a beautiful young woman coming down the steps, her hair glamorously waving in the breeze.

When Benjamin realized it was Samantha, he coughed on his beer. Her beauty captivated him. Except for the time he saw her almost naked body, this was the first time he had seen her outside of her maid's attire. He gave an appreciative nod. He never took his eyes off her, measuring her from head to toe. For a moment, time seemed to stand still for him. Benjamin was absolutely smitten. He couldn't believe how beautiful she was. He knew she was stunning, but how could she have concealed such beauty? Benjamin stood there in mute wonder until she reached the foot of the steps, and he nearly fell over his own feet on his walk over to greet her.

"You look beautiful. Stunning!" he murmured, barely able to find his voice.

Samantha flushed and shifted her attention away from him.

Benjamin realized he was close to her, so close that he could smell her exquisite perfume, which was alluring. He loved nothing more than cradling her in his arms and hugging her close. He would kiss Samantha passionately if it weren't for a hundred pairs of eyes staring at them. Samantha was ecstatic, and Benjamin's complete attention to her enchanted her again.

As his brothers and cousins crowded around them, the air around Benjamin got dense and foggy until his mother grabbed Samantha's hand in hers. She toured her around and introduced her to the rest of their family, including their business partners. Benjamin appeared disgruntled, as he thought he had Samantha all to himself. He sighed heavily.

"Your nanny is gorgeous! Beautiful! If she's available, I'll propose to her right away," Tim stated.

"Not if I can help it. I'll make the first move and propose to her." Justin, Benjamin's younger brother, stated.

Eric, Benjamin's third and eldest brother, was about to join his brother's discussion when he spotted his wife staring at him from a distance. He knew he should stay out of it and keep his mouth shut.

Benjamin's brow wrinkled as his gaze became more intense.

"I'm sorry to disappoint you, brothers, but she is off limits," he said.

His brothers scowled.

"What do you mean, she's off limits? Wait a minute. Is she the reason you've been smiling and having a good time since you arrived? You don't even give Cassandra or any other female here the right time of day anymore. What's the problem, bro? Are you crazy in love with Samantha?" Tim asked. "But if nothing else is going on between you, I'll ask her out tonight."

"I'm warning you, Tim, and that goes for all of you," Benjamin remarked, pointing to his brothers and cousins. "Samantha is off-limits. Do you understand?"

"That will be difficult," Tim said, as he patted him on the shoulder. "Look at those teens. They're drooling over her, not to mention Uncle Vernon, Uncle Dudley, and the rest of our uncles. They can't keep their eyes off her."

It was the deciding factor. Benjamin exploded with outrage. He wanted everyone to know Samantha belonged to him. He walked over to her. Meanwhile, as soon as Cassandra noticed Benjamin, she sashayed her way to the dance floor and blocked Benjamin's path, asking him for a dance. Benjamin declined, and without looking at her, he said they'd dance later and left, leaving Cassandra enraged.

Benjamin motioned for Samantha to dance. He approached her, took her hand in his, and led her to the dance floor. Samantha continued looking down at the ground as they danced slowly. When she lifted her head, she found Benjamin grinning at her. He had a glint in his eyes she had never seen before. For a moment, time stood still, as if they were the only two people in the universe. Her pulse pounded as Benjamin leaned in closer. He gave her a smile. Their lips met, and they kissed.

"Bravo!"

Everyone applauded when they kissed.

Mrs. McClain jokingly elbowed her husband in the ribs. "I did not know our son was so romantic," she chuckled, shaking her head.

"Like father, like son," Mr. McClain answered, grinning as well.

Benjamin grasped Samantha's shoulders and kissed her firmly, and Samantha allowed him to do so. She was surprised why his family cheered and allowed him to kiss another girl in front of them. She also noticed that no one had addressed Rosalie's mother. The actual score between Benjamin and his wife intrigued her.

That little exhibition enraged Cassandra. She stood there for a moment, watching them dance and kiss. Then she walked to the bar, drank her martini, and ordered vodka straight up, which she also drank. She was green with envy as Benjamin and Samantha danced too close together. She had never witnessed Benjamin act in that manner before, not even with her. When Cassandra saw them kissing again, she snapped and threw the glass on the ground.

"That crone," she remarked.

"Did you notice what she's wearing?" her friends said when they came over to see her. "She is dressed in Jimmy Choo shoes and designer jeans. How could she afford to buy them?"

"She's a gold digger. I'm sure Benjamin purchased it for her," Cassandra said. "I can't let this happen."

Cassandra and her friends plotted to beat Samantha at her own game. They devised a scheme to humiliate her in the most terrible way possible. Her pals suggested a swimming competition the next day.

"But I don't feel like swimming," Cassandra commented.

"It's not about swimming, girl! It all boils down to showcasing your attributes," her friends elaborated. Cassandra had the most beautiful physique they'd ever seen. They were confident she would win. "Besides, you were the best swimmer in high school. You'd easily defeat a nanny."

"Oh, I see," Cassandra remarked slyly. "You're all so diabolical!"

They all busted out laughing.

Cassandra surprised everyone the next morning by announcing a new event.

"Swimming competition for women aged 20 to 25 years old. Anyone who can beat me will receive an ultimate shopping spree in Beverly Hills."

As expected, many participants signed up for the contest to show off their swimming ability. Cassandra and her friends went through the long list of names, but Samantha's name was missing.

"Oh, Cassie, she needs to compete. What's the point of this competition if you can't show everyone that you have a better figure than she does?" Her pals said.

"You are correct," Cassandra responded.

Cassandra approached Samantha after being persuaded by her friends to do so.

"Come on, Samantha. Don't you want to win the ultimate shopping spree? With your paycheck, I'm sure a new wardrobe is out of the question. This is your chance."

Samantha didn't like the tone of her voice. A raging rush of rage was rising within her.

"For your information, I have shopped all over the world. In fact, I despise shopping locally. I'd rather visit Paris. That is the place to be right now."

"Oh, my goodness," Cassandra said. "What a vivid imagination you have. As if! What about a friendly wager between the two of us? The winner takes it all. What's the prize? So, if you defeat me, I'll leave you and Benjamin alone. I vow I won't bother you, and I'll never set foot in his house again. But if I win, you'll resign from your job and leave his house. Deal?"

Cassandra's proposal surprised Samantha.

Why are people so obsessed with wagering? And why does Cassandra act as though Benjamin is single? Is she willing to be a mistress?

"Well?" Cassandra asked.

"What difference does it make whether I compete with you or not?" Samantha asked. "I will not participate in your stupid games. Remember, I'm the nanny. I have to watch Rosalie."

"Are you terrified of competing with a little old me?" Cassandra challenged her with narrow eyes.

"I think she realizes you're more attractive and better than her, Cassie," Cassandra's pals mocked.

Samantha knew well that she was being bullied. On the other hand, the opportunity presented itself, and it was too good to pass up. Lately, she had thought of moving on with her life. She'd been staying at Benjamin's house for nearly two months and had outstayed her welcome. Samantha knew that last part was a lie. She was only making excuses for her actions. Perhaps she was trying to convince herself that it was time to leave. Samantha knew she needed to protect herself. Rosalie informed her that her mother would return home soon. They couldn't possibly share a house. Three's a crowd. Samantha needed to leave before she arrived. Her life was becoming more challenging than she expected. She escaped an arranged marriage, but then found herself in a love triangle. She was looking for an impossible love relationship with Benjamin. She would have had a different perspective if Benjamin had been single. It was now time for her to focus on resolving her issue with her father. She'd been putting it off for far too long. It was time for her to return home.

"OK, Cassandra, you've got a deal!" Samantha decided without giving it any more thought.

Cassandra and her friends exchanged a sly grin and a sidelong glance.

"It's a deal!" Cassandra stated.

The two women clasped their hands in agreement.

CHAPTER THIRTEEN

Benjamin's cousins and nieces signed up to compete in the swimming event, but they could not do so because it was only open to individuals aged 20 to 25. They were underage or overaged.

Samantha and Cassandra were two of the six competitors that met the age requirement. Cassandra's companions stayed behind to carry out Plan B—a backup plan if the first failed.

The contestants formed a line and took turns walking around the pool, presenting themselves as if they were in a beauty pageant. Cassandra was first, and everyone applauded. She was a vision of perfection: tall, blonde, and beautiful. Cassandra was not shy about flaunting her stunning figure. She was wearing a high-cut, black one-piece swimsuit that showed off her toned form and plenty of cleavage, confident that no one could match her beauty.

Samantha was the last to appear, and when she walked out to the poolside, she turned heads, and all eyes were on her. She was the center of attention, and everyone nodded in approval. She looked gorgeous in a purple two-piece, showcasing her stunning bikini body with amazing abs and a tiny waist.

Cassandra's cheeks reddened, and she gnashed her teeth in wrath. She didn't expect a nanny to have a killer physique. How could that be?

"That witch! She always spoils my plans!"

Meanwhile, Benjamin was in the barn talking to the ranch caretaker when his nephew, Chuck, raced up to him.

"Come on, Uncle Ben. You should see Samantha in her two-piece bikini. She's a knockout!"

"What are you talking about, Chuck?" Benjamin asked.

"Samantha, Cassandra, and some friends have entered the upcoming swimming competition. Come on, let's go! It will begin shortly."

Benjamin followed Chuck, with the caretaker close behind. They heard groups of people growing louder around the pool area. Benjamin pushed his way to the front of the crowd. It was a sight to behold as the six finalists strolled around the pool and posed for photographs with Grandpa McClain.

Benjamin's eyes widened as he focused on Samantha. It was refreshing to see her enjoying herself. His mouth dropped open and his brow wrinkled. Samantha, sultry and alluring, raised Benjamin's and everyone else's temperature as she strolled by them. She was stunning!

Cassandra spotted Benjamin in the crowd watching the event, and she made a point of passing by him, giving him her most sensual grin, while her hips playfully swayed back and forth.

Tim elbowed Benjamin in the side. He smiled and winked at him.

"One thing you could say about Cassandra is that she isn't shy," Benjamin said, shaking his head.

"She is. It's obvious she likes you!" Tim chuckled.

"No, thank you," Benjamin said.

The announcer then introduced the judges, Grandpa and Grandma McClain, as well as Benjamin's parents, Mr. and Mrs. McClain.

"Woo-hoo! Go, Grandpa!"

Everyone cheered.

The six participants were ready for the race. Samantha faced the pool in her assigned section, while Cassandra was next to her. Cassandra winked and smirked, as if to imply she couldn't defeat her. Samantha ignored her.

Finally, the announcer remarked, "On the count of three, I will blow my whistle, and the race will begin. One, two, three!" He blew the whistle.

The contestants jumped into the pool. They each swam across the pool and back. Cassandra was several yards ahead of everyone, and Samantha was close behind. Cassandra could taste victory as she advanced more boldly. All eyes were on Samantha as she continued plowing through the water as if she didn't have a care in the world. She stepped up her game at the last second, determined to beat Cassandra. Cassandra didn't expect Samantha to be a skilled swimmer. She didn't want to be outdone by an ordinary nanny. In desperation, she signaled her pals to proceed with Plan B. Cassandra's friends quickly positioned themselves behind the crowd, creating a distraction. They screamed so loudly that everyone shifted their attention to them for a minute. It was long enough for Cassandra to pretend she had calf pains and cry to Samantha for help. Samantha was almost to the finish line when she noticed Cassandra struggling in the water. She knew things were moving fast at this point. She didn't have time to think. Samantha swam over to Cassandra to save her, before she plummeted to the bottom of the pool. At least, that's what she thought. Cassandra swam to victory the minute Samantha dove below, leaving Samantha at the pool's bottom, still looking for her. Samantha ascended to the top and saw Cassandra holding the winning ribbon and her friends laughing at her. She knew they had duped her. They crowned Cassandra, the swimming champion.

Cassandra approached Samantha after the event and reminded her of their wager.

"You didn't play fair," Samantha said.

"A bet is a bet. You lost, and I expect you to honor our wager. Don't worry. I'm giving you a few days to pack your things and leave. Oh, and by the way, you will tell no one about any of this, okay?" Cassandra pouted and twisted her head sideways.

Samantha narrowed her eyes. Cassandra was cunning, but why did she allow herself to get sucked into her cruel games? Why did she let Cassandra walk all over her? The old Samantha would never let Cassandra get away with something like that. How could she have been so trusting? She had definitely matured.

THE ENTIRE FAMILY GATHERED in the family room to view old home movies. There were films of family picnics, Disneyland visits, and other activities. When Benjamin and his brothers were younger, they had a lot of fun torturing their cousins in the video. Except for Samantha, everyone had a great time. She was sitting in the corner, thinking about her impending departure. Samantha couldn't believe she let Cassandra fool her. She intended to leave, but she loathed being forced to do anything against her will. It should still be her decision.

It was getting late, and everyone was leaving. They heard about a new nightclub in town and wanted to check it out. Cassandra and her pals were the first to go. Benjamin's siblings and cousins followed a few minutes later.

"Sam, are you sure you don't want to go nightclubbing with us? It'll be fun," Benjamin speculated.

"It's OK, Ben. I'm exhausted. I'm ready to go to bed and have a good night's sleep."

Benjamin walked her to her room and kissed her on the lips.

"Should I stay here tonight?" he joked.

Samantha gave him a perplexed look.

"I was kidding, Sam. Please don't frown." Benjamin laughed.

Samantha merely nodded and remained silent.

Benjamin raised his brows, confused. "Sam, are you all right? Do you want me to stay?"

"Don't be silly. I'm fine. I'm just tired."

"Okay, I'm going to go now, but I'll be back soon."

Samantha said nothing. She entered the room quietly after Benjamin had left, closing the door behind her.

Benjamin was on his way out when he ran into his nephew, Chuck, who was holding a DVD. He spent the night in his room putting the video together.

"Anyone want to see Grandpa's 85th birthday event?" he asked.

"I'm leaving now, but maybe tomorrow," Benjamin said as he messed up his hair.

"How about you, Grandpa?"

"Sure, I'm not sleepy yet."

Chuck inserted the disk into the DVD player and sat next to his grandfather. Grandma McClain asked what they were watching.

"Grandma, it's today's event footage," Chuck said.

"Oh, how wonderful!" Grandma McClain said as she sat in the chair next to her husband.

"Can you fast-forward to the swimming competition? That was the highlight of the day," Grandpa McClain commented.

"Somehow I knew you'd want to see those bikini-clad candidates again. Don't deny it. You were drooling as you watched them compete." Grandma McClain chuckled.

"I may be old, but I'm not dead," Grandpa McClain said, laughing.

Chuck yawned. "Grandpa, I'll watch it tomorrow. I'm exhausted. Good night, Grandma and Grandpa." He mumbled as he kissed his grandparents and proceeded to his room.

Cassandra was strutting and showing off her physique when Grandma McClain entered the room with a glass of milk in hand, but Samantha was the obvious winner in a bikini competition.

It was becoming late, and Grandma McClain yawned. Grandpa McClain decided it was time to retire to bed and watch the home video again in the morning. He was about to turn it off when they noticed Cassandra struggling in the water.

"Was that Cassandra?" Grandma McClain asked. How could they have missed this part of the event?

Grandpa McClain replayed the tape, and they watched it. He paused the video. He locked his gaze on his wife. Before Grandma McClain could say anything, Grandpa McClain placed his fingers over her lips.

"Don't say anything. We'll talk about it later," Grandpa McClain stated. He didn't want to disrupt any of the scheduled activities for the children the next day. On the last day of the family event, he hoped to resolve the issue as a family.

The next day, they went about their business as normal. They went to the barn to see the animals, fed the ducks, and swam in the pool. A few adults cruised around the lake in boats. Following that, they went on a vineyard tour for wine tasting. After the kids had gone to bed, Benjamin's parents invited everyone to the lake, where they continued the celebration by telling amusing stories around the campfire. They provided toasted marshmallows, hot dogs, hot chocolate, and wine from their vineyard.

Samantha had a troubled expression on her face. She excused herself and informed Grandpa and Grandma McClain that she wasn't feeling well. Cassandra gave her an odd look. Grandpa and Grandma McClain shook their heads when they saw it. They had a clear idea of what was going on.

Benjamin was sitting on a tree stump, and Samantha didn't even look at him as she passed by. He couldn't help but wonder whether there was something wrong with her. Since the swimming competition, she had been acting strangely. He went after her.

Samantha was getting ready for bed when she heard a knock at the door.

"Sam, are you awake?"

"Good evening, sir," she murmured, trying not to yawn in front of him as she opened the door.

"Sir? Since when did you call me Sir?" Benjamin chuckled, but came to a halt as he noticed her standing in front of him, her hair messy but still looking beautiful. He admired her wholeheartedly. Benjamin couldn't believe how quickly his heart rate increased simply by gazing at Samantha. She was all he had wished for in his life. As his hands cupped her face, his lips met hers softly. He kissed her lips again, more passionately this time. He broke the kiss and drew back.

"If I keep going, I can't promise I'll stop," he added.

"Perhaps you're right. We should stop," Samantha sighed heavily. She wanted him to kiss her and put his arms around her, but she didn't want anybody to see them in such an awkward position, especially since they were at his parents' house. What would they say if she had an affair with their married son? Mrs. McClain was nice to her, and she couldn't hurt her. But she couldn't figure out why her entire family didn't protest when Benjamin kissed her on the dance floor. Did they disapprove of their daughter-in-law?

Benjamin didn't want the night to end.

"Get ready," he advised. "I'll meet you downstairs in five minutes."

Samantha unconsciously nodded, startled by the surprising twinkle in his eyes. After Benjamin had left her room, she went to the bathroom to freshen up. She changed into Mickey Mouse pajamas and walked downstairs, where she found Benjamin drinking coffee on the countertop. As soon as he spotted her, he smiled.

"Do you want coffee, tea, or hot chocolate?" he asked.

Samantha frowned, perplexed why he was acting in such an unexpected and enjoyable manner.

"I don't want to bother you. I'll get my own."

"No, no, it's not a problem."

"Whatever you're having, it's OK."

Benjamin offered her a cup of coffee.

"It's our night, just the two of us," Benjamin explained.

"Our night? What do you mean?"

"It means I need to spend some time alone with my girl."

Benjamin grasped Samantha's hand and tried to lead her away. "Come on, let me show you another of my secret hideouts here at the ranch."

He brought a pillow, a blanket, a thermos of hot coffee, and a bag of freshly baked bread. Benjamin held Samantha's hand as they strolled along the lake, stopping at a secluded spot surrounded by trees, bushes, and tall plants. He placed the blanket on the grass and laid the pillow on it. He sat down and reached for her hand. Samantha smiled as she sat next to him.

Samantha asked about his upbringing, and Benjamin's face lit up as he retold memories of his youth. He told stories about how his family spent Christmas with the McClain's in Aspen, Martha's Vineyard, and other places. Benjamin's eyes twinkled, and he never ran out of stories to tell. His large family captivated Samantha because she was an only child. It was intriguing to hear his story. They stayed up late talking and laughing.

Moments later, she yawned.

"It's no wonder you're sleepy. Look at the time. It's three in the morning. I guess I'm ready for bed as well."

Benjamin gathered everything, and as they returned to the house, they saw Cassandra and her friends arriving from the nightclub.

"What are you people up to?" Cassandra asked, her brow furrowed and her gaze suspiciously riveted on them.

"Just staring at the stars," Benjamin replied as they walked toward the house, holding Samantha's hand.

Cassandra exploded in anger as they watched them leave.

"I'm going to pluck every hair from that cunning little witch's head."

"Don't worry, Cassie," her friends reassured her. "In a few days, she'll be gone from Benjamin's life, and you'll have him all to yourself."

"I can hardly wait." Cassandra said with a devilish grin.

CHAPTER FOURTEEN

Samantha felt tired, but she poured herself a bath. She needed to decompress after her date with Benjamin at the lake before going to bed. She stepped into the hot, foamy water with her favorite gardenia bubble bath. The warm water relieved some tension. The lovely scent filled her senses, and she closed her eyes and fell asleep.

A faint tap at the door jolted her awake. Samantha checked the clock on the wall; it was 7:30 a.m. She couldn't believe she'd fallen asleep in the tub.

"Just a moment," she said.

Samantha grabbed her towel and wrapped it around herself. She rushed towards the door and flung it open, and what a sight it was. Benjamin was wearing blue shorts and a white shirt, leaning against the door, smiling at her.

If only she'd known. Benjamin had the shock of his life when he saw her with a little towel wrapped over her. He could smell the sweet-smelling soap all over her body. The sight of her roused him. He fixed his attention on her. He wanted to touch her, embrace her, and kiss her, and he wasn't sure he could resist making love to her now.

"Yes? What is it?" Samantha questioned Benjamin when he remained silent.

"Do you realize you're driving me crazy, woman?" he said.

Samantha gave him a false grin. "I didn't know I'd done that."

Benjamin was in a daze, staring at Samantha.

"Ben, uh... Do you mind if I don't join you and your family today? I know we're leaving tomorrow, but I'm not feeling well."

Samantha reasoned that it was best if she separated herself from him. She had to accept that they didn't belong together. Samantha intended to quit her job as soon as they got home. Not because of Cassandra, but because she knew it was the right thing to do. She adored Rosalie too much to allow herself to become involved with Benjamin. It was time to put a stop to her foolishness.

"Are you ill? What's the matter? Do I need to call a doctor? Tell me," Benjamin asked, concerned about her.

Samantha shook her head and smiled tiredly at him. "Ben, you're overreacting. I'm OK. It's simply that I overworked myself. I'm exhausted."

Benjamin stood there, studying her as if to ensure himself that she was OK. "Alright, get some rest. I'll check in with you later."

Samantha smiled, but with a mournful look in her eyes as she looked up, and it didn't escape him.

"Are you certain you're okay, Sam? You appear paler than usual. Maybe I should stay with you."

"Don't be silly, Ben. I said that I was OK. Don't worry. I'm a big girl. I can take care of myself."

Benjamin tilted his head, his gaze locked on her. A kiss on the lips was his last act of affection before walking away. Samantha fought back tears as she watched him walk away.

"BECAUSE THIS IS OUR last night, I'd prefer to spend the rest of the time together. If you have a date or need to go somewhere else tonight, cancel it." Grandpa McClain gave the command.

"Yes, sir," everyone said as they laughed and saluted him.

Grandma McClain brought some popcorn and lemonade, and they all settled in to watch the home video. Everyone laughed at their shenanigans during Grandpa's birthday party. Chuck even recorded the event's preparations and Benjamin's dance with Samantha. They shouted and applauded when they kissed.

Cassandra scowled and pouted.

Everyone cheered each girl in her bathing suit. Cassandra's walk around the pool garnered rousing applause. She smiled at them, but glared when they cheered louder when Samantha appeared and strolled around posing for everyone. Cassandra smirked loudly this time.

The swimming competition started. Except for Cassandra and her friends, everyone cheered again. Cassandra's eyes widened. She turned pale and terrified. Her heart was pounding frantically. Her friends exchanged looks. How could they have failed to see this coming? They thought they had everything perfectly planned, but they didn't expect someone to record the event. Sweat droplets formed on their brows.

"Wow! Samantha had gained the upper hand. She is going to win. Come on, you're almost there," Tim cheered, although he knew Cassandra had won the event. Suddenly, the room was deafeningly silent. How did they miss this part of the event? Samantha was only a few feet away from the finish line. They saw Cassandra struggling in the water and watched as she went under. They saw Samantha dive in search of her, but Cassandra came to the surface quickly, swimming faster to the finish line and declaring herself the winner. Cassandra cheated. That was clear to them.

Cassandra's cheeks became scarlet. They caught her in the act, and she couldn't deny what she had done. As revealed by the video, she faked her drowning incident. She didn't know what to say.

Benjamin stated strongly that one thing he loathed was liars and cheaters. "If you're not being honest with us, Cassie, we'll have to talk to your friends to sort this out."

"I'm not sure why you think I cheated," Cassandra questioned.

"Are you suggesting my nephew Chuck tampered with the video?"

Cassandra maintained her denial of any impropriety in the swimming competition.

"You leave us with no choice except to turn this over to the police so they can investigate," Benjamin continued. He reasoned that by scaring Cassandra, he might get a confession.

His parents and grandparents looked at Benjamin with trepidation. They didn't expect to involve the cops, but before they could protest, they saw Benjamin shaking his head at them. They read his mind. Benjamin was entrapping Cassandra to persuade or frighten her into confessing. And it paid off.

"I love you, Ben. I've been in love with you for years, but you've never given me the chance to prove it. I was looking forward to becoming Mrs. Benjamin McClain after this celebration, but it disappointed me when you showed up with that witch, Samantha. I tried to seduce you, but you continued to reject me. I grew irritated when you portrayed her as the nanny while lavishing her with special attention. My pals and I conspired to destroy whatever relationship you may have had with her. I planned the swimming competition so you could see that I'm better than Samantha. I intended for you to fall in love with me, but the plan went awry. We didn't expect a nanny to beat me in this game. I didn't expect her to be a skilled swimmer either. I hate losing, especially to a nanny, so when I realized she was going to win, I improvised and pretended I was drowning. When Samantha jumped in to help me, I seized the opportunity and swam to victory. Don't you see? I needed to win. I made a bet with her that if I lost, I would stop bothering you, and if she lost, she would quit her job and leave your house immediately."

Benjamin took a deep breath before speaking. "Cassie, we welcome you and your friends to our house, since our families have known each other for a long time. I'm glad you found me appealing and even fell in love with me, as you have with so many of your boyfriends, but this is not the way to go about it. And I've already told you before that I love you as my younger sister. That's all. Putting someone's life in danger solely to get your way is irresponsible and reckless. What if Samantha drowned while trying to save you? Did you ever think about that?"

For a long time, Cassandra remained silent, staring at the floor.

Grandma McClain sprang to her feet, visibly disturbed. "Cassie, I'm sorry, but you and your pals are no longer welcome at the ranch. We will not tolerate such a horrible act. Pack your stuff and leave as soon as possible. Our driver will take you and your friends to the hotel."

Cassandra sobbed as she hurried to her room, her pals trailing behind her. They packed their belongings and left without saying goodbye.

"So, now that the troublemaker is gone, why don't you call Samantha and let's celebrate? That's probably why she's been cooped up in her room all day. What do you think, Ben?" Grandpa McClain asked.

Benjamin had a devilish smirk on his face. "No, Grandpa, I've got a better idea. Let us continue as if nothing had happened. I'd want to play along with her."

Everyone's faces were filled with apprehension. Benjamin burst out laughing.

"Don't worry, I cordially invite you to our wedding."

"Did you propose yet?" his parents asked.

"Soon, I promise," Benjamin said with a chuckle.

"Well, hurry along and give me another grandchild," his mother jokingly said.

Everyone laughed and giggled as Benjamin reddened at the comment.

"Soon, I promise, Mom," he said, laughing. "Very soon."

Benjamin approached Samantha's bedroom door and knocked. There was no answer, so he waited a few seconds before trying again, but the result was the same. He turned the doorknob and opened the door.

"Sam, are you awake?"

She didn't answer.

Benjamin struggled for a light switch in the dark and knocked something over. He eventually located the light switch and turned it on. Benjamin noticed Samantha in bed, her covers drawn up to her chin, fast asleep.

Benjamin continued looking at her while she slept. He kissed her on the lips as he knelt. The kiss jolted Samantha awake. When she recognized who it was, she returned Benjamin's kiss. She protested at first, but it didn't stop him from clinging closer and kissing her deeper. The intensity of the kiss took her breath away. For a while, she relished the warmth of his embrace, but immediately regained her composure and drew away.

"Samantha, what's the matter?" he asked, his arms around her, not wanting her to break away from him.

"Ben, this isn't right," she said as she turned away from him.

"But why?"

Samantha returned her attention to him, tears running down her cheeks. "I can't let myself fall in love with you," she trembled.

"Sam, I'm not sure I understand. No matter how much you deny it, I know you have feelings for me. I know it."

"That's true, Ben. I admit I have feelings for you, and it pains me to keep them hidden anymore, but I'm not desperate to be your mistress. I love Rosalie so much, and I didn't want to break your family."

"Mistress?"

Benjamin was trying hard not to laugh, and Samantha fought to remove her hand from his because he clutched it so strongly.

"This is precisely what I mean. You're still holding my hand. You keep throwing your arms around me and kissing me for no apparent reason. I'm not that kind of girl. Your daughter is sleeping next door, and who knows where your wife is? I'm not sure what kind of family you have that would allow a married man like you to have an affair with the nanny."

Benjamin couldn't help but chuckle.

"What's so funny about it?"

"I'm drawn to your innocence. For the record, my dear Samantha, I do not plan to make you my mistress. I thought you knew about Rosalie. If you had asked me sooner, you would have realized I had never been married! "

"Are you a single father?"

"No, not at all. Rosalie is my goddaughter. Bradley, my best friend, and his wife, Lacey, were killed in a car accident a few years ago. Rosalie's legal guardian is me."

"Oh, my gosh! Rosalie knows this? Does she know anything about her parents? "

"Yes, she knows. I hid nothing from her."

"I'm confused. Rosalie told me her mother is in France."

"She must be referring to her godmother, Courtney," Benjamin said. "Rosalie was five when her parents died. We told her I was going to be her new father and Courtney was going to be her new mother. It was tough for her to accept it at first, but she ultimately became accustomed to it. I believe it is still illegal to marry your cousin."

Samantha's heart skipped a beat as she realized there was something between them after all—he wasn't married.

"Oh, yeah, I see. This is awkward. I thought you were..."

Benjamin cut her off in the middle of her sentence with a passionate kiss on the lips, and Samantha couldn't stand it anymore, so she leaned forward and kissed him. It felt good to be loved by the man who had taken over your heart.

AFTER A HEARTY BREAKFAST, everyone packed up early the next morning to avoid rush hour traffic. Samantha was mystified why Cassandra and her friends hadn't joined them. She asked Benjamin's cousins and nephews, but they didn't give her a straight answer.

"We've all been sworn to secrecy. All we can recommend is that you speak with Grandpa before leaving. It's critical," Chuck suggested.

"All right, gotcha," she replied.

Samantha searched for Grandpa McClain and found him in the kitchen.

"Where are Cassandra and her friends, Grandpa?" she asked.

"We discovered your little bet, Samantha," Grandpa McClain stated.

Samantha's eyes widened. "How did you find out about that?"

"Well, thanks to Chuck, he recorded the family gathering by mounting the video recorder on a tripod. Cassandra and her companions were unaware of it since it was hidden. We saw how Cassandra deceived you to win the bet. We caught her red-handed, and she confessed. Grandma McClain booted her and her friends from the residence last night."

"She did?"

"Yes, so don't worry about your bet. She's probably trying to get you out of Benjamin's house. Cassandra must be jealous of you for doing this. She knew well that you posed a threat to her. And she was right. Benjamin adores you."

"Grandpa!"

When they heard Benjamin's voice behind them, Samantha and Grandpa McClain turned around.

"Grandpa, do you recall what I told you a minute ago?" Benjamin asked.

Grandpa McClain burst out laughing. "Oh, you mean you won't tell Samantha about what happened to Cassandra?"

"That's correct, Grandpa, but what did you do? You told Samantha, anyway."

"I'm sorry, Ben, but I couldn't help myself. Samantha seemed concerned. I'm sure you had something heinous planned for her. We like Samantha. I believe she has proven herself to the family."

"Grandpa, remember that's a secret, too? You're killing me right now!" Benjamin pouted like a toddler.

Samantha gave Benjamin a scathing look. "So, you were cooking something awful for me, weren't you?" she joked. "You'll get it if you don't confess."

Benjamin shook his head and shut his mouth.

"So, you're not talking, are you?"

Benjamin shook his head again.

"OK, I'm done." Samantha feigned to walk away and was ready to grasp Benjamin's arm to pinch him, but he was faster than she was, withdrawing it from her reach in time and smiling gleefully as she chased him outside the house as he ran in circles.

"Go, Samantha, go!" shouted everyone.

"Wait a second! Why are you rooting for her? I'm your family?" Benjamin busted out laughing.

"Sorry, dude. We love Samantha more," Tim stated.

"Traitor!" yelled Benjamin.

Benjamin called it quits and raised his hands in surrender. He lifted Samantha off the ground and swung her around several times, laughing like children.

It was time to go. Everyone hugged their grandparents and expressed thanks for a wonderful family reunion. Samantha was taken aback when Benjamin's parents and grandparents told her they were looking forward to seeing her again at the next get-together with a child in tow. She found the conversation odd. What were they saying?

Moments later, one by one, the cars pulled out of the driveway, preparing for the long journey home.

CHAPTER FIFTEEN

It was time to leave Santa Barbara after a relaxing and enjoyable family vacation. In his brand-new Lexus LX 570, Benjamin took the first turn onto Highway 101. Rosalie sat in the middle, next to Samantha, while Jack sat up front. Rosalie kept them entertained by telling them about her school, the animals at the barn, and a Disney movie she wanted to see while taking photos of the places they passed.

They took the next exit to San Francisco and ate lunch at a restaurant on the waterfront. They wandered about and browsed at various stores, taking advantage of the pleasant weather. After a quick stop at Ghirardelli Square, they were back on the freeway, occasionally stopping at one or two wayside fruit stalls along the way.

Benjamin said he needed a break after traveling for several hours. Jack took over the driving after a brief break at a rest stop and some stretching to loosen up. Benjamin sat next to Samantha, who kept looking out the window and avoiding eye contact with him. Benjamin's mouth made a cute little twist, as if he was trying to hide his grin. He redirected his gaze to Rosalie in the third row. She was fast asleep.

"Could you please pull over at the next gas station, Jack?" Benjamin stated.

When Jack looked at the fuel gauge, he noticed they had more than half a tank left. "We still have gas, Sir Benjamin."

"No, I need to get something to drink."

"We have drinks in the back. I can pull over to get it."

"No, don't bother. I'd like a hot cup of coffee. Just pull over to the next gas station. Let's also get some gas and possibly some hot dogs and potato chips."

"All right, sir, you're the boss."

When he spotted a gas station sign, Jack exited. Benjamin handed him a $100 bill for food and gasoline.

As soon as Jack walked inside the store, Benjamin glanced at Rosalie. He flashed a devilish grin when he saw she was still sleeping. He noticed Samantha peering out the window. Benjamin startled her by laying down on her lap and saying nothing. He reached up and softly touched her lips. He drew her face down and kissed her. Samantha gasped with delight as she reciprocated his kiss. It struck them with a bolt of electricity, a spark that ignited a fire in their hearts. Benjamin kissed her lips again, as if he couldn't get enough of her, and their kisses became more passionate as they sighed. When the door swung open, it startled them. Samantha straightened up, and before she could catch her breath, Jack handed the cup of coffee to Benjamin, who didn't bother to get up. He remained in her lap, smiling.

"Are you okay, Samantha? Do you want me to get you a drink? You appear out of breath," Jack said.

Samantha was dumbfounded. She was blushing, mortified, and embarrassed. As Benjamin struggled to hold back his laughter, she felt like a teenager caught by her parents making out on the porch swing.

"Don't worry, Jack. She was just exhausted," he explained.

Jack nodded and handed him the hot dogs and chips. He returned outside to fill the gas tank.

Samantha clutched Benjamin's side. "You know, you're a sneaky little devil, don't you? That's why you sent Jack away."

Benjamin gave her a sneaky grin. "They've called me worse." He laughed. "Can you blame me? I'd want to spend some time with you."

As Jack returned to the car, Benjamin drew her head down to his and kissed her long and lingeringly. By the time Jack got in the car, Samantha had already placed a pillow behind her head and was preparing to nap, while Benjamin remained resting on her lap, grasping her hand, no longer concealing his affections for Samantha. Jack grinned. He could tell that a special bond was developing between them.

The drive back to Seattle was uneventful, with glorious weather the entire time. They arrived home before midnight. Linda, Nancy, and Lucy were waiting in the driveway.

"They want to see you all at our next family reunion," Benjamin said as he handed Linda a few bottles of wine from his grandparents.

"Oh, how wonderful! I'll make sure we come along the next time," Linda answered.

It overjoyed Samantha to tell everyone about her vacation. Jack would periodically interrupt to tell his story.

"I wish we could have been there," Nancy said.

"Don't worry, Nancy. We'll all be there next year. The McClain's have invited us," Linda said, beaming.

"I can't wait. I'd never been to the McClain family retreat in Santa Barbara before," Nancy said.

"I've been to Santa Barbara many times and had never appreciated how beautiful it is until today. Santa Barbara is beautiful," Samantha said, a grin on her face.

"Samantha, you sound as though you've been everywhere. You're only fantasizing. How could a maid like you afford a vacation? Who is deceiving whom here?" Lucy spoke up.

Linda merely had to give Lucy the nasty look to silence her. Lucy walked away, enraged. Samantha stood there watching her walk away, wondering how long Lucy would be upset with her. She had no idea what she had done to irritate her.

BENJAMIN WAS AT THE airport, waiting for his flight to New York for a two-day conference. He was irritated and anxious as he repeatedly tried to call Samantha at home, but no one answered the phone. Lucy answered his last attempt.

"What happened to Samantha?" he asked.

"She's entertaining a visitor out on the patio," Lucy stated.

"Who is this visitor?" he asked again.

"Samuel came to see Samantha," Lucy stated. "I overheard him inviting Samantha to his parents' anniversary dinner tomorrow night."

"An invitation to a party? Please call Samantha right now!" He gave the order.

"Yes, Sir Benjamin," she said, but Lucy didn't move. She waited for a few minutes before picking up the phone again.

"Please hold, sir. I'm still looking for her," Lucy remarked. When she heard Benjamin grunting and yelling at the other end of the phone, she broke into a wicked smile.

Samantha was talking to Samuel in the garden when Lucy came.

"Hello Samuel, what are you doing here?" Lucy asked, making sure she said it loud enough for Benjamin to hear. She pointed the receiver at Samuel.

"I was hoping Samantha would accept my invitation to my parents' anniversary dinner. I didn't have a date, so I figured I'd ask her out."

Benjamin could hear it clearly. He was infuriated with jealousy and kicked the chair next to him.

"I'm sorry, Samantha. I almost forgot about it. Sir Benjamin wants to speak with you," Lucy said as she handed her the phone.

Samantha narrowed her eyes and gave Lucy a suspicious look, before grabbing the phone from her.

"Please excuse me, Samuel. I've had to take this," she remarked as she headed back inside the house. "Hello, Ben. Are you still at the airport?"

"Yes, I'm still at the airport, but never mind that. What's the deal with Samuel inviting you to a party?"

"How did you know?" she asked, annoyed with Lucy. "Yes, it is true. Samuel invites us all to his parents' anniversary party. Isn't that nice?"

"I don't want you to go anywhere when I'm not there, Sam."

"What are you talking about, Ben? He invited all of us."

"It was clear what he wanted from you."

Samantha grinned. "Are you sure you're not jealous?" She made fun of him.

For a while, Benjamin remained silent.

"Are you jealous?" Samantha questioned again.

"You bet I am," he answered.

Samantha smiled when she heard this.

"Okay, Sam. I must admit I am jealous. Actually, it's more than that. I'm canceling my trip and going home right away. If Samuel is still at the house when I arrive, I will smack him across the face."

"Don't you think you're exaggerating, Ben? You should continue your business trip. I promise I'm not going with Samuel, okay? Rosalie expressed a desire to visit the park tomorrow, so Linda and I would accompany her."

"Do you promise?"

"I promise."

For a while, there was silence between them.

"Sam, please put Linda on the line."

Samantha grimaced before passing the phone to Linda, who was getting ready to serve them lemonade and cookies.

"It's Ben," she whispered.

Linda took the phone from her. "Yes, Ben. What is it?" She murmured into the phone, frowning as she listened.

"Make sure Samuel is out of the house in two minutes. As soon as he leaves, lock the gate and the doors. Call security and tell them he is not allowed to enter the gate anymore. I don't want that bastard coming back to the house. Do you understand?"

Linda choked on her saliva. Benjamin was acting childish.

"Yes, Benjamin. I'm going to have Jack toss Samuel out on the street right now."

"I'm not kidding, Linda," he yelled. "Do precisely what I tell you."

Linda heard him slam the phone down, saying something she couldn't understand, while Samantha struggled to hide her emotions, wondering whether to laugh or get upset at Benjamin's abrupt reaction.

"What is going on with Benjamin? He is acting like a jerk," Linda said, shaking her head.

"I don't know, Linda. Your guess is as good as mine," Samantha replied.

Two days had passed. Benjamin arrived at the airport and jumped into the car as soon as he spotted Jack waiting for him at the curb.

"Drive as fast as possible," he told Jack.

"Linda asked me to stop by the drugstore to pick up her medication, because it's on the way home," Jack said.

"Is it urgent?" asked Benjamin.

"No," Jack answered.

"Jack, drive me home first, and then pick up the medication," Benjamin remarked.

"OK, sir. You're the boss."

As they drove home, there was an awkward stillness in the car. Linda was waiting for them as their car pulled into the driveway.

Ben's first question was, "Where's Sam?"

"She's in the garden. Where else?" Linda spoke up.

Benjamin put his briefcase on the chair and searched every corner of the garden before he walked to the greenhouse. Samantha was busy trimming rose bushes and planting fresh seedlings. Samantha seemed surprised to see Benjamin standing next to her, especially when he grabbed her hand, drew her behind the tree, and kissed her on the lips. He kissed her again, deeper and harder, with a ferocious intensity that made Samantha feel weak as she kissed him back with a flaming passion of her own. They were both trembling as he ended the kiss.

"Ben, what was that for?" Samantha inquired when she had regained her breath.

He smiled. "I missed you."

Samantha burst out laughing. "Cute, Ben, adorable!"

Now that Benjamin was back, the sexual tension between them became stronger, as if time and sound had stopped for them. They were at it whenever they could, but they'd never gone beyond a kiss. Benjamin respected Samantha and wanted to take their relationship carefully until she was ready. They took great care not to raise suspicion, and no one at home noticed their flirty moments.

Samantha was in the kitchen to make a snack for Rosalie when she got home from school. Rosalie impressed her when she showed her progress report card. Rosalie outperformed the rest of the class. Samantha was in a good mood and didn't realize Benjamin had arrived until he cleared his throat as he leaned against the door.

Samantha let out a tiny gasp, taken aback by his abrupt appearance, as she hadn't expected him home at that hour. She also did not hear his car arrive in the driveway. Was he trying to catch her off guard?

"Sorry, Sam. I didn't want to startle you. You looked adorable in your bare feet, singing and humming," Benjamin stated.

Samantha said nothing and paid little attention to him. She put the finger foods on the plate and poured orange juice into a glass to take it to Rosalie out on the patio when Benjamin held her hand. When he saw no one was around, he put the plate and glass on the counter, reached his hand to her chin and lifted it. Benjamin dropped his head and kissed her softly on the lips. He threw his arms around her waist and drew her in tight against him. Benjamin let her go, but he took her hand and headed toward the door.

Samantha was perplexed and inquired. "Ben, where are we going?"

"You'll see," he said. He opened and locked the bathroom door.

"Ben, what are we doing here? I have to serve Rosalie's snacks."

"Shh... Benjamin lifted her up and placed her on the bathroom counter. He bowed his head and kissed her lips. His kisses get more daring with each passing moment. The kiss made her weak because of the pleasure he sent through her body. Suddenly, they heard a knock on the door. The interruption irritated Benjamin.

"Are you in there, Sam?" Rosalie asked.

Benjamin and Samantha were both sweating hard and panting furiously, but neither said anything.

"Sam, are you in there?" Rosalie asked again.

Samantha and Benjamin heard Rosalie's anxious voice from outside the bathroom, as well as the repeated banging on the door when she did not respond within the minutes that had passed.

Samantha attempted to calm down. "Rosalie, I'm here. I'll be there in a moment. Why don't you wait for me on the terrace, dear, and I'll get you your snack?"

"OK, Sam," Rosalie said.

Samantha could hear Rosalie's footsteps as she walked away. She spoke in hushed tones to Ben. "Wait till I'm gone before you exit, okay?"

Benjamin smiled wryly at her. He grabbed her and kissed her hard on the lips, before letting her go. Samantha opened the door and shut it behind her, leaving Benjamin inside, trying not to laugh at Samantha's awkwardness.

"Yay!" screamed Rosalie when Samantha brought her snack.

"How's school today, Rosalie?"

"Sam, are you forgetting already? I told you we had an award ceremony this morning. I even showed you my report card."

"Oh, that's right," she said. "Sorry, Rosalie. I'm a little distracted today. I have no idea why."

Samantha fanned her face with both hands, occasionally turning her head towards the kitchen door, waiting for Benjamin to show up. She eventually saw him emerge from the kitchen. She gave him a kind grin.

"Hello, Ben," she greeted. "Rosalie, look who's arrived!"

Rosalie smiled and said, "Hi, Dad," as she ate her finger food.

Benjamin kissed Rosalie on the cheek. He drew a chair from the table and straddled it backward, crossing his arms over his back.

"Hello, Sam," he said casually.

"Would you like to join us for snacks?" Samantha asked.

"That's not what I'm hungry for," he whispered in her ears.

Samantha choked and gave him the side eye. Rosalie cast glances at Benjamin as he laughed aloud.

"You are a true original, Samantha," he said. "And your innocence is driving me insane," he muttered.

Samantha grimaced, but tried to hide it with a grin. She didn't want to show any signs of delight at his words. When he was around, her heart rate increased, and the mere sight of him caused her breathing to quicken. She wasn't sure how much longer she could resist his charm.

"Rosalie, let's go upstairs. It's time for your bath," Samantha said as she fumbled to gather the crayons and papers on the table.

"Leaving so soon? I just got here," Benjamin teased.

"Just never mind that. Let's go, Rosalie," Samantha said as she pulled her hand in a hurry, leaving Benjamin laughing at her nervousness and a puzzled look on Rosalie's face.

SAMANTHA COULDN'T SLEEP, no matter how hard she tried. She stood up, opened the door, and went downstairs to the kitchen to get something to drink. Samantha didn't bother turning on the light switch, since she didn't want to wake anyone in the house. When she opened the refrigerator door, a hand covered her mouth to keep her from screaming.

"Shh, it's me," Benjamin whispered softly.

Samantha smacked his arm. "Ben, you scared me half to death. Never do that again."

"Sorry, Sam. It was dark, and I didn't want to scare you."

Samantha sighed heavily. "Well, it's too late for that. What are you doing here, anyway?"

"Sam, let's go outside."

"What? Do you know what time it is?"

"Yes, I understand, but we cannot do anything in the house. So, let's head into the greenhouse. I have something to tell you."

Samantha gave him a sidelong and serious glance. She opened her mouth to object, to say something, anything, but Benjamin had already seized her hand and led her to the greenhouse. He wasted no time, and as soon as they stepped inside, he pressed her back against the wall, trapping her with his weight. He teased her body. Samantha groaned in delight. It was hard for her to resist what Benjamin was doing to her.

"Sam, you're a beautiful woman. I've never felt like this before. You resurrected the lost piece of me and made me whole again. I know I'm ready to take our relationship to the next level."

"Not until I know more about what type of relationship you have in mind," Samantha teased.

"We'll discuss that at length. In the meantime, I would like to enjoy this newfound relationship with my girlfriend."

My girlfriend! Samantha felt giddy.

Benjamin stared her in the eyes as they entered a small room in the greenhouse.

"You truly have an impressive collection of orchids here," Samantha commented as she heard him shut the door behind him.

Benjamin did not respond. Samantha turned around to see him leaning against the door, staring at her. She wasn't sure what to make of his intense stare, but his expression said it all. He wasn't interested in small conversation. Benjamin approached her, grabbed her into his arms, and dropped his kiss onto hers, brushing his lips along hers. She glanced up into his eyes, and their lips touched again. She watched as he stroked her arm and hand. This time, it was more sensuous, causing her body to tremble. He kissed her ears and neck, and then returned to her lovely lips.

Meanwhile, Samantha couldn't help but wonder where all this flirtation was heading. Sometimes she would tell him not to kiss her again, but she hoped he would ignore her. Samantha couldn't resist his charm. She could sense him yearning for her. Was she prepared to give himself over to him?

They kissed again, their breathing becoming hot and heavy. Samantha had become engrossed in the stolen moment of passion when the above sprinklers triggered, drenching them both. They hurried outside, laughing as they shook off the extra water from their clothes.

"There you are! I wondered where you'd gone," Linda said as she walked to the greenhouse, Lucy following behind. "Rosalie woke up and was looking for both of you."

"We'll be right there," Benjamin remarked, his voice irritated, as Samantha bowed her head in shame. Her face flushed deeply with humiliation.

Linda raised an eyebrow. She glanced at them with skepticism, but nodded before turning around to leave. Benjamin and Samantha trailed after her.

"To be continued," Benjamin muttered to Samantha, his annoyance evident.

"You mean saved by the bell? Fortunately, that spared us from the embarrassment of being seen having sex in the greenhouse," she mumbled.

"That's true. We'll do better next time," Benjamin teased, and Samantha pinched him on the side.

"Ouch! That hurt," he laughed.

Lucy scowled at them as she walked behind them. She had a feeling that something was going on between Benjamin and Samantha. She kept her jealousy hidden with her hatred and gave Samantha the evil look.

Samantha, you'll wake up one day and find it was all a dream. I'll make sure you go back to where you came from.

CHAPTER SIXTEEN

Lucy couldn't help but feel envious of Samantha, not just for her beauty, but also for the attention she received from Benjamin. She had feelings for him, since her mother worked with his parents in Santa Barbara. When her mother grew ill, she took over her job as head housekeeper when she was seventeen, right after high school. Benjamin took her in when he moved to Seattle and built his home there. He sent Lucy to culinary school, and hired her as his cook.

Lucy's feelings for Benjamin grew more intense and profound with each passing day. But Benjamin never found out how she felt about him. Lucy kept it a secret. It was now too late. She blamed herself for not telling him. Every time Benjamin gave Samantha special attention, her heart broke into a million pieces, and each piece hurt more than the one before. She knew something about Samantha was fishy. Samantha was concealing something, and she needed to find out what it was so she could expose her and get rid of her once and for all. Consumed with jealousy and irresistible curiosity, she investigated.

Lucy sneaked into Samantha's room and snooped around like a thief. It was the first time she'd ventured inside, and her envy grew as she discovered Samantha's room was the finest she'd ever seen. Lucy narrowed her brows, but she put her personal sentiments aside for a minute and focused on finding anything she could use against her. She looked around. There wasn't much of her personal stuff in the room, but a Hermes suitcase and handbag caught her eye under the bed. She pulled them out and examined them, her eyes wide open. They were genuine.

If she isn't a thief, how can she afford such expensive luggage and handbags?

Lucy unzipped the purse in search of Samantha's wallet to check her identity card. There were none. She found a little gold trinket box wrapped in a soft cloth. She opened it and discovered priceless jewels. Lucy had seen nothing like that in her life. She thought they were real gems. Lucy confirmed her suspicions and grew more certain than ever when she held it in her hand, eyes wide open.

Samantha is a thief, she told herself, smirking maliciously. She took the sapphire ring and put it in her pocket to check it. If her suspicions were correct, she now had the proof she needed to expose her.

She looked around, and the closet door caught her attention. She reached out to turn the doorknob and relaxed as the door swung open. Inside, clothing hung that differed from what Samantha wore daily. She checked them all, and each one had a label from a high-end designer or well-known department store in New York or Paris. She'd seen and read about them in a magazine. Lucy couldn't believe her eyes.

Are these Samantha's clothes?

She then opened the bedside drawer and pulled out a silk kimono robe and silk undergarments. She knew they were expensive. They were silky and smooth. She was about to open another drawer when she heard a noise outside. She placed everything back in the drawer, frightened that someone might see her snooping.

It so happened that Cassandra dropped by the mansion that afternoon to apologize to Benjamin for what she had done at his grandparents' ranch in Santa Barbara. She hoped to persuade him to forgive her. Lucy opened the door and found an ally in her. She brought her to the side and told her what she had discovered, describing Samantha's clothing and each piece of jewelry to her.

"Perhaps Benjamin gave it to her," Cassandra said. "She was wearing designer clothes and shoes when they went to Santa Barbara."

"How else can you explain the Hermes suitcase and handbag? Sir Benjamin didn't give it to her. When Samantha arrived at the mansion with Linda, she had them with her," Lucy stated. "I'm telling you, she's a thief. Inside an old trinket box, there were more jewels, and they looked expensive. This morning I took the sapphire ring to a friend who works at a jewelry store in town to get it appraised. I couldn't believe it when my friend told me it was worth at least $50,000. Tell me, if she didn't steal it, how could she afford to buy it? What should we do, Miss Cassandra? Should we call the cops and have her arrested? I want her out of here," Lucy said.

Cassandra glanced at her with a wicked smile on her face, and behind that smile, her brilliant, devious mind was devising a plan to get even and get rid of Samantha once and for all. She was confident that things would work out in the end, and Benjamin would forgive her for her transgressions.

"Leave everything to me, Lucy. I have a better idea." Her sly grin appeared again. She told Lucy to put everything back in Samantha's bag and clean her fingerprints off of it.

"Why?" she asked.

"I'll tell Benjamin I went shopping and will describe each piece of jewelry. We'll know he gave it to Samantha if he reacts. If not, I'll pretend to show them to him just to discover they've vanished. Of course, I'm going to check everyone's rooms. Viola! We'll find it in Samantha's purse. When Benjamin learns he is harboring a criminal in his house, he will be furious and call the cops right away."

"That's a brilliant plan, Miss Cassandra. I can't wait to see Samantha's expression when she is forcibly hauled out of this house."

They bore a similarly nasty grin.

BENJAMIN PARKED HIS Mercedes-Benz in the driveway. He reached into the back seat and grabbed a couple of take-away bags from Haley's Chicken Delight, Samantha's favorite restaurant. She enjoyed their chicken spaghetti and Caesar salad. As he walked into the house, it surprised him to find Cassandra waiting for him in the living room.

"What are you doing here?" he asked.

"Ben, dear, I apologize for my behavior. I promise I will never hurt you or your family again. Can you please forgive me?" Cassandra cried and pleaded in a child's voice.

A flash of irritation crossed Benjamin's face again. He walked to the kitchen, disregarding her and remaining silent.

He gave Lucy the takeaway bags. Cassandra followed him as he washed up for supper, but Benjamin ignored her. She followed him to the dining room and was surprised to see Samantha sitting next to Rosalie. She came to a halt, her eyes narrowed.

"Ben, you've changed. When did you allow the servants to eat with you and Rosalie?"

"Cassie, watch your manners. Samantha is not a servant at this house. She is welcome to sit with us. However, I believe I already said you are not welcome in my house. What are you still doing here?"

Cassandra didn't respond, but she smiled slyly at Samantha. Samantha grimaced when she noticed it.

What is she up to?

"Cassie, I'd want to invite you to dinner, but as you can see, I only bought enough for the three of us. Why don't you apologize and then leave?" Benjamin stated.

"Of course, I was in the area and thought I'd stop over to say hello. I went to see a friend at a jewelry store in town and purchased a few pieces. And I can't wait to show them to you. I bought a sapphire ring, a diamond necklace with a rose petal pendant, and a few other things."

Samantha, who was listening in on their conversation, couldn't help but wonder. Cassandra was describing her jewels.

Cassandra observed Samantha's reaction to her description of the jewelries, and Benjamin did not show any hint of interest. Lucy was right. Samantha stole them. A mischievous grin appeared on her face.

"Is that your apology? And what makes you think I'd be interested in your jewelry?" Benjamin asked with irritation.

"Come on, Ben, for old time's sake? This will be the last time I bother you. And do you want to know what I'm wishing for right now? I wish I could sit here at this table and dine with you and Rosalie," Cassandra murmured, eyeing Samantha's Caesar's salad. "Let me have the salad and let Samantha eat whatever leftover food you have."

Cassandra had invited herself to supper, which didn't surprise Benjamin at all.

"Sorry, Cassandra. The salad is for Samantha," Benjamin said this while calling Lucy from the kitchen.

"Sir?" Lucy asked.

"Put another plate on the table for Cassie, please? She'll be joining us for supper. We don't have enough food here, so just give her what you're eating."

"Sir?"

"You heard what I said. I only purchased enough food for three people, and Cassie insisted on eating supper here, so she'll eat whatever you're having."

Lucy went to the kitchen, scratched her head, and returned with a fresh place setting.

"So, Lucy, what are we having for dinner? I'd love to try one of your famous dishes," Cassandra inquired.

Lucy did not respond. She reappeared from the kitchen, holding a plate with two pieces of pepperoni pizza on it.

"I'm sorry, Miss Cassandra. Sir Benjamin told me to buy pizza for us while he ordered supper for them," she said as she quickly left.

Cassandra had a disgusted expression on her face. She didn't do it on purpose. Pizza, hot dogs, and hamburgers were not her favorite foods. She thought they were all wrong for her figure.

"Is there a problem, Cassie?" Benjamin asked.

"No, no problem," she said.

Cassandra took a nibble of her pizza. She swallowed hard, trying to push the food down. Cassandra felt like she was about to gag. She pushed her plate aside without taking another bite. Meanwhile, Samantha took pleasure in eating her salad, which made Cassandra envious. She arched her brow and grumbled.

After supper, Cassandra grabbed Benjamin's arm and brought him to the living area.

"All right, now tell me what you think of the new jewelry I bought."

"Why do you keep insisting I look at them?" Benjamin asked, his voice tinged with annoyance.

"Come on, Ben. Will you please just humor me? This might be my last visit. Before I buy it, I'd like your honest opinion."

Benjamin scowled. "I thought you had already bought it and wanted to show them?"

"Yes, I purchased it, but if you don't think it's nice, I'll return it and not buy it," Cassandra stumbled with her words as she continued to tell lies. She pretended to glance inside her handbag and appeared shocked.

"Oh, my God! They're not here? I put my purse here, and now it's gone."

"Perhaps you left them at the store," Benjamin said.

"No, I had them with me. I even showed them to Lucy."

Benjamin called Lucy. "Have you seen the jewelry Cassandra was talking about?"

"I did," Lucy said.

Cassandra pretended to be concerned and went through Lucy's room as planned. Samantha followed them, intrigued. Cassandra searched through Lucy's belongings and cried when she couldn't find it.

Lucy silently grinned. She did not know that Cassandra was also a talented actress. She was great at faking tears.

Meanwhile, Benjamin was in the living room when his phone rang. He had an emergency in the office that he needed to attend to. He departed, with no one knowing where he had gone.

Cassandra and Lucy were unaware Benjamin had left. Cassandra resumed her search, checking through every room in the house. She went to Samantha's room last, and she was furious when she discovered it was upstairs, separate from the servants. Cassandra threw things around when she realized how lovely and spacious they were—fit for a queen. She saw Samantha's handbag and opened it. She acted surprised when she saw the gold trinket box with the jewelry inside.

"Here it is! This is my jewelry."

"What are you talking about? It's mine," Samantha said.

"Yours? Really?" Cassandra stated in a sarcastic tone. "How can a nanny afford such pricey jewels? These are the pieces of jewelry I purchased and showed Lucy earlier."

Cassandra dragged Samantha downstairs and into the living area with no warning. She looked for Benjamin, but couldn't find him.

"Where is Ben?" Cassandra asked Linda.

"Ben called from his car," Linda replied. "There is an emergency in the office. What's going on?" She asked when she noticed Cassandra gripping Samantha's arm tightly.

Cassandra and Lucy exchanged concerned glances.

"Should we go forward with it, Miss Cassandra, given Sir Benjamin isn't here?" Lucy hushed.

"We don't have a choice. We have to do it now," Cassandra whispered. "We may never have another chance again."

"Linda, I'm not a thief. Cassandra and Lucy accuse me of stealing her jewels, although they are mine. I'm not sure why they're claiming it's Cassandra's," Samantha explained.

"I believe you, Samantha," Linda answered confidently.

"I didn't ask for your opinion, Linda. I'm calling the cops right now," Cassandra said as she dialed the phone.

"Please call, Ben, Linda. Tell him what happened," Samantha urged.

Cassandra glanced at her in disbelief. "How dare you call your boss by his nickname? You are disrespectful, ambitious, a liar, and a thief. You'll rot in jail."

"Don't worry, Samantha. I'll call Benjamin immediately," Linda remarked as she dialed his number.

SAMANTHA WAS IN THE police station and didn't know what to do. She was in more trouble than ever. She had no idea how long they had held her. When Benjamin arrived, his lawyer accompanied him. Benjamin dashed to her side and encircled her in his arms. He had to console her as she sobbed and clung to him.

Benjamin's attorney returned a few moments later and handed out all the evidence against Samantha, stating he planned to negotiate a deal. Cassandra was adamant about filing charges against her.

"Is there anything you could tell us that would help your case? Where were you when Cassandra came to the house?" the attorney inquired.

"Before I say anything, I just want to say that Cassandra and Lucy are lying. And to answer your questions, I spent the entire day in the garden. I didn't even realize Cassandra was in the house until I came in. Rosalie took a bath, and we stayed in her room until Ben came home and had dinner. I haven't even been in my room since this morning."

"Are you suggesting someone put the jewels in your handbag? Why?"

Samantha shook her head and glanced down at the ground. "No one put the jewels in my bag. The jewelry is mine, and it's been in my purse since I left home," her voice faded.

The lawyer scowled. "Samantha, I checked the jewelry personally, and it's worth at least $200,000, if not more. The judge will wonder how a nanny could afford expensive jewelry on your salary. And why would Cassandra lie and claim they were hers?"

"I'm not sure why Cassandra would lie like that. As for why I had the jewels, I forgot they were in my bag. They were gifts from my parents, and I kept them in my trinket box to play with them. When I packed my clothes, I guess I just threw them in my bag without thinking."

"$200,000 worth of jewelry and you play with them?" the lawyer asked, his eyes wide.

"I used to play with them when I was a little girl, but not anymore. If possible, I don't want to reveal my identity since—"

"Since what?" the attorney inquired.

"Because I ran away from home," Samantha choked on her words.

Benjamin was shocked to hear it.

Samantha couldn't look Benjamin in the eyes. She had betrayed his trust. She was not truthful with him and hoped he would forgive her for concealing her identity.

"I'm sorry, Ben. I didn't tell you the truth about myself since I'm at war with my father. All I can say is that I can prove the jewelry is mine. My name is inscribed on the trinket box, and there is a hidden compartment underneath. There's a photo of me with my parents. I was wearing the necklace."

The attorney checked the compartment and found the photo Samantha was referring to. "This pendant is worth roughly $100,000," the attorney said.

"It was a gift from my father on my tenth birthday, along with the trinket box made of pure gold. He custom-made it for me."

The attorney was in disbelief. "That was your father's tenth birthday gift to you?" the attorney nearly coughed. "And who is your father?"

Samantha stared at Benjamin and swallowed hard before responding. "Artemus St. James."

Benjamin remained silent. He was still in disbelief.

"The multi-millionaire? The same Artemus St. James from Los Angeles?" the attorney asked, confused.

"Yes, that's him. He is my father," Samantha said. "My real name is Samantha Isabella St. James of Beverly Hills."

The attorney shook his head in a way that expressed understanding. He exited the room and informed the police captain of the information he had gathered from Samantha. They checked the police database and found Samantha's driver's license record.

Meanwhile, Benjamin was mute. He had no way of knowing Samantha hailed from a hugely influential and rich family. Maybe he had a hunch that something was wrong. He should have connected it when Samantha said her last name was St. James. Benjamin knew well that Samantha had never done any work in her life, not with her delicate hands and lovely skin. He didn't know Artemus St. James directly, but his father conducted business with him. Benjamin grasped Samantha's hand as she cried. He held her close and dropped kisses on her forehead.

"I can't comprehend what it must be like to go through what you have," he murmured. "It had to be something serious for you to work as a gardener and nanny. Don't worry, Sam. Everything will be OK. I promise."

Samantha's chest tightened. She wanted to say something to him, apologize, anything, but the words wouldn't come out.

The attorney returned moments later with the captain. He corroborated everything Samantha had stated. Her driver's license was also verified, as were some articles and photographs of Artemus and Samantha from a benefit event they found on the internet. They also came across a news report about Samantha fleeing the wedding on the day of the ceremony. Benjamin realized Samantha was the runaway bride he saw in Los Angeles. He knew they were connected the moment their eyes met in front of the church.

Benjamin's counsel asked the captain not to reveal Samantha's identity.

"Family troubles are separate, and we don't need to become involved in family squabbles," he said.

The captain agreed not to release any information about Samantha's whereabouts for the time being, especially when she assured him that she needed a few days to sort things out before contacting her father.

THE DETECTIVES PUT Cassandra and Lucy in separate interrogation rooms. Lucy expected it. Cassandra had already explained how investigations worked.

"They'll attempt to gain the specifics of the occurrence, evaluate it, and regurgitate it. Don't worry, stick to our plan, and this will be over soon," Cassandra encouraged her.

Lucy hesitated at first. She did not know that their little scheme would cause them to be questioned by the police or detained at the police station, but Cassandra was convincing. Lucy felt at ease.

Cassandra was the first to be interrogated by two investigators.

"When did you buy the jewelry?"

"I bought it that afternoon," she said.

"Do you have any proof?" he inquired.

Cassandra promptly changed her story. She explained she bought it from a local jeweler friend, and she had the documentation.

"Can you give us the name of the person you bought it from?" the second investigator asked.

Cassandra's carefully crafted plan unraveled, forcing her to improvise. She couldn't think of anyone who would collaborate with her on her story. Cassandra informed the cops, "My friend departed Seattle a few hours ago, bound for Honolulu. I can ask her to contact you as soon as she returns from her trip."

Cassandra believed she had ample time to call her friend Judy, who had gone to Hawaii, to back up her story. Another issue was proving her friend owned a jewelry business, but for the time being, she felt this would suffice.

Both detectives nodded simultaneously.

"Thank you, Cassandra. We'll talk to Lucy right now. Please wait a moment."

Cassandra nodded.

The investigators moved into the next room. Lucy closed her eyes and took a few long breaths while the cops questioned her.

"When did Cassandra show you the jewelry?" one detective asked.

"She showed it to me that afternoon," Lucy responded.

"Do you have a grudge towards Samantha?"

Lucy paused for a moment before responding, "No."

"Do you realize lying to the police is a crime?" the second detective questioned.

"Yes, I never lied to the cops," Lucy said.

The detectives nodded.

"Okay, Lucy, this is your last chance. We know the jewelry does not belong to Cassandra. We're not sure why you both lied and want an innocent person imprisoned. If you do not cooperate with us, we are talking about incarceration for a long time. So, what will it be?" the first investigator asked.

Lucy felt there was no use in lying anymore. A sense of helplessness overtook her. She sobbed when she revealed her role in the crime.

"We made up the story to retaliate against Samantha. I have no proof she stole the jewelry, but I know she's a thief. She is bad for Sir Benjamin. I had to do it since I despise her so much.

The detectives shook their heads. It was a simple case of jealousy.

As the cops were about to charge Lucy, Samantha stopped them in the corridor and informed them she was not pressing any charges. Her swift action surprised the captain, but Samantha was more surprised at her reaction. She knew she had changed. Samantha would never hear of it if it happened when she was still the spoiled, rotten person she was a few months ago. She would condemn Lucy and make sure she paid for her wrongdoings.

"No one is pressing charges, so you are free to go," one of the cops informed Lucy.

Benjamin told Lucy, "I'm disappointed with your conduct. I couldn't believe you were capable of such a thing. I'm ending your employment. Pack your belongings and leave."

Lucy sobbed. "I'm sorry, Sir Benjamin. Please forgive me."

"Despite your wrongdoings against Samantha, she asked me to advance six months of her wages and give you that money to help you. Perhaps if you'd only given Samantha a chance, you'd discover she's a good friend," Benjamin said.

"Do you mind if I ask where Samantha got all those jewels if she didn't steal them?" Lucy inquired.

"As it turned out," Benjamin said. "Samantha had fled from home. She came from a wealthy family in Beverly Hills."

Lucy wept ceaselessly. She was embarrassed of herself. Lucy couldn't believe Samantha would do such a thing after what she had done to her. She didn't take the time to recognize her for what she was: a good person with a kind heart.

"I hope you'll learn to forgive me, Samantha," Lucy said when she saw her in the waiting area.

"I think it's a blessing that you're leaving Benjamin's house," Samantha said. "Maybe now you'll find the love you are looking for. I heard Samuel is looking for someone to help him at the fish market."

Lucy smiled. "Seriously?"

Meanwhile, Cassandra couldn't believe it when the police showed her the gold trinket box with Samantha's name inscribed on it.

"That's impossible. Samantha likely had that made after she stole it. If she didn't steal it from me, she stole it from someone else. She's a nanny, for heaven's sake," Cassandra said, insisting she was the victim. "I know I lied, but it was for a good reason. She is a thief. She belongs in jail. Tell me how a nanny could carry $200,000 in jewels and a $50,000 purse. Something fishy is going on with her."

"Let's say we investigated and discovered the jewelry belongs to Samantha," the investigator said.

Cassandra couldn't believe it. Did Samantha outsmart her again?

The detectives informed her that filing a false police report was a serious crime with significant implications.

"You might look at more than a year in jail," the second investigator added.

"No," Cassandra yelled and cried as the officers took her into custody, but Samantha did not press charges against her. If she brought charges against Cassandra, Lucy would be an accessory, which she did not want.

Cassandra ran into Samantha in the corridor. She showed no guilt and did not even thank Samantha for dropping the charges against her. But Benjamin had enough of Cassandra's childish behavior. He informed her she could never return to the mansion again. She was not permitted to enter the gate.

Cassandra cried.

"It's difficult to accept that I lost you to a simple servant. I'm not sure how Samantha got away with it, but I can tell you she's a thief and liar."

Benjamin let out a long, exasperated sigh. "Cassie, there was no "we," therefore you never lost me. Stop fantasizing and start living your life. Be grateful for Samantha. If it were up to me, you'd be in jail for putting us through hell. Samantha is not a servant. We found out who she was thanks to you—an heir to a multi-million-dollar fortune who had gone into hiding. She is 100 times wealthier than you and your pals combined."

Cassandra stared in shock, her jaw fell, and her heart beat hard in her chest. She had trouble accepting the truth about Samantha's identity.

I can't believe Samantha defeated me again.

"So, what do you have to say about yourself?" Benjamin asked.

"I'm sorry, Ben." Cassandra choked on the words.

"Is that all you have to say? How about apologizing to Samantha for what you've done to her?"

For a brief period, the two ladies locked gazes. There was a long pause between them. Neither of them showed any emotion. Cassandra showed no regret for what she had done. She immediately departed without saying a word and never looked back.

As for Samantha, it relieved her that it was all over.

CHAPTER SEVENTEEN

Benjamin phoned the head of his security department to gather as much information as possible about the financial condition of Artemus Industries and Chandler Corporation, as well as their connection. He relayed all of Samantha's details and stated that it was a top priority. Unfortunately, there wasn't much to go on. Samantha knew very little since her father didn't tell her everything. Benjamin, on the other hand, had his reservations. Artemus St. James was one of the most successful businessmen in the country, although he had never heard of Chandler Corporation, Robert Chandler, Sr., or his son, RJ, before.

Why an arranged marriage? What could persuade Artemus to agree to such a deal? Benjamin was intrigued by what he had pieced together.

Harry Zanini, a short, balding man in his late forties dressed in a tan trench coat and a gray hat, was the head of security at McClain Enterprise. He and Benjamin were having Irish coffee in the study. After a few moments, Harry Zanini opened his file.

"Not only did our investigators look into Artemus Industries, but they also looked into any companies or individuals who could have an interest in it. One name in particular, Robert Chandler, Sr., popped up. He had been studying Artemus Industries' financial strength for some time, which was odd given that he was broke."

"Broke?" Benjamin questioned as he gulped the last of his coffee.

"According to my sources, Mr. Chandler's company had suffered a setback. Their staff dropped from thousands to hundreds, and he had to float the payroll himself. To save his company, he took out high-interest mortgages on several of his properties. He had relied too heavily on his business and had failed. His stock was falling in value, and he was on the point of declaring bankruptcy. Meanwhile, I learned from another source that Mr. Chandler had discovered a gold mine. He's rumored to be back in the game. We don't know what it signifies yet, but we're digging."

Benjamin moved his head back and forth a few times. He wondered what Artemus and Mr. Chandler had in common, other than being old friends. Why would Artemus persuade Samantha to marry RJ if Chandler Corporation was struggling? What would he gain? Samantha's arranged marriage piqued his interest.

"Tell me about Artemus."

"Aside from being a multi-millionaire retail entrepreneur, he was active on the social scene. He was involved in several activities and charitable events, but we haven't been able to learn anything about him since his daughter ran away a few months ago. According to rumors, he hired private detectives to track her down, but they were unsuccessful. He has one daughter, Samantha Isabella St. James, 22, a Beverly Hills socialite who is a typical pampered brat. She has a penchant for overspending. We poked about their mansion, and one of the domestic servants informed us that Mr. St. James had lost his desire to live. He remains reclusive in his home, seldom leaving his room. He's given up hope of ever finding his daughter. Meanwhile, word on the street is that Robert Chandler, Jr. has set up a million-dollar cash reward for anyone who can find Samantha."

"What is Robert Chandler, Jr.'s relationship with the St. James?"

"According to society pages and newspapers, Samantha Isabella St. James and Robert Chandler, Jr. were engaged when Samantha ran away on their wedding day. They haven't found her yet. We know very little about Robert Chandler, Jr., except that he is the biggest playboy in history, flashing his money in everyone's face, especially ladies. He brags about his wealth, appears to lack business acumen, and lets his charm pass for credibility. According to another rumor, the young Chandler's extravagant lifestyle and fondness for lavish spending on wine, women, and fancy automobiles drove the family into shame and debt. Unfortunately, this is only a rumor, and we were unable to confirm it, but we are currently investigating."

"Thank you, Harry. Excellent work! Just keep me updated on how things progress. Please get Artemus' phone number for me."

Harry Zanini nodded his head before he stepped out of the room. Benjamin was on his way to the kitchen to get another cup of coffee when he saw Samantha waiting for him in the doorway. Benjamin could tell she had overheard his conversation with the head of his security because of her surprised expression and stiffening.

"Did I hear it correctly? Why were you looking into my father's affairs?" she asked.

"How much of our chat did you hear?"

"Not much."

"Don't be mad at me, Sam. We know your father was pressing you to marry RJ, and we want to know why. I had Artemus Industries and Chandler Corporation investigate. We may presume the connection is between the two companies. There are far too many things that don't add up."

Benjamin paused for a moment before he spoke again.

"There are other things to consider, Sam. RJ has offered a million dollars in cash to whoever can find you."

Samantha sighed. "He is desperate to find me. But why? We'd never dated or been friends before. My father never explained why he wants me to marry RJ. I don't understand. Ben, I'm scared."

Samantha's situation troubled him, but Benjamin didn't want to show it. He didn't want to worry her any more than she already was. He kissed her on the lips as he lifted her chin.

"Just stay close and never leave this house without telling me. Promise me, Sam? Can you do that for me?"

"OK, Ben. I promise."

"I'd want to meet RJ. I don't think our paths have ever crossed in the business world."

"Trust me," Samantha said. "You don't want to know him. I've been trying to avoid that jackass since the first time I met him."

Benjamin chuckled sweetly at her. "Don't worry, Sam. You'll never see that jackass again. Not while I'm around."

A phony giggle accompanied Samantha's false grin. She knew better. RJ was attempting to exert control over her even before they planned their wedding. He would never leave her alone. Not in this lifetime!

BENJAMIN AWOKE TO SEE Samantha in the kitchen having a serious talk with Linda, while Rosalie sat on a chair, weeping. When he noticed her bags on the floor, he frowned.

"Sam, what's going on? Are you going somewhere?" he asked.

"Yes, Ben. I should have gone a long time ago, but it wouldn't be fair to leave without saying goodbye. Thank you for your hospitality, but it is time for me to leave. I have a cab waiting outside to take me to the train station."

Benjamin sighed heavily. "Linda, please take Rosalie to her room. I need to speak with Samantha alone."

He waited until Linda and Rosalie were out of sight, before speaking to Samantha.

"What happened to our conversation yesterday? I thought we agreed you'd never leave my sight." Benjamin asked.

"I did some soul-searching this morning. This is my problem, Ben. I should never have involved you and everyone else in this house. If I leave, you'll be safe. No one will harm any of you."

"I don't want you to go, Samantha. I will not allow it!" Benjamin murmured as he gripped her.

"Ben, I have to get going. RJ is powerful and influential. He is a deceitful and vicious person. I'm sure he can make someone vanish if he wants to. It'll only be a matter of time until he tracks me down."

Benjamin remained silent. Instead, he stepped outside, paid the taxi driver, and sent him on his way. When Benjamin returned to the house, there was a long stillness during which he kept his gaze locked on Samantha. He took her hand and led her to the study. Benjamin gently squeezed her upper arm as he drew her closer to him as he closed the door behind him.

"Please, Samantha. This is something we need to discuss. You don't have to go anywhere. I will protect you. I care for you. Believe me, we'll get through this together," he whispered. His arms reach around her and hold her as if he didn't want to let go.

"Ben, I don't want to leave, but I have to. Now that my true identity is known, it's only a matter of time before my father or, worse, RJ finds me."

"Oh, Samantha," he mumbled, making her heart skip a beat inside her chest.

Samantha exhaled a deep breath. "This is what I mean," she said.

"What are you talking about?"

"This!" Samantha said, looking into his eyes. "You and me, the hugging, whispering, teasing, kissing, and..."

"Sam, will you marry me?" Benjamin asked, enunciating each syllable.

Samantha's eyes widened in surprise. Her heart pounded a little faster.

"What did you say?"

"I asked you to marry me, Samantha Isabella St. James," he repeated.

Samantha stared at him, wondering whether he was expressing a message to her in those words. But when she glanced up at him again, she saw genuine concern, not because he was in love with her.

"I thought that's what you said," Samantha said, sadness in her voice. "Why would you marry me, Ben?"

"You said it yourself. Your father is forcing you to marry this guy, RJ. They can't compel you to marry if you are already married."

Samantha was dissatisfied with Benjamin's response. She was hoping he'd tell her he wanted to marry her because he loved her. Samantha gave him the saddest look she could manage. She took a deep breath and swallowed hard before speaking.

"But it won't solve my problem," she responded, finding her voice.

"No, it's not, but it's the first step. Would you rather marry RJ or marry someone as attractive as me?" he laughed.

"Please, Ben, stop making fun of me. I've got a real problem here."

"You hated it when you thought I was planning to make you my mistress. Now I'm proposing marriage, and you still despise it. What would it be?" he asked, chuckling.

"I'm sorry, but your joke isn't funny."

"I'm not kidding. Rosalie loves you, and I am a handsome twenty-eight-year-old bachelor ready to marry you. This might also be a marriage of convenience. We may annul our marriage as soon as your problems with your father and RJ are resolved. There are no strings attached."

He's already talking about an annulment before we've even had our wedding, Samantha told herself. "And you? What do you get from this marriage?" she asked.

Benjamin was silent for a moment. "I've got my reasons. I'll tell you about it someday, but for now, let's focus on your problem, okay?"

Samantha was unsure about Benjamin's intentions for her. He kept giving her conflicting signals, but since there were no strings attached, maybe it was the only way she could get rid of RJ once and for all. She no longer had to hide. If she marries, RJ and his family would have no reason to pursue her. Benjamin's suggestion was not a bad one. But what about her father? His debt? How could she help him? She let out a long, deep sigh.

IT WAS TWO O'CLOCK in the morning, and Samantha still could not sleep. She was pondering Ben's wedding proposal and wasn't sure if she should accept it. Samantha strolled across the garden, her heart heavy, and when she reached the pool, she sat on the edge, her feet dangling in the water. She took long breaths to relax.

"Marriage for convenience" and "debt" kept popping into her head, and she tried to block them out.

Benjamin was on the balcony, thinking of ways to help Samantha with her situation, when he saw her sitting on the edge of the pool, troubled. He didn't want to make her upset by proposing, but it was the only way he could think of to keep her from leaving. Benjamin admitted he had feelings for her. Something about her appealed to him, and he looked forward to coming home early, something he had never done before. He didn't want to go a day without seeing that beautiful face. Benjamin knew deep down, that he loved her. Yes, he confessed. He was madly, deeply, and completely in love with Samantha. He didn't want to rush her and frighten her. Samantha's mental state was not good at the moment. He had to be there for her and support her in resolving her problems before they could go forward in their relationship.

It had been a restless night for both of them.

The next morning, Benjamin saw Samantha waiting for him in the kitchen.

"Ben, why do you want to marry me?" She asked, hoping he would finally reveal his true intentions... his true feelings for her.

Benjamin glanced towards Samantha. It tempted him to tell her how much he loved her, but he resisted. It was not the right time. Samantha was frightened and vulnerable. He didn't want to put her under strain or confuse her.

"Like I said yesterday, would you rather be married to RJ or me? With me, we can get our marriage annulled or divorced whenever we choose. I don't think you have a choice with RJ, especially if he's desperately trying to find you. He would not go through the trouble of finding you and offering reward money if he were to allow you to get a divorce later. You're safe with me."

Samantha became frustrated by Benjamin's incapacity or unwillingness to convey his feelings to her. She had a feeling there was more to it than what Benjamin was saying, as if he was withholding something from her. She could see he cared about her as much as she cared about him, but she didn't want him to feel pressed into anything. What if he merely cared for her, but did not love her? He was sending her mixed signals. But then again, Benjamin was gracious enough to help her with her problem. She should not make any assumptions.

Samantha sighed in frustration. "I want to say yes, Ben, but I'm frightened."

"You have the option of declining. It was only a suggestion. It is not a legally binding agreement."

"Okay."

"Okay, what?"

"All right, I'll marry you, Ben," Samantha stammered. She had no clue what was going to happen next, so she chose to simply go with it.

"What exactly did you say?" Ben asked.

"I said I'd marry you, Benjamin McClain," she said.

Benjamin chuckled as he drew her closer to him and laid a passionate kiss on her lips. Samantha grew numb, and as their lips parted, she stumbled back, unable to maintain her footing. She was at a loss for words. All the signs were there. The timing was perfect, yet Benjamin could not say the one thing she wanted to hear. She could tell Benjamin wasn't ready for a serious commitment. If he were, he would have proposed to her without limitations or reservations.

"Keep in mind this union is purely platonic. The two of us will continue to sleep in separate rooms," she said to ease Benjamin's anxiety.

"All right, Sam, whatever you say. I assure you that our marriage is simply on paper. I will not ask you for my right as your husband unless you give it voluntarily," he answered before he grabbed and kissed her on the mouth.

Benjamin had long since left, leaving Samantha alone in the living room, pondering. Was she so special that Benjamin would go to such lengths to protect her?

CHAPTER EIGHTEEN

Artemus agreed to meet Benjamin in a tavern on the outskirts of Pomona, away from the crowds and Chandler's men. But it was tough to leave his residence unnoticed. He was aware he was being monitored. Artemus knew the Chandlers were behind it. He thought he could have stopped them, but he didn't. Instead, he remained reclusive in his home, seldom leaving his room. He refused to have any contact with the Chandlers, no matter how hard they tried. But when Benjamin McClain phoned, he grew intrigued when he mentioned his daughter.

Artemus, dressed as Miguel, his chauffeur, put on a gardener's hat and dark sunglasses and drove the station wagon to the Chinatown fish market. He parked the car and strolled inside. Artemus made his way through the crowd, took a deep breath, and calmed his nerves. He kept his gaze concentrated on the front door, on the lookout for dubious people. His jaw stiffened. Two scruffy-looking men walked in, paused, and peered around as though looking for someone. Artemus suspected they were looking for him.

He went inside the restroom, where Miguel was waiting for him. It was part of their plan to divert the attention of whoever followed him. Miguel slipped out of the house unnoticed, rented a car the day before, and slept at a nearby motel. He gave Artemus the key to the rental car parked on the other side of the building. Artemus removed his red flannel shirt, gardener's hat, and sunglasses. He gave it to Miguel, who handed him his Lakers baseball cap.

Miguel strolled outside, bought the fish, and drove away a few minutes later. He pulled up to a nearby gas station and checked the area to see if anyone was tailing him. They were. He went inside the mini market and called Artemus while he watched the door. He informed him that their plan had worked. The thugs who had previously followed Artemus were now trailing him.

Artemus proceeded through the rear of the market to a car Miguel had rented. Artemus was trembling and nervous as he drove to their meeting place in Pomona. He arrived early at DJ's Pub. He ordered scotch and consumed two by the time Benjamin arrived.

"Mr. St. James, it is my pleasure to meet you, sir, but I wish the circumstances were different," Benjamin remarked.

Artemus stood up, and they shook hands.

"It's a pleasure to meet you, too, Mr. McClain."

He took a closer look at the tall, young man sitting next to him. Benjamin was a lot younger than he expected, and he was also attractive. Artemus was worried about their meeting. He'd heard about McClain Enterprise and their reputation. He was well acquainted with his father. When Benjamin called Artemus and informed him he had a way to get the Chandlers off his back, he had to admit it piqued his interest and agreed to meet him. He was interested in whether he knew anything about his personal affairs with the Chandlers or where Samantha was hiding. Artemus waited for the young man to speak.

"How are you, Mr. St. James?" Benjamin inquired.

"Fine, thank you, and why do I have the pleasure of your acquaintance?" Artemus asked. "To be honest, it surprised me when you called, especially since you mentioned my daughter and the Chandlers."

Benjamin glanced towards Artemus. "Mr. St. James, I'll go straight to the point. I am fully aware of your current situation with the Chandler family, and I am here to assist you."

Artemus arched his brow. "I'm not sure what you mean. How did you find out about my business with the Chandlers?"

Benjamin noticed a slight change in Artemus' demeanor and realized he'd hit a nerve. He sensed Artemus' problem was more than a business arrangement, but he played along to see what information he could get from him.

"I know you're being pressured to force your daughter's marriage to the younger Chandler."

"Did they send you here to intimidate me, or are you here to blackmail me?" Artemus screamed in rage as he asked.

Blackmail? This is getting better by the minute, Benjamin thought to himself.

"Let me put it this way, Mr. St. James: Would you let me marry your daughter if I made a better offer?"

"What?" Artemus asked, his voice tainted with rage. "You should be careful what you say, young man."

"Calm down, Mr. St. James. I know you're in trouble," Benjamin remarked. He drew in a deep breath and let it out quickly with a sigh, before continuing to talk. "Mr. St. James, how much do you owe the Chandlers?"

Artemus peered deeply into Benjamin's eyes, as if trying to read his mind. Something about him made him answer his question. "Would you believe I don't owe them anything? I'm referring to money."

Benjamin grimaced and raised an eyebrow. "What is it, Mr. St. James, if you don't mind me asking?"

"I'm sorry, Mr. McClain. I know your father, but I don't know you well enough to trust you."

"Believe me, I don't want to intrude on your life, but this is crucial... for Sam."

"For Sam?" Artemus' eyes glowed. "Do you know my daughter? Do you know where she is? Please tell me, I implore you," he said.

"Sam is safe, Mr. St. James. She is fine, but before I tell you about her, I need to know what transpired. You may be uncomfortable talking about that, but I am here to help you, not to condemn you."

Artemus stared him in the eyes, attempting to reread him. He felt he could trust this young man in front of him, but it terrified him. What if this was all a set-up by one of Chandler's men? He paused, shook his head, and sighed heavily.

"What you're saying sounds good, Mr. McClain, but what if you're here to trick me?

"There will be no trickery, Mr. St. James," Benjamin stated. "I promise." He took out his phone and showed pictures of Samantha and Rosalie feeding and petting the animals at the ranch when she wasn't looking. She looked happy.

Artemus sobbed when he saw images of his daughter. "Oh, Samantha."

"Mr. St. James, I love your daughter, and I believe she loves me too," Benjamin explained.

"And you know this because?"

"She's been living with me for the past three months."

Artemus was stunned and said nothing. He waited for Benjamin to finish.

"Samantha met our housekeeper on the bus. I paid for Samantha's dinner when she lost her wallet at a coffee shop. My maid brought her over to the house, since she didn't have a place to stay, so I hired her as a babysitter for my nine-year-old godchild," Benjamin stated. "I don't believe in coincidences. I think our paths are meant to cross. It's a long story."

Artemus's eyes widened when he noticed his daughter was wearing a maid's outfit in the photographs.

"A nanny? Oh, my goodness! What have I done?"

Samantha's decision to work as a babysitter rather than marry RJ made Artemus' heart race. He sipped his scotch.

"Can I see my daughter?"

"Soon, Mr. St. James, soon, but first, we must deal with your problem with the Chandlers. We must ensure they do not bother you or Samantha again. I don't want to see them once we're married. If they do, I pray they don't come across my path because I'll take it personally."

"What do you intend to do, Mr. McClain?"

"Please call me, Ben, sir."

"OK, Ben. What do you suggest we do?"

"Why don't you tell me what happened? I am not here to criticize or condemn you, sir, as I already stated. I'm here to help you."

Artemus took a deep breath and swallowed hard. He drank the last of his scotch. He ran his hand through his hair, shook his head, and exhaled a sigh. The guilt had nearly squeezed the life out of him, and he finally confided in Benjamin.

"I realize it appears like I'm a horrible father for forcing my daughter into an arranged marriage, but Robert tricked me into doing so, and I can't prove it. I felt dirty and ashamed. I failed my daughter, and now I'm going to lose everything I've worked so hard for... for something stupid I did. If I could only remember everything that happened that night, it could shed some light on this bizarre series of events. My daughter is more important than any amount of money in the world. That's something I've realized. I'm no longer concerned with anything. I want to see my daughter and apologize to her. I'm hoping it's not too late. I love her. She is the only family I have left."

Benjamin scowled. "I'm sorry, sir, but I don't understand what you're saying."

"I woke up in the hotel room with a headache, not to mention I was naked," Artemus said, his voice breaking. "A young lady who had been brutally beaten was lying next to me, and a young man was photographing us together. I don't even recall getting a room at the casino. They threatened to contact the cops and have me arrested, but Robert Chandler took care of everything."

"Wait, Mr. Chandler was with you?" Benjamin asked, confused.

"Yes, we had a drink the night before. I respected him as a close friend, and I trusted him when he took care of everything for me. He bribed those individuals for their silence. I felt Robert was a sincere friend who wanted to help me, but he was deceptive. Unfortunately, it was too late for me to realize he was devious and untrustworthy. He entrapped me and drove me into disgrace. Two weeks later, he and his son, RJ, paid me a visit at the office. They got copies of those images without my knowledge and were blackmailing me. That was their intention all along. Robert stated that we would arrange for my daughter to marry his son. I told him it wasn't up to me and that I couldn't compel Samantha to marry anybody, but Robert persisted. He and his son continued coming into the office and pressing me to agree to the marriage or hand over my business to them. When I declined, they threatened to publicize the photos and expose me, which I couldn't have. It would ruin me. That was the reason I had to consent to my daughter's arranged marriage."

Artemus exhaled a sigh of relief and felt much better after sharing the specifics with Benjamin. However, Benjamin was suspicious of the circumstances of Artemus' blackout and Mr. Chandler's involvement at the time of the incident, leaving him perplexed about this unexpected turn of events.

"My father told me about you, Mr. St. James. He had nothing but positive things to say about you. You're a decent man. I'm glad you're doing your best to deal with the situation," Benjamin said.

"I had already planned to go to the police station and report the incident before you called. I've had it with the Chandlers. I will not let them bully me. Whatever happens, I'm ready to deal with it. I can no longer withhold the truth from my daughter."

"No, Mr. St. James. Not yet. Mr. Chandler himself set you up from the start."

"What? Do you think so?"

"I'm guessing Mr. Chandler started the contact and invited you out for a drink?"

"Yes, that's right."

"And did he choose the location for the meeting?"

"That's correct."

Benjamin continued to nod his head. He had a pretty good idea of what happened, and he knew the reason Mr. Chandler and his son, RJ, went through the extremes to trap Mr. St. James.

"Mr. St. James, please call the Chandlers and schedule a meeting with them. How about this Friday at 10 o'clock at your office? Inform them that you have finally agreed to hand over your company to them. I'm sure they'll be thrilled to hear you've changed your mind, but mention nothing about what we discussed. Just schedule the meeting, and I'll take care of the rest."

"What is the significance of this Friday?"

"I only need a few days to gather sufficient evidence against the Chandlers, and I know where to start," Benjamin said. "Money talks, Mr. St. James. I also have a great team of investigators. We will get the evidence we need. Don't worry. The Chandlers will be apprehended and charged with their crime. Oh, and one more thing, Mr. St. James. I'd like to ask for your daughter's hand in marriage once this is over, but please don't tell her yet since I'm planning a surprise wedding for my bride."

Artemus realized what was going on. "I will not object if Samantha loves you. Thank you, Ben. Thank you for taking in my daughter and helping us get out of this jam. Do you know how difficult it is to watch everything I do and every move I make because someone's spying on me?"

"Don't worry, Mr. St. James. That will be taken care of as quickly as possible."

"When do you suppose I'll see my daughter?"

"Saturday morning, after we take care of this little situation with the Chandlers. Meanwhile, while I conduct my investigation, I believe it is best if you stay at home until everything is clear. From now on, we have to be careful. We need to trap the Chandlers, and I don't want them to have any communication with you until you see them Friday morning. Then we'll fly to Seattle."

"Seattle? Is that where she's been all this time?"

"Yes, Samantha lives at my house, which will soon become our home."

"THAT'S RIGHT, I WANT you to take care of this matter personally." Benjamin was overheard saying on the phone early Thursday morning. "Robert Chandler, Sr., and his son, RJ, should be prosecuted for conspiracy to blackmail. I met with the manager at Bayview Casino and the bartender at the casino bar, and they showed me videos from before and after the incident," Benjamin said to Jordan Morris, a childhood friend and college roommate now the Beverly Hills police chief.

"How did the Chandlers persuade Mr. St. James to cooperate and not contact the police?" Jordan asked.

"The Chandlers believed they had a brilliant plan, but I have the best team of investigators in the country," Benjamin explained. "Here's what happened: Mr. St. James met Mr. Chandler in the Bayview Casino bar at the latter's request, but Mr. St. James was unaware that Mr. Chandler's son, RJ, and two associates were hiding in the back of the bar. They set everything up the day before. Surveillance video from the casino showed Mr. St. James seated at the bar with Mr. Chandler until Mr. St. James went to relieve himself. Mr. Chandler remained at the bar. Mr. St. James returned, and minutes later, he was falling from his chair, staggering as if intoxicated. Mr. Zanini, the head of my security, spoke with the bartender who worked that night, and he remembered seeing Mr. St. James drunk and virtually incoherent. He stated he remembered it so well because Mr. St. James gave him a big tip. He wondered why Mr. St. James appeared to be wasted when he had only served him one drink—a martini. Before he gave him the drink, the bartender mentioned that Mr. St. James was drinking hot tea, friendly, even chatty, and a good tipper. He claimed to have seen Mr. St. James leave the bar to use the restroom. The bartender went to the back room for a moment, and when he returned a few minutes later, he saw Mr. St. James had returned from the restroom, but he observed how weird it was. Mr. St. James was slurring his words and acting strangely while he spoke until he passed out. Two young men struggled to help him up. The bartender was concerned, so he followed them to the elevator. He found it odd that the two men knew just where to take him. But he dismissed it, believing they may be his friends. The footage also showed RJ as one of the men. Everything, according to Mr. St. James, was a haze. He had no recollection of RJ being with him that night. We don't know if Mr. Chandler or RJ slipped something into his drink at the bar or elsewhere, and we can't prove it. Mr. St. James blacked out, and when he awoke, a young woman was lying in bed with him, brutally assaulted. Another man in the room was photographing them together. That was the part they screwed up.

They were apparently preparing Mr. St. James for blackmail and didn't expect him to wake up so quickly. Mr. St. James spotted the person snapping photographs, but because he didn't ask who or why the guy was there and just assumed he bludgeoned the woman in the room, they felt they got away with it. What they didn't realize was that they had been captured on tape days earlier, entering the casino together. We had a face to work with, thanks to the footage we gained from the casino. My team of investigators reviewed security footage from all the businesses within a five-mile radius of the casino hoping to find something."

"How did you convince them to hand them to you?" Jordan asked.

"Money talks, my friend."

Jordan nodded his head in understanding.

"My team were looking for a needle in a haystack. But, as chance would have it, all three—RJ, the male friend, and the lady beaten up in Mr. St. James' room—had lunch together days before the incident at a nearby restaurant. The waitress who served them remembered RJ. She'd met him at a friend's party two years before. It upset her that RJ didn't even remember her because they dated for a short time. She covertly snapped a photo of them while they were dining, and uploaded it on her social media account with the title "Never date this jerk!" Surveillance video also showed the three entering the casino together. They pretended they didn't know each other once inside, but their body language suggested otherwise. The Chandlers had arranged everything."

"But why go through all that? Chandler Corporation is a well-known firm in the country. My cousin, Fred, works there."

"My research department verified their present financial status, and they are on the edge of bankruptcy. Mr. Chandler and Mr. St. James had been friends for years, but it was a well known fact that Mr. Chandler had always been envious of Mr. St. James' success. Mr. Chandler and his son, RJ, devised a scheme to take over Artemus Industries through blackmail in order to salvage their firm and avoid bankruptcy. They knew that Mr. St. James was worth millions of dollars. They wanted him to believe he had battered a young lady so they could easily blackmail him into letting his daughter marry RJ, which would eventually give them access to Mr. St. James' money. After all, his daughter, Samantha, is the heir to his business empire. Since Mr. St. James' daughter had fled, the Chandlers continued with Plan B, pressuring Mr. St. James to turn over his business to them in exchange for the return of the photos. Unfortunately, Mr. St. James lived in utter seclusion after his daughter fled. He'd never left his house and had severed ties with the outside world, so the Chandlers couldn't reach him. They kept an eye on him and his staff, waiting for the right moment to strike," Benjamin said.

"This will not sit well with my cousin Fred. He'll be out of a job soon," Jordan stated. "What happened to the beaten woman? Is she all right?"

"I forgot to mention that their female companion was one of RJ's playmates. He told her to pose naked with Mr. St. James while intoxicated or drugged. There were graphic images of her battered body, but they were all fabricated. They had an adjoining room at the hotel, and that's how easily they set up everything—makeup, camera, everything."

"So, the photos show Mr. St. James with a naked, battered woman?" Jordan asked.

"Let's just say that several images, although fake, were unsuitable for public viewing. Mr. St. James was photographed in various compromising poses with the woman. It will damage his image, especially with his daughter. He had to agree to the Chandlers' terms. He had no idea he was giving up all he cared about: his daughter and his company."

"Please tell me you have all the evidence with you?"

"I can do better than that," Benjamin said. "Everything is on its way to you right now. We had security footage and sworn affidavits from the bartender at the casino bar and the waitress at the restaurant. My investigators found the woman who posed naked and battered in the room. She confessed immediately because she was so terrified when they spoke to her. The woman even provided them with the original copies of the photos they took. She agreed to testify against the Chandlers in return for leniency. With the help of the Beverly Hills Police Department, the woman provided proof in the form of a sworn statement detailing her role in the Chandler extortion. She is currently in your custody. My security chief is now collaborating with your detectives. Oh, and by the way, Mr. St. James' hotel bill was in RJ's name, not Mr. St. James'. The Chandlers' plan was so stupid that you had to laugh."

"This is excellent investigative work, Ben. As soon as we receive the evidence you supplied, along with the sworn statement from the woman and the bartender, I will review everything, and we will issue an arrest warrant for the Chandlers right away."

"You may arrest them at Mr. St. James' office at 10 o'clock tomorrow morning. Following my directions, Mr. St. James set up the meeting with them. They will demand Mr. St. James sign agreements handing over his business to them in exchange for the photographs. You have time to set up a trap, don't you? I'll email you all the specifics in a few minutes."

"Yes, I'll get right on it. How can I reach you?" Jordan asked.

"Just call me on my private number. Do you still remember it, Captain Morris?" Benjamin made a remark.

"How can I forget, Mr. McClain?" Jordan laughed. "You've had that phone number since high school."

"And I bet you're still wearing your short-sleeved football jersey, my friend."

"You bet!" Jordan responded.

They both burst out laughing at their silliness.

CHAPTER NINETEEN

The morning was chilly, and the air still smelled like rain from the night before. The sun was rising and attempting to break through the clouds. Artemus arrived early at Benjamin's mansion. He scarcely slept because he was so excited. His mind was racing. After three months apart, he would finally see his daughter today. A cool breeze touched his face as he walked into the garden. Artemus had come to a standstill. A familiar sound, a woman's laughter, filled his ears. He looked around to see where it was coming from, but saw no one until he observed a magnificent yellow butterfly hovering around a woman working in the garden, landing on her and flying away, only to return and perch on her again. Artemus blinked and rubbed his eyes to make sure they weren't playing tricks on him. He focused his attention on the woman. He pricked himself. His mind raced. Was it possible? It couldn't be, could it?

It was clearly his daughter who was doing the manual job. Samantha was crouching in the dirt with her gardening gloves on. Her forehead wrinkled in concentration as she removed growing weeds from the flowerbeds. She seemed happier and in better shape than she had previously. He approached his daughter with zeal.

"Samantha!" he cried.

Samantha was digging in the garden when she heard her name called. She turned around and looked up at the old man in front of her. Samantha froze, an incredulous expression on her face. She was speechless, especially when her father fell to his knees and wailed. He sobbed as he held her fiercely. Samantha couldn't hold back her emotions any longer and burst into tears.

"Oh, honey, I'm so sorry for putting you through this. You mean the world to me," he eventually said.

"Dad, I'm sorry I left," she replied quietly and solemnly.

"I'm the one who should apologize. I was protecting my reputation and our good name, and I had forgotten about the most important thing to me. Sam, I've missed you so much."

"Dad, you know I love you, but I don't want to marry RJ."

"You don't have to marry that jackass anymore. Both Robert and RJ will go to prison soon."

Samantha frowned. "What do you mean?"

"I'll tell you later. I'm thrilled to see you. Do you know how long I've been looking for you and hoping to see you?"

"Dad..." Samantha paused a moment. "I meant to call, but... how did you find me?"

"Finding you has been my greatest wish in life, but it was Benjamin McClain who brought us together."

"Ben did that?"

"Yes, he did. It's a miracle your paths crossed, because he's a fantastic guy."

"I know. Benjamin is both my angel and my savior."

The father and daughter hugged again, both weeping hard as they finally reunited. Benjamin stood nearby, quietly observing them, his heart pounding in his chest as he witnessed their joyous reunion. As he neared them, he grinned. Samantha smiled and hugged him the instant she saw him. Artemus offered his hand, and Benjamin accepted the handshake.

"Thank you, Ben. It's good to see my daughter again. I still can't believe she's here with me. We can finally put this nightmare behind us."

Artemus wrapped his arms around his daughter again as she returned the hug. They laughed as they walked to the house to celebrate this happy occasion.

"IT WAS INCREDIBLE. Perhaps it was fate that brought us together." Linda nearly choked on the words as Samantha told the truth about why she had fled on her wedding day. She couldn't put into words how thrilled she was right now. Samantha was like a daughter to her.

Artemus grinned. Linda's stories fascinated him. His eyes widened as a sense of familiarity raced over him. He felt the same way the first time he met his wife.

Linda had prepared a special meal in honor of their guests, so the night was one big feast of eating and drinking. When Rosalie went to bed, Jack and Nancy joined them. The conversations got louder, and soon they were laughing and crying. They talked and laughed till midnight.

Soon after, Artemus became tired and decided it was time to rest, because he had a flight with Samantha scheduled for early the next day. Artemus was eager to visit his doctor for a complete check-up before returning to work, and handing early Christmas bonuses to his staff was at the top of his priority list now that they didn't have to worry about the Chandlers anymore. He was similarly overjoyed when Samantha informed him that it was time for her to help him run the family business.

Benjamin and Samantha escorted him to the guest room. Artemus opened the door, pleased with the spacious and comfortable chamber. The furniture complemented the bed, and an open fireplace kept the room warm. He yawned, put his hand over his mouth, and tapped it. He kissed his daughter goodnight, before closing the door behind him.

Benjamin and Samantha walked in silence until they reached her room.

"So, this is it. We'll return to our normal lives tomorrow," Samantha mumbled, easing the tension between them.

Benjamin purposely ignored her. He was ready to put his plan into action—to make Samantha believe his feelings for her had changed. In reality, he planned a grandiose surprise wedding for her in Beverly Hills.

Samantha was growing agitated with Benjamin's silence. She stood there for a long time, staring at him. She leaned forward to kiss him, unable to hold back her tears. Both were breathing heavily as their lips separated. Samantha didn't want the night to end. She kissed him again, more passionately this time. She extended the kiss, probing, teasing. But, to her surprise, Benjamin broke the kiss, drawing back to look into her face, and she nearly cried out at the loss of that delightful touch, leaving her breathless.

"Ben," she said. "What's wrong?"

"You surprised me, that's all," Benjamin murmured as he moved back, his eyes glinting above a smile.

Samantha's face reddened. She felt she was being overly forceful, but she couldn't bear the thought of being away from him. She was certain Benjamin felt the same way.

But why do I have the unpleasant feeling that I'm missing something here?

That concept irritated Samantha much more than before, but Benjamin's next move surprised her even more.

"Good night, Samantha. Sweet dreams," Benjamin said as he kissed her lips one more time and walked away.

Is that it? Why had Benjamin's manner shifted toward me, as if he didn't care that I was leaving? Was this his way of showing that he was also in anguish, that he didn't know how to deal with his feelings for me, and that he was still in denial?

Samantha sighed as she entered her room and closed the door behind her.

It was three a.m. Samantha leaned against the door, unsure whether she should make a move. She'd be returning to Los Angeles in a few hours, and she didn't know if or when she'd see Benjamin again. She knew in her heart that the moment they parted, she would miss him more than anybody else in her life.

It's now or never.

Samantha tiptoed her way out of her room. She knocked on Benjamin's door.

"Ben, are you awake?" she asked, but received no answer.

She listened through the door to see if she could hear anything, but there was no movement inside the room. She turned the doorknob, and it opened as if Benjamin was waiting for her. With her heart beating fast, she went in. Samantha saw Benjamin lying in bed asleep.

She locked the door and proceeded to the bed. She took off her nightgown, dropped it on the chair, and threw herself on top of him. Samantha kissed him deeply until Benjamin woke up.

"Sam, what are you doing here?" he asked.

"I am leaving tomorrow, Ben. I want to give myself to you before I go."

"Sam, you don't have to do this."

"Shut up, Ben. Just kiss me and hold me tight."

Samantha didn't need to say another word. Benjamin wrapped his arms around her. He kissed her lips, and he moved to her neck. Samantha didn't protest. Benjamin took off his clothes and let them fall to the floor. He got on top of her and kissed her hard. Samantha moaned with pleasure. She was feeling the electricity pulsing through her veins. They kissed again, and they were both breathing heavily when their lips finally parted. Benjamin caressed her cheeks and ran his hand through her hair. He looked into her eyes and kissed her hard again. Their tongues swirled around in each other's mouth. They both gasped at the pleasure as their bodies touched. Samantha closed her eyes, ready to surrender herself to him, and she bit her lips when they became as one. Showers of sparks flew into the night. It was magical!

Still steeped in the sensations of their lovemaking, Samantha sighed blissfully and snuggled deeper into his embrace. She lay peaceful and content in his arms, clinging to every minute, every second with Benjamin—her one true love. Samantha ached with the wish the night could last forever. They made love all night, and when they finally slept, she had a smile on her face.

Samantha had a hard time getting up the next morning. The time had come for her to go home. She dreaded the thought of leaving. She had trouble saying goodbye to Rosalie, Linda, Nancy, and Jack, but most of all, to Benjamin. She choked back her tears, but felt the sudden coldness from him. He was acting strange again, and she prayed it wasn't because she had given herself to him. Benjamin seemed distant around her... uncomfortable. She had no idea what she had done to cause this change.

Artemus shook Benjamin's hand and thanked him again for all he had done for them. He reached for Linda's hand and kissed it.

"I am confident, Linda, we shall see each other again," he said.

Linda smiled; her eyes glowing. They looked at each other for a long time. There were no words spoken, but they knew something magical was happening between them.

Meanwhile, the awkward silence between Samantha and Benjamin continued. For a long moment, neither said anything.

When Samantha couldn't stand it anymore, she broke the silence.

"I guess we don't have to worry about getting married anymore, and we don't have to worry about an annulment or a divorce."

Samantha's heart broke into small pieces. She felt guilty of doubts about Benjamin's strange behavior. Samantha waited for Benjamin to say something, but he didn't say a word. He gave her a look she couldn't define. The two of them fell silent again and stared at each other. They were only inches apart, but with the distance of years between them. Samantha grew increasingly frustrated.

Benjamin blew out a sigh and looked at her. "Sam, about last night...

"Ben, stop. Don't give it another thought. What happened between us was my idea." She forced a straight face. "I don't regret what we did last night."

"Take care of yourself, Sam. Don't forget. We had a fun time together." Benjamin pulled her face close and kissed her. He left without saying another word. A sly smile broke over his face as he walked away. He purposely left her alone without looking back, leaving Samantha confused.

Fun time?

Those words stabbed Samantha's heart as deeply as a knife blade.

While she admitted they had never discussed a future together, like a real marriage, she thought that was where they were heading. Apparently, Benjamin didn't care what happened between them. He didn't want a commitment—a no-strings-attached affair. Everything was clear to her now. Benjamin wasn't serious about her. He only wanted her for a good time, and she fell for it. Now she was leaving, and their affair was ending. She was such a fool.

Samantha was angry with herself for being so gullible and vulnerable to Benjamin. She ran out in a hurry and climbed into the back seat of a black limousine where her father was waiting for her. Samantha heard Rosalie scream as she left. It broke her heart, but she didn't look back when the car drove away. She knew it was the end of her summer love story and her first love.

Samantha stayed silent on their way to the airport to board their private plane until they reached Olive Way, where she recognized the local bus stop and coffee shop. She motioned for the driver to stop.

"Are you hungry, Sam?" Artemus questioned her as they came to a halt.

"No, Dad, but I have some unfinished business here." ‑

Samantha exited the limo and entered the coffee shop, her father behind her. The restaurant was packed. Samantha looked around for a familiar face. She recognized the cashier who had previously insulted her, and a devious smile appeared on her face.

"Table for two, please," she said.

The cashier looked at her, trying to recall where she had seen her, but quickly glanced away when she noticed Samantha was gazing back at her.

"Is there a problem?" Samantha asked, her brow wrinkled at her.

"Of course not," the cashier said.

Samantha rolled her eyes and pursed her lips. Her behavior bothered the cashier and glared. She motioned for someone to come, and a server with purple hair emerged, seated them at the last table, and handed them the menu.

Samantha remembered the young waitress who had previously served her. She smiled at her, and she smiled back before walking away.

"Dad, try their pot roast here; it tastes like the one mom used to make," Samantha said.

"Is that true? You're making me hungry."

The server reappeared to take their order. Samantha ordered two pot roasts and two black coffees.

"What's the deal, Sam?" her father asked when they were alone.

"I'll tell you in a minute," she promised.

Samantha turned around to find the cafe's owner scolding Felipe. She made a clicking gesture with her tongue. Nothing changed. Felipe's hand slipped to the side, knocking a dish off the table. It smashed on the floor. The owner yelled at Felipe even louder this time.

Samantha took a breather before turning to face her father. "That's Felipe. He's the busboy here," she said, pointing to him. She then told him everything that had happened to her on her bus ride into the city.

"And I'm assuming we're here to help Felipe? Is that right?" Artemus asked.

"You are correct, Dad! He did not know who I was, and I'm sure I was rude to him, yet he still tried to help me. I think it's my turn to reciprocate the kindness he's shown me."

Artemus focused his attention on his daughter. He had to admit that fleeing was the best thing that ever happened to her. She had matured since she left home. "So, what are your plans?"

"I'm thinking of giving Felipe his restaurant. He is an excellent cook, and if given the chance, I believe he might succeed. Did you know he made the pot roast?"

"He did?" Artemus asked. "I thought he was the busboy."

"The waitress informed me that Felipe had to arrive early in the morning to prepare the food, and after the restaurant opens, he is the day-shift busboy. Felipe is genuinely pleasant, and the owner pays him the bare minimum. He does not know that the owner is taking advantage of him."

"It's a shame," Artemus said, shaking his head. He scratched his chin and thought for a bit. "We own a couple of buildings in Seattle, Sam. I'll have to call the office to find out the exact location. If you are serious about helping him, we may use a space in one of our buildings to launch Felipe's restaurant, if that is what you want to do."

"Yes, Dad. That is precisely what I aim to do."

Artemus took out his cell phone and dialed his secretary, who was at the office working overtime. Artemus smiled as he hung up the phone after recounting the details of the conversation.

"How about it, Dad? Where's the building?" Samantha asked.

"I know strange things happen from time to time, but this is crazy," her father commented. "Would you believe we're sitting in one of our own buildings right now? We own this building and the one next door."

Samantha's eyes widened. "Oh, my God, Dad. What a coincidence."

"What's strange is that I only paid a few hundred thousand years ago for this structure. Who would have predicted this building would be in the financial area, within walking distance of the Convention and Cultural Center? It is now worth millions of dollars. I believe our office is on the fifth floor. My secretary confirmed the lease at this place, and the owner has not yet renewed his contract. It is up for renewal at the end of next month."

"Oh?" she murmured. "That's perfect."

A few seconds later, the server brought their food and placed the pot roast with mashed potatoes and string beans on the table. Then, they poured each cup of coffee, putting an end to their discussion.

"Will there be anything else?" the waitress asked.

"I'm glad you asked. Would you mind calling the owner to come here, please?" Samantha requested it.

"Is there a problem? I mean, is my service not satisfactory to you?" asked the server.

Samantha shook her head. "Oh no, you're fine. It's only that we have a personal matter to discuss with the owner."

The waitress nodded. "Please give me a moment."

Samantha observed the server converse with the owner while pointing in their direction. She noticed the owner nod, and he moved up to them, smiling.

"Good morning. My name is Hank, and I am the owner of this establishment. What can I do for you?"

"You don't recognize me, do you?" Samantha asked.

"No, ma'am, I'm sorry. Have we met before?" Hank asked, hardly audible, staring at her.

Samantha paid little attention to him until she had a query for which she needed an answer. "I understand you haven't renewed your lease for this building yet."

Hank's eyes widened. "How did you know?" he asked, raising his brows.

Samantha made a clicking gesture with her tongue. "This is Mr. Artemus St. James, your landlord and the owner of this building."

Hank turned to face the man in the chair opposite him. He wiped his hands on a towel, before shaking Artemus' hand.

"Sure, Mr. St. James of Artemus Industries. I'm glad to meet you, sir. I recognized you from a photo in our monthly tenants' newsletter."

"Speaking of tenants, Mr. St. James has decided not to renew your lease. I thought I'd let you know right away so you could make other plans."

"I know I haven't submitted the lease agreement yet," Hank said, "but I thought I had until next month to do so."

"Yes, but we elected not to renew the contract."

Hank covered his face with his hands. He took a deep breath to calm himself down. "May I?" pointing to the empty chair next to her.

"Please do," Samantha said.

"I hope to retire soon, but I'm still waiting for this individual who showed interest in buying my business. He's out of town, but he'll return next week. I'd appreciate it if you could spare me some time—"

Samantha cut him off in the middle of his sentence. "How much money do you need?"

"Excuse me?"

"How much are you asking for your business?"

"My asking price is $80,000, which includes all the store's furniture and equipment. I'm not keeping anything. Of course, the price is negotiable. Someone offered me $50,000, but we are still haggling."

"I'll tell you what. I'll give you $100,000 if you turn over the key and sign the paperwork today, but only on one condition."

"And that is?" Hank held his breath, waiting for Samantha's response.

"The condition is that you stay until next month to train the new owner on how to run this restaurant."

Hank couldn't believe his luck. He got more than he bargained for. "You've got a deal, ma'am. It will be my pleasure."

"Dad, please call your secretary again to contact the property management of this building to arrange all the—"

"Can you wait till I'm done eating, Sam?" Artemus spoke with his mouth full. "I'm hungry, and this pot roast is wonderful and delicious, exactly as your mother made it for me."

"I'm sorry, Dad." Samantha laughed as she took up her fork and ate.

Hank let the father and daughter have their meal. He excused himself and grinned as he entered his office. Hank couldn't believe his luck. He called his wife and told her to pack. "We're going to Disneyland this weekend."

FELIPE WAS CLEANING tables when he spotted Artemus lifting his cup. Because the server was busy, he quickly took the pot of coffee from behind the counter and headed to his table.

"Would you like me to refill your coffee, sir?" he asked.

"Thank you, another cup would be wonderful," Artemus said, smiling at Felipe.

"Are you enjoying your pot roast, sir? I made it myself." Felipe commented as he poured coffee into their cups.

"That's why I'm back," Samantha stated.

Felipe looked at Samantha and felt she seemed familiar, but he couldn't remember when or where he had seen her before.

Samantha snatched her Hermes purse off her lap and pulled out her compact mirror.

Felipe remembered where he had seen her. "Miss, it's you. How are you? You haven't been here in a long time. I hope your situation has improved since your last visit."

"Indeed. In fact, it changed my life." Samantha smiled.

She introduced her father, and the two men exchanged handshakes. They spoke for a while, until Felipe excused himself to return to work.

About an hour or so later, the building's property manager and Artemus' attorney arrived at the coffee shop. They provided all the documents Artemus had requested, and the last details of the shop's sale, a new lease, and a contract agreement for training new staff were ironed out relatively promptly. Hank was overjoyed, especially when they informed him that his check would be ready for pick up the next day. He was amazed at how quickly everything moved.

"I'm intrigued, Miss St. James. Who will take over my company?" Hank was curious.

"I bought this coffee shop for him," Samantha stated bluntly.

"Felipe?" the owner asked, perplexed.

"Yes, Felipe," she confirmed.

Felipe, who was wiping tables, turned his head when he heard his name. "Yes?" he said, his face bright.

"Felipe, did you hear me? I said I bought this shop for you," Samantha explained.

"Miss, did I hear you correctly? Did you say you bought this coffee shop for me?" He was perplexed.

"Yes, for helping me on that day. Felipe, you're gifted. You're a fantastic cook. I bought this coffee shop for you. Not only that, but I'm also giving you $100,000 to help you set up and run your business the way you want it."

Hank's jaw dropped open. How did Felipe get so lucky?

"Why would you do that for me? You don't even know who I am?" Felipe asked. His hands were shaking.

"Felipe, I used to spend hundreds of thousands of dollars on one shopping trip on items I didn't even need, but when I was broke and helpless, you proved that you don't need to know someone to assist them. You, a complete stranger, helped me. Felipe, please take this gift from me. Buying this business for you is my way of repaying your kindness."

Samantha's unexpected gift surprised Felipe. He couldn't believe what he was hearing.

"Is this correct? Is this coffee shop mine?" he inquired.

"Felipe, it's all yours," she responded.

"Do you mean my wife can stop working at the factory and help me here?"

"If that's what you want to do."

Felipe shifted his gaze to Hank. "Are you okay with this, boss?"

"Felipe, I'm OK. I've been wanting to retire for a long time, and now I can."

Felipe extended his hand to Samantha and Artemus. He cried as he conveyed his appreciation for the opportunity they had given him.

"Thank you for taking advantage of this once-in-a-lifetime chance, Felipe. Don't waste it," Samantha explained. She handed the paperwork over to Felipe, the new owner of the coffee shop.

"It is entirely up to you whether you want to hire new staff or keep the ones you have. I will transfer the funds after you have set up your business account. Hank will stay on until next month to train you and help you get your business license and anything else you'll need to run this coffee shop. Isn't that right, Hank?"

"Felipe, I'll be here to show you everything I know. And thank you for everything, Miss St. James and Mr. St. James. For a moment, I thought it would force me to close my business without recompense. I can finally relax now," Hank expressed this.

Samantha gave Felipe her father's business card.

"I'll send someone to help you set up everything to ensure the transfer goes well," she continued.

Felipe nodded. He couldn't believe his wonderful fortune.

Artemus gave Felipe a $10,000 check to open a business account.

"I'm so happy, I don't know what to say." Felipe said.

He joyfully hugged Samantha and Artemus and promptly called his wife to tell her the good news. They could hear happy screams in the background. Samantha and her father both burst out laughing at the same time.

Samantha looked around, and when she spotted the young waitress with purple hair, she motioned for her to come over.

"Do you need anything else?"

"Would you mind taking a seat for a moment?"

"OK. What is this all about?"

"Do you remember me?" Samantha asked. "You waited on me three months ago. I simply wanted to thank you for a job well done."

The young server stared at Samantha and recognized her.

"Oh, you've returned. I apologize for what occurred the last time you were here. I didn't have any money to assist you because I just worked part-time here."

Samantha shook her head. "Oh, don't worry about it."

Samantha shocked the waitress by giving her ten $100 dollar bills to pay for their meal. Samantha's generosity didn't end there. She handed the server her father's business card and added, "Call me when you're ready for a career change or want to return to school. We'll talk about your future."

When the waitress read the name on the card, she exclaimed in surprise. She kept up with business news and was familiar with Artemus St. James of Artemus Industries. She couldn't believe how fortunate she was at the moment. Samantha was so tightly embraced by the server that neither of them could breathe.

Hank stopped Samantha and her father as they were ready to depart. "I'm intrigued, Miss St. James. Why would you do that for Felipe? You don't even know who he is."

Samantha turned around and glanced at him. "On the contrary, I am familiar with him. You don't remember me, Hank, even though I was here three months ago. I lost my wallet and could not pay the bill. Not only did you threaten to call the cops, but you and the cashier ridiculed and humiliated me in front of your customers. Felipe was a poor busboy with little money, yet he volunteered to pay for my meal. I regained control of my life, and I'm repaying the favor. I am giving Felipe and his family the opportunity to live a happy life."

Hank paused for a while, vividly reliving the events of the day in his mind. He gazed at Samantha and recognized her. He blushed with embarrassment. Hank couldn't look her in the eyes. He was ashamed of himself, and all he could do was apologize for his harsh and inappropriate behavior. Samantha opted to remain silent and said nothing. She and her father hopped into their waiting limousine to take them to the airport, eager to return home. Hank realized he had learned an important lesson that day.

As the last customer left the coffee shop, Hank gathered his workers and informed them that he was retiring and Felipe would be the new owner. Before anybody could ask, Hank told them everything that had happened that day. He began by telling them about a customer who couldn't pay her bill because she had lost her wallet. Everyone was in disbelief as he concluded his narrative. They congratulated Felipe and the waitress on their good fortune. The cashier envied them and wanted to kick herself for being such a jerk.

If she'd just shown sympathy and tried to be kinder to Samantha, maybe... just maybe...

CHAPTER TWENTY

So here she was, back home again. Samantha walked around the house, looking at familiar places and objects, but she was uneasy, as if this wasn't the house she grew up in. Everything was still the same as she had left it, but she didn't feel at ease here. Even being back in her room and sleeping in her bed wasn't enough to lure her to return to the life she'd left behind.

Samantha was still irritated that Benjamin had moved on so quickly. They didn't have an understanding, and they hadn't even labeled their relationship, but she felt it was something unique, something more than a fling. She had never felt such an overpowering attraction to someone before. She missed him and wished she could feel his warmth and his hot, sweet breath on her skin. When she was at her most vulnerable, Benjamin showered her with attention, love, and compassion. She was eager to rejoin Benjamin and live the life she was now free to enjoy, because her father had given her the freedom to choose her own path in life. Samantha was ready to confess her actual feelings for Benjamin when he vanished into her life. She needed to see him. She needed to tell him she loved him, but what if the man she loved never wanted to see her again?

Samantha tightened her fists, sickened by the notion of Benjamin pretending to like her to get his way with her. She was hurt and disappointed, and she was angry with herself for allowing him to fool her. His betrayal upset her, since she had fallen in love with him. How could something so lovely have turned into something so agonizing?

Why did he have to make me fall in love with him? What did I do that was so terrible that he would do that to me?

Samantha wanted to yell and chastise him for causing her such misery. She stifled a sigh, knowing she was feeling sorry for herself. Samantha looked in the mirror.

If you miss him, go see him one last time to get closure. Samantha posed a question to herself.

A little voice inside her answered. *Maybe you should pay one last visit to Ben. Perhaps meeting and conversing with him would be good. If he doesn't want you, it's time to accept it and move on. You can end the fantasy that you'll be together forever.*

She grumbled and looked out the window. Loneliness filled her heart and brought tears to her eyes.

Samantha remained in her room for several days, weeping as softly as she could. Her first week at home had left her pale and restless. She knew it was absurd, but she couldn't get Benjamin out of her mind, no matter how hard she tried. Samantha thought about him every minute of the day, and when she closed her eyes, she could see his gorgeous face, even when she was sleeping, dreaming about him, missing him far more than she had any right to. She was in tears. She'd loved Benjamin with all her heart and soul. And she prayed that maybe, just maybe, he'd realized how much he loved her too.

If only she had known. Benjamin enlisted the help of Samantha's best friends—Jennifer, Stephanie, Vanessa, Rachel, and Alexandra—to arrange the most beautiful and unforgettable romantic wedding of the season. They, as expected, participated in this classic romance. Benjamin had arranged every detail to surprise Samantha with a secret wedding, and they couldn't wait to see how she reacted.

Benjamin also colluded with Linda, Nancy, Jack, and Rosalie to ignore Samantha's calls. They collaborated on where, when, and how they would pull it off.

Even Artemus was in on it. It tempted him to tell his daughter that everything was a ruse, that Benjamin was planning an opulent surprise wedding for her, and that they would marry in a few days. Artemus had made a promise, and he didn't want to dishonor it. All he could do was bite his tongue and watch his daughter sulk.

SAMANTHA'S NATURAL spark in her eyes returned a week later as she put her failed love affair behind her. She realized that what she and Benjamin had was a fantasy that would not survive in the real world. But when she sought solace, answers that would make her life worth living again, none were forthcoming. Her father was frequently at a business meeting, and Nanny Lorraine was busy or out of the house. Even her fellow SBPs did not pay her a visit. She hoped at least one of them had been there to comfort her in her hour of need, someone to help her sort through her thoughts and decide what to do next. She tried calling her friends many times to discuss her problems, but no one was home. Everyone ignored her. She felt alone and abandoned.

Samantha heard a car pull up in the driveway. She looked out the window. Samantha couldn't believe it. Her friends had finally shown up. Rachel was the first to get out of the car, followed by Jennifer and Alexandra. Stephanie was the last, and she grinned as she glanced at her bedroom window.

Samantha smiled from ear to ear. Her eyes glowed with enthusiasm as she dashed out the front door to welcome them. She approached them, arms wide, and gave them a joyous hug, tears running down her cheeks. Then she gave them the evil eye.

"Humph!" Samantha scoffed. "It's about time you showed up. Do you realize how long I've been calling you? I left messages, but no one returned my calls. I thought you'd deserted me and I was becoming concerned."

"I'm sorry, Sam. I had made an earlier commitment that I couldn't back out of," Stephanie stated.

"I was preoccupied. I had to leave town," Rachel clarified.

"I was too busy with problems at home," Jennifer stated.

"I'm sorry, Sam," Alexandra said, fumbling with her fingers.

Samantha stared at them in a way that made them wonder what she was thinking. They took a deep breath and crossed their arms, waiting for her to respond to their comments. Samantha arched her brow, folded her arms, and glared at them. Her friends swallowed hard.

Samantha burst out laughing. "I'm sorry, I couldn't stop myself. I'm just messing with you. What matters is that you're here now."

Her friends nearly collapsed from relief.

"You scared the hell out of us, Sam," Stephanie said.

The friends all laughed simultaneously.

"Listen up, you guys," Alexandra remarked. "I apologize for the short notice, but I'd like to invite you all to a wedding tomorrow. I'm one of the bridesmaids."

"I'm sorry, Alex, but I can't." Stephanie said. "I already have an earlier engagement."

"I'm sorry, Alex. I told my brother that I'd assist him in shopping for a project he was working on that was due on Monday," Rachel explained.

"I'd like to go, but I can't. It's my mother's birthday, and my father plans to surprise her. Guess who's in charge of organizing it?" Jennifer rolled her eyes.

Alexandra turned to face Samantha. "How about you, Sam? I'd like you to accompany me to this wedding."

"I can't."

"And why not?"

"I don't think I'm feeling well enough to be around people right now."

"Sam, you need to get out more. You need fresh air."

Samantha locked her gaze on her friend. "Why are you asking me to go, Alex?"

"Does there have to be a reason? I'd like you to accompany me. That's all," Alexandra answered, her hands trembling.

"You've never asked me to any of your gatherings before. Is it because I'm your last resort after everyone else has said no?"

"Sam, don't be like that. I thought you needed a change of pace. It's fine if you don't want to go. You are not obligated to do so. I will not yank your arm. I'll go by myself. I'm sure I'll enjoy sitting alone in the corner."

"I'm sorry for putting you off, Alex, but I'm not in the mood to go out," Samantha said, her voice shaking with sorrow.

The friends exchanged a subtle glance, and each pushed Alexandra to continue before returning their attention to Samantha.

"Please come with me, Sam," Alexandra begged. "I need your help. I told my family that I would bring one of you to the wedding. I promise I'll make it up to you."

Samantha softened as she sensed her friend's despair. She exhaled. "I know I'll be sorry, but since you put it that way, okay. I'll go."

"Great, I knew you'd say yes," Alexandra said, exhaling a sigh of relief. "It's a Hawaiian theme, and I've already bought your dress and matching shoes. I'll be here bright and early tomorrow morning with a makeup artist, so you and I can dress up together. This is a pretty formal event, Sam. I'm sure you'll enjoy it. I'd also like to show you off to my cousins. They don't believe me when I tell them about my gorgeous friends. It's important that you look beautiful," Alexandra said.

"Alexandra!" Samantha expressed her dissatisfaction by shaking her head. "Don't hook me up!"

"Well, someone should," Jennifer pointed out. "How are you going to find someone if you're sitting in your room by yourself? I think it's a terrific idea."

Samantha paused for a moment to contemplate. She didn't mind if her friends set her up on blind dates every now and then. They used to do it all the time for one another. But that was before, and this time, the idea offended her. Was she expecting Benjamin to appear and whisk her away?

"Just don't set me up—Wait, what do you mean you already bought my dress and shoes, Alex? How did you know I'd be going?"

"Um, well..." Alexandra faltered. Her eyes widened. She turned to her friends with a gaping mouth, screaming for help, but they were just as horrified as she was.

"Uh, heh, don't be ridiculous, Sam." Alexandra feigned a chuckle. "It's only that I asked them earlier, and they had already told me they couldn't go. You were my last hope, and I knew you'd say yes," she said, with a beautiful pout on her lips.

"Alex! I think there's a conspiracy going on here," Samantha observed.

Alexandra looked up at her and shook her head feebly. Her skin became paler. Her upper lip quivered, and her hands trembled as she pressed her fingers together. Samantha was staring at her.

"You don't have to go, Sam, if you don't want to. I bought the dress knowing you wouldn't let me go alone. That's all."

"All right," Samantha finally said. "Perhaps going out is good for me, but I'll ask my father's permission first. He's been acting weird since I got back."

Alexandra and her friends exhaled a sigh of relief as the tension dissipated.

"Don't worry, Sam. I've already asked your father. He said he thought it would be a good idea for you to leave the house," Alexandra said.

Samantha took a step back, her eyes wide as she struggled to grasp what Alexandra had just said.

"What? I can't believe he allowed me to go out so fast," Samantha said.

"Don't be foolish, Sam. Your father trusts me, OK?" Alexandra took a deep breath and licked her lips nervously.

The friends sucked on their bottom lips, occasionally biting their nails to mask their anxiety. They weren't sure how much longer they could put up with Samantha's endless questions and suspicious looks. They had never been good at lying.

The day started brilliantly. Samantha spent the morning getting ready for the wedding by showering and grooming herself. She did not know why she had agreed to go along with Alexandra. Samantha wasn't ready to mingle or meet new people, but her friend needed her support. So, for one day, she'd keep up appearances and pretend she was happy, and maybe, just maybe, she'd forget her sorrows.

Samantha got into a hot foamy bath scented with her favorite gardenia bubble bath with a hint of lavender. She had to admit that the soothing scent of lavender had made her feel more at peace than she had since Benjamin had departed her life. Samantha closed her eyes and imagined herself with him... their shared moments, their kiss in the water, and the intense sensation of his body next to her. She shook her head, trying to rid her mind of the conflicting thoughts.

This is ridiculous, she thought to herself. *Forget about him. Forget Benjamin McClain.*

Alexandra and two makeup artists arrived early. Samantha insisted on doing her makeup, but Alexandra didn't want to hear it.

"Sam, please let them pamper you, okay?"

"Alex, you're the bridesmaid. You need to look good. I'm just here to support you. I don't have to get dressed up."

"Come on, Sam, please work with me. There are two makeup artists in this room. Allow the other person to work on you. Give her a job. She needs the tips."

Samantha locked her gaze on one of the makeup artists, who returned her stare with a desperate expression on her face. Her heart softened.

"How can I say no now that you've worded it like that?" Samantha stated.

The makeup artist smiled and nodded her thanks.

"Don't worry, ma'am. I'll make you look even more beautiful. I will take care of you."

A BLACK LIMOUSINE PULLED into a circular driveway in front of a ranch-style home with an impressive brick facade and stucco accents. The driver emerged from the car, dressed in a black suit and cap. Alexandra, dressed in a peach floral gown, stepped out as he opened the door. They styled her hair in a messy, yet lovely updo.

"Shall we go?" Alexandra inquired.

Samantha stepped out of the car after a long wait. She was dressed in a lovely strapless silk Hawaiian dress with a blue and green floral design on a white backdrop, highlighting her exquisite proportions. A wide green bandeau hid her bust slightly, and she wore matching five-inch blue sandals with ankle straps to show off her gorgeous, shapely legs. Samantha went for a light, natural-looking makeup tone and a peach tint for her lips. She looked stunning in a half-updo, with flowing curls and white flowers behind her ear. She was gorgeous!

"Alex, I fear I am overdressed for the occasion. I believe I will outdo the bride. You should wear this dress instead of me," Samantha said.

"Shh, you look lovely. Quit fidgeting. Oh, I nearly forgot. It's also a masquerade ball. We need to wear masks," Alexandra said as she took one of their masks from a velvet box and handed it to Samantha. "Here, put this on."

"A wedding masquerade ball? Who came up with that?"

"The groom came up with the concept. He thought it was the ideal icebreaker, because the bride and groom's families had never met."

Samantha made a tongue-clicking motion. "I guess I'll have to give it to the groom. He considered the details. This might be a fabulous wedding, if you ask me."

Alexandra smiled.

Samantha slipped on her mask and transformed into a princess from a fairy tale. She wore a classic Venetian half mask surrounded by lace, gold, and diamonds. Alexandra donned a simple feather mask adorned with gold and white glitter.

"Are you sure this is what I'm supposed to wear?" Samantha inquired.

"I picked that mask for you to match your dress, Sam. I told you I wanted you to look stunning when I introduced you to my cousins."

"Alex, please don't pair me with one of your relatives!"

"Of course not. Don't be silly," Alexandra said. She had a goofy smile on her face.

They walked into the home. The room fell silent, and all conversation came to a standstill. Samantha felt uneasy as she looked at the women dressed in Hawaiian attire and feather masks. Their eyes were the only visible, since it entirely obscured their faces. Nobody would recognize anyone in their costumes.

Samantha didn't care what Alexandra said. She was clearly overdressed. Samantha should berate herself for allowing her friend to persuade her to come. Everyone was gazing at her, which made her anxious. She felt something was wrong, but she couldn't put her finger on it.

The wedding was a magnificent backyard garden affair with a stunning sunset backdrop. It was a gorgeous property with panoramic views of downtown Los Angeles and some of the best ocean and mountain views in Southern California.

Samantha explored the backyard and discovered the most magnificent flower garden she had ever seen, even better than Benjamin's garden. They created the garden in a circle, with pebble paths running through the rose bushes. She sat on the gazebo bench, taking a deep breath and inhaling the blooms. She did not know how much she cherished and missed those smells. Samantha took another look around and noticed the wedding was well guarded. There were uniformed security officers on duty, and all entrances and exits were barred. She looked around to see if there was any sign of who was getting married, but it was impossible to tell because everyone was wearing masks covering their full face. She found it strange that there were no wedding banners or invitation cards lying about, as if she were a member of a secret organization.

Fresh roses, lilies, and orchids, her favorite flowers, were selected to decorate the altar. There were a few potted plants bordering the aisle. They draped a white tulle canopy stretched from a tree limb down to the altar's corners with cascading flower arrangements. Soft chiffon fabric was used to cover each chair. Beautiful strands of lights were strung throughout the yard and wrapped around the trees. There was also a large tent with a dance floor and exquisite table settings for the reception.

"Hmm... I'll hand it to the wedding planner. This is exactly what I would want for my wedding: simple but elegant. If this was the bride's idea, then we had a similar sense of style."

Samantha looked over her shoulder when someone tapped her on the back.

"Hello, Sam. It's just me. Are you having a good time?" Alexandra asked as she removed her mask.

"Alex, where have you been? I've been looking for you."

"I'm sorry, Sam, but I was helping the bridesmaids get ready."

"Whose weddings are this again?" Samantha inquired. "Is it a famous person? What's up with the security guards?"

"A dear friend of mine," Alexandra stated sincerely. She swallowed hard before speaking again. "Um, Sam, I know I'm imposing too much, but the maid of honor was running late and couldn't make it to the wedding on time. The wedding is about to begin, and we need a proxy for her. I volunteered you because you're already dressed for the occasion. I hope you don't mind."

"What? Why would you do such a thing? Alex, you're putting me in a bind here. What has gotten into you?"

"I know. I swear this is the last thing I will ask from you."

Alexandra grabbed Samantha's hand before Samantha could say anything, and they hurried to the room to get ready.

Meanwhile, everything appeared in order, and the guests took their seats. The officiant, the groom, and the best men were already waiting at the altar. The wedding planner made sure everything was perfect, and they lined everyone up, ready to walk down the aisle. The flower girl and ring bearer were standing in line. The bridesmaids stood to the right, while the groomsmen stood to the left. Samantha, the maid of honor, was last.

"We're waiting for the signal to begin the wedding march," the wedding planner stated. "Take your time walking down the aisle. You don't have to rush."

"Alex, why are we still wearing masks?" Samantha murmured.

"Just keep the mask on, Sam, until they tell us to take it off. Just go with it, OK? Don't forget to walk slowly."

"All right, I'll do it, but this wedding is becoming weirder by the minute, as if everyone wants to keep their identity hidden," Samantha commented, pointing to the full-head masks everyone was wearing.

Alexandra chuckled. "Don't worry, it will be over soon."

The music started playing as the flower girl walked down the aisle, throwing red rose petals on the ground, followed by the ring bearer, bridesmaids, and groomsmen. Samantha kept turning her head to get a glimpse of the bride, since she was certain she was dressed better than a bride would be. Even the mask she was wearing was overkill. It seemed pure gold.

Alexandra certainly went to the great lengths with dressing me up just to meet her cousin. She shook her head, but giggled a little. She had to admit it was one crazy day.

Moments with Benjamin raced before Samantha's eyes as the bridesmaids and groomsmen began their long walk up the aisle. She wondered what would have happened if Benjamin hadn't phoned her father. Would he have followed through on his wedding proposal to marry her? Would he have fallen in love with her and never let her go after the wedding?

A dignified older man approached and took her arm, wearing a satin eye mask that entirely covered his face. Samantha believed he was her partner. She nodded at him, recognizing his presence, but he said nothing and made no eye contact with her. Samantha shrugged her shoulder. She thought the man was rude. She looked behind her to see if she could see the bride, but she wasn't there.

This wedding is closely guarded, but when will the bride arrive? Perhaps she had second thoughts about the wedding. Samantha answered her own question. She was now keen to learn who the bride was. The tension was killing her.

The wedding coordinator motioned them to begin walking.

"Do you think it's strange for us to go ahead when the bride hasn't arrived yet?" she said to the man next to her. Samantha waited for him to respond, but he didn't even turn to face her. He didn't say anything.

How rude! She mumbled to herself.

The organist played "Here Comes the Bride" as they walked down the aisle.

Someone messed up big time. The bride is still not here, but the music has started. Samantha chuckled a bit.

The guests stood up and smiled as she passed.

Wearing this silly mask confuses everyone. They think I'm the bride. She giggled while covering her mouth. *Okay, I'll play along, but they're going to be surprised.*

As she got closer to the altar, Samantha had flashbacks of her friends convincing her to go to the wedding, the makeup artists who showed up at her house, the dress and shoes Alexandra chose for her, and the extravagant mask. She felt her heart stopped. She looked to her left shocked to see her friend Vanessa waving at her. Michael, her husband, held Clarissa Belle, her godchild. They waved, and she reluctantly waved back.

Samantha frowned when she saw Nanny Lorraine, Linda, Nancy, and Jack waving at her from the next row. Mr. and Mrs. McClain, Grandpa and Grandma McClain, as well as Benjamin's brothers, nieces, nephews, and relatives, were also there.

She was confused at this point. Samantha came to a halt.

The music suddenly stopped. Samantha stood there and watched as everyone removed their masks. She couldn't believe what she was seeing. The bridesmaids were Jennifer, Rachel, Stephanie, and Alexandra. Rosalie was the flower girl. She screamed in disbelief as her partner removed his mask.

"Dad? What is the meaning of this?" Samantha asked.

"Oh, Samantha, you look so beautiful," he murmured as he hugged her.

Samantha looked around, and it instantly drew her gaze to a tall guy standing in front of the altar. The groom gently removed his mask, exposing Benjamin, who was as gorgeous as could be. Tim, his brother, stood next to him as best man. Samantha broke into tears. She had finally figured it out. She was the bride, after all!

"Dad?" she said, tears streaming down her cheeks as she removed her mask.

"Please, honey, don't cry. Isn't this what you wanted? I am happy for you. Benjamin is a wonderful person. He's perfect for you."

The officiant took his place behind the podium, and Benjamin waited for her.

"Ben, what did you do?" she asked, sobbing as she approached the altar.

"Shh, don't cry, my runaway bride. Can't you see? I'm here to marry you for real."

"I don't understand. I thought you didn't want me."

"I'm sorry to put you through this, sweetheart. I asked your father for your hand in marriage the day I met him, and he said yes. I've been planning our wedding for a long time."

Samantha turned to face her father, who nodded and smiled.

"Dad?"

Artemus approached the altar and hugged his daughter again. "I apologize for not saying anything, Sam. Benjamin came up with the idea. He asked me not to say anything to you when we were in Seattle. He wants to give you the most amazing wedding possible."

Samantha couldn't believe it. He stared at Benjamin with all the love she felt for him.

"I did it for you, darling. I conspired with your father, your friends, and everyone else here to keep you confined to your house. I wanted to make sure you were safe while organizing and planning our wedding. My uncle, Judge Perry McClain, is here. He will officiate at our wedding," Benjamin explained.

"Welcome to the family, Samantha," Judge Perry said as he reached out to shake her hand.

It rendered Samantha speechless. Overjoyed, she sprang to her feet and wrapped her arms around Benjamin.

"Oh, Ben," Samantha exclaimed as she kissed him lovingly and affectionately.

"Oh, sweetheart, you don't know how long I've wanted to taste the sweetness of your lips again," Benjamin muttered as he kissed her passionately.

Everyone applauded and screamed.

"Ahem," Judge Perry interrupted. "I haven't yet proclaimed you husband and wife. Could you just wait a few minutes before kissing?" He said, amused, trying not to laugh, as he witnessed them confess their love for one another right in front of him.

"Would you...?" Judge Perry got things started.

"Wait," Benjamin said, interrupting him.

"Yes, Benjamin?" Judge Perry asked.

"Do you mind if I first ask Samantha a question?"

"Now?" Judge Perry asked again. "Very well," he said, motioning for him to proceed.

"Do you remember when I proposed to you back in Seattle, Sam?"

"How could I have forgotten? Yes, I remember."

"What I didn't tell you was that I truly meant it. I fell in love with you on the night you spilled milk all over the kitchen floor. I couldn't get you out of my mind after that. My wedding proposal to you in Seattle was sincere. So, sweet woman, would you marry me right now and live in this beautiful house with its own greenhouse for you?"

"Did you purchase this house for me?"

"Yes, I bought it for you on the day I asked your father for your hand in marriage, so you could be close to your friends and family when we're in Los Angeles. I knew you'd fall in love with this house, garden, and huge greenhouse the moment

I saw it. Remember, we still have unfinished business in the greenhouse." He whispered in her ear.

Samantha caught up on it quickly. "Naughty boy," she responded.

They kissed for what seemed like an eternity, and everyone thought it would never end.

"Ahem," Judge Perry interrupted again. "Could we perhaps proceed with the ceremony now that we've straightened things out? I'm famished." He busted out laughing.

"I love you with all my heart, Sam, and I need your response. Will you marry me?" Benjamin pleaded.

"Yes, Benjamin McClain, I will marry you! I love you with all my heart and soul." Samantha stated.

"All right, Uncle Perry. Now you may marry us," Benjamin said, reaching for her hand. "Please continue," he said, chuckling.

The judge couldn't stop laughing with Benjamin. He had never thought of his nephew as a hopeless romantic.

The ceremony went off without a hitch. Benjamin recited his vows properly and accurately. Samantha answered in a gentle voice, making promises while lovingly glancing at Benjamin. They signed the marriage license in front of the court clerk, Benjamin's niece, as the guests looked on.

When the ceremony was over, everyone stood up and cheered, clapping their hands and whistling as the happy couple shook everyone's hands. Samantha Isabella St. James and Benjamin Julius McClain tied the knot.

They waved to everyone as they climbed into a waiting limousine to take them to the airport for their honeymoon getaway to Hayman Island, Australia.

"WHAT ARE YOU DOING with my shoes, my sweetheart?" Samantha inquired. They were on their honeymoon on a luxurious boat at sea.

"My love, I don't want to see any more running shoes around you. I'm tossing them in the water," he joked. "Never wear them again. You are no longer a runaway bride!" Benjamin chuckled.

Samantha burst out laughing as she watched her husband throw her running shoes into the ocean. She wrapped her arms around him as they peered out at the breathtaking scenery of the island. Her eyes shone with love and excitement as she gazed at her husband—her one true love.

Benjamin kissed and scooped up his new bride as he closed the cabin door behind him and gazed into her eyes, vowing to love her "until the end of time."

EPILOGUE

Following spectacular undercover footage from a sting operation headed by Captain Morris of the Beverly Hills Police Department, they apprehended Mr. Chandler and his son, RJ, after an unsuccessful attempt to blackmail Artemus St. James. They also charged their male and female accomplices, who admitted to having a role in the father and son's scheme. They recovered all the photographs they had taken.

In an unexpected turn of events, a thorough investigation uncovered the father and son's involvement in several illegal business activities. They froze any remaining assets they had. Mr. Chandler and his son were convicted and sentenced to prison for their crimes. Mrs. Chandler fainted and collapsed on the courtroom floor. Mr. Chandler threw a tantrum, and three bailiffs hauled him out of the courthouse, his yells echoing throughout the room, while RJ pleaded for mercy and sobbed hysterically as the bailiff dragged him away.

FELIPE'S MENU INCLUDED many exquisite dishes he learned from his father, and he was an instant hit with his customers. Felipe's restaurant was a huge success because of his hard work, positive attitude, and dedication, as well as his strong connections with the local community. He extended his business even further by offering secure online ordering and free delivery. His wife had quit her job at the factory, leaving her with nothing to do but care for Felipe and their children in the four-bedroom house they had purchased.

ROSALIE WAS OVERJOYED when Samantha and Benjamin adopted her, and she couldn't wait to be an older sister to her baby brother.

ARTEMUS MERGED HIS company with McClain Enterprise. He stepped down as CEO and intended to retire and enjoy life. He befriended Linda, and they discovered they had similar interests. They spent time together and took a romantic vacation to Hawaii. Artemus proposed to Linda shortly after, and they planned to marry in December.

AFTER LEAVING BENJAMIN'S estate, Lucy began working at the fish market alongside Samuel. They ended up getting married and having twins. Lucy and Samantha reconciled and ultimately became good friends.

CASSANDRA HAD NOT BEEN seen or heard from since leaving the police station, and her whereabouts were unknown.

BENJAMIN HAD FINALLY found the love he had been searching for. He couldn't imagine his life without Samantha. She was the best thing that ever happened to him. With Rosalie and a new baby on the way, he and Samantha were looking forward to having more children fill their home with joy for many years to come.

SAMANTHA, AN OPINIONATED, obstinate, and rebellious spoiled wealthy brat, eventually learned the true meaning of love and self-respect. And it just took a handsome and charming man named Benjamin McClain to change her life for the better. They both believed they were meant to live happily ever after.

ABOUT THE AUTHOR

Marissa Marchan writes young adult, new adult, middle grade, and short story fiction for younger readers. Her grandson, Ray Angelo, was the inspiration for *A Ray of Sunshine* and *Ray and Haley in the Kingdom of the Gobtrolls*. It tells the incredible story of a young boy full of love, faith, hope, and courage, filled with heartwarming stories that will lift your spirits and warm your hearts.

Each of us has our own way of expressing our grief and loss. When Marissa's father died many years ago, she discovered she had an incredible ability to create the most wonderful world of pure imagination. She squandered hours fantasizing and making up stories. This was her way of dealing with grief.

Another tragedy struck Marissa's family shortly thereafter, with the death of her sister, Mirla. Marissa struggled with grief and loss for a long time. Ray gave her the strength she needed to move forward. He was a source of love and inspiration for her. Ray instilled in her the courage and ability to persevere in the face of adversity and fear.

Marissa took up writing and could finally put her thoughts into words. Not only did writing help her heal, but it also gave her a sense of stability. She can finally let go.

Since then, Marissa has pursued a writing career, and she is the author of two Spoiled Brats book series: Forbidden Love and Runaway Romance. This series continues with four other novels. A dream she had inspired the character of Mrs. Millionaire, as well as her story.

Read more at https://marissamarchan.com

CONNECT WITH THE AUTHOR

WEBSITE:
Marissamarchan.com[1]
EMAIL:
marissa.marchan@yahoo.com
TWITTER:
@marissamarchan[2]
FACEBOOK:
booksbymarissamarchan[3]
LINKEDIN:
linkedin.com/in/marissa-marchan-41474854[4]
INSTAGRAM:
instagram.com/marissamarchan[5]
PINTEREST
@designbymarissamarchan
TUMBLR
https://marissamarchan.tumblr.com

---

1. http://www.marissamarchan.com/

2. https://twitter.com/marissamarchan

3. https://www.facebook.com/Booksbymarissamarchan/

4. https://www.linkedin.com/in/marissa-marchan-41474854

5. https://www.instagram.com/marissamarchan

MRS. MILLIONAIRE SHORT STORY BOOK SERIES

M rs. Millionaire Short Story Book series is a collection of fictional stories. Each story focuses on an unlucky family or individual who crosses paths with Mrs. Millionaire.

Matilde "Tilly" Jane Parker begins as a jet setter known for her rebellious streak and reputation as a party girl. When Tilly suffers a personal tragedy, it changes her perspective on life, and her experience has shaped her in many ways. Rather than living her life as a victim, she uses her power and wealth to help those who cannot defend themselves. Tilly finds herself in various situations and occasionally works as an amateur detective who helps people in need solve the problems she is involved in.

MRS. MILLIONAIRE SHORT STORY BOOK SERIES VOLUME 1

Mrs. Millionaire and the Homeless Woman Book 1

∞

MATILDE, OR TILLY TO her family and friends, is well-known for being a party girl. She enjoys unnecessary trouble despite being born into a wealthy family, and her wild behavior worsens as she gets older. Tilly meets Dusty, the man of her dreams, and learns for the first time what it means to give in and when to leave a relationship. But events, even the most uncontrollable and tragic ones, can play tricks on us, change our lives forever, and teach us lessons that we will never forget. Someone attacked Tilly in the underground parking lot, but fortunately a homeless person came by and saved her. That event alters her perspective on life and helps her become a better person.

∞

Mrs. Millionaire and the Bad Father Book 2

∞

Matt Calderon is a caring husband and father of two children. His wife Maria suffers from a condition that limits her ability to perform manual work, forcing Matt to work two jobs to support his family. Despite their difficulties, the family is optimistic. But every now and then life throws a curveball. Matt's boss accused him of stealing money from him. To make matters worse, Matt is in a gas station when a robbery occurs. He is trapped inside, surrounded by police, while his family waits for him to return home. What chances do they have now? Is there hope for them?

Mrs. Millionaire and the Waitress Book 3

∞

Lucy was only two when her mother died. Her father married a widow with two children. Lucy's father never told her the truth about her upbringing, so Lucy assumed her stepmother was her biological mother. Her father died several months before graduating from high school, leaving Lucy with the only family she knew, and they revealed their true colors. Lucy's stepmother secretly transferred her inheritance to herself, and told Lucy that her father had left them penniless. Lucy left school to work as a waitress to support her family. Her stepbrother stole money and valuables from Lucy's work. The owner accused Lucy, and the police arrested her. Will Lucy ever uncover the truth of her past?

∞

Mrs. Millionaire and the Runaway Kids Book 4

∞

After his wife's death, Dexter Curtis accepts a supervisory position at a textile company and moves to Connecticut, determined to provide a better life for his four children. His new job went well, but a colleague was cruel and jealous of him. He ruined Dexter's reputation, resulting in Dexter losing his job. Dexter became depressed after he could not find work and turned to alcohol to relieve his stress. A tragic accident left him unconscious and in a coma. Child Protective Services placed the children in a temporary shelter until they could make other arrangements for them. They wanted to split them into two separate households. The youngsters have escaped because of this chain of events. Will Dexter get out of his coma? Is there a chance to reconcile and mending the family?

Mrs. Millionaire and the Delivery Girl Book 5

∞

The last thing Nancy wanted was to work as a delivery girl. She had high goals in mind. After holding off dating until she got a job, Nancy made it a priority to stay in school and participate in as many activities as possible. Her perception of bad boys and bikers changed when she met Julius. Nancy's ambition to pursue a prosperous career shattered in an instant. They married at City Hall with just a few friends present. Nancy's parents disowned her. When Nancy moved in with Julius's parents in Wisconsin, things turned for the worse. His mother was vengeful and tyrannic. She kept track of every detail of her stay, which irritated Nancy even more. This has caused friction in their relationship. Julius' wandering eye persisted. Nancy discovered her husband was cheating on her and threatened to leave him. Julius begged her not to go. Will Nancy forgive him? Will they continue after the betrayal?

MRS. MILLIONAIRE SHORT STORY BOOK SERIES VOLUME 2

Mrs. Millionaire and the Thief Book 6

∞

HAVE YOU EVER BEEN taken by surprise and had no idea what was going on? To propose to his fiancée, Dan Collins, an advertising account executive, worked hard to get the promotion he wanted. However, a colleague threatens to sabotage his plans for a happily ever after. He sabotages Dan's career, leading to his dismissal, and his life spirals out of control. Will Dan ever prove his innocence? Is a wedding for him still on the horizon?

Mrs. Millionaire and the Housekeeper Book 7

∞

Lesley is a single mother of her seven-year-old daughter Haley. Her boyfriend Stanley disappeared after she gave birth. With nowhere else to go, Lesley makes amends with her mother and returns home. Everything was fine until her mother married Jacob, a man ten years younger, and Lesley's life turned into a massive battleground. Lesley does not get along with him, which leads to friction between her and her mother. Lesley and her daughter moved out of the house after her mother chose her new husband. What will happen to them? Will she be able to support her daughter?

∞

Mrs. Millionaire and the Reluctant Hero Book 8

∞

Ray Griffin is an unfortunate street musician. His wife divorced him and left with their eight-year-old daughter. He has had nothing but bad luck and a series of misfortunes since leaving Texas. Ray became homeless and moved away. He wants to get his life back on track and find a permanent job, so he can regain custody of his daughter. Will Ray overcome the seemingly insurmountable obstacles on his path? Will he see his daughter, whom he has not seen for a long time, and reunite with her?

∞

Mrs. Millionaire and the Elevator Man Book 9

∞

Carlos Angelo, a sixty-two-year-old Italian man, works as an elevator operator in the Lower Manhattan neighborhood of New York City. It was his first and only job in the United States, after nearly four decades in the country. He is known throughout the company as a dedicated, loyal and likeable employee who has received numerous "Employee of the Month" awards over the years. When his employer adapted to new technologies and fired him, he became depressed. What future would he have if he didn't know how to do anything else?

∞

Mrs. Millionaire and the Taxi Driver Book 10

∞

Regie Adams, a forty-year-old dairy farmer, has worked all his life. After several years of feeding, cleaning and milking cows every day, he had had enough and tried his luck elsewhere, despite his mother's protests. Regie boarded a bus outside the city and finds himself in the midst of a series of disasters. Eventually, he found himself in Las Vegas, Nevada. He was content with his simple life as a taxi driver until one fateful night when everything changed. Two men followed a woman who signaled for him to stop. Would this event change his life for the better or for the worse, given his history of bad luck?

SPOILED BRATS BOOK SERIES

The Spoiled Brats Book series is a new adult novel that follows the lives of wealthy teenagers in the affluent city of Beverly Hills. These stories chronicle their extravagant lifestyle, including socializing with the elite and attending private parties, their growth from childhood to maturity, and a serendipitous encounter with love in an unexpected place.

FORBIDDEN LOVE
Spoiled Brats Book Series Book One

VANESSA FLORENCE GRANDEVILLE, a Beverly Hills socialite and infamous spoiled brat, celebrated her 21st birthday with her wealthy friends in Honolulu. By chance, she ran into Michael, a fisherman from a nearby island, the same day. Vanessa humiliated him, but Michael fell in love at first sight.

Vanessa and her friends had rented a yacht for a weekend cruise when complications arose. Their boat capsized in a fierce storm and swept them overboard. The Coast Guard rescued everyone except Vanessa, who drifted away. Michael found her at sea suffering from a head injury and amnesia. He saved her life, but did he deserve to be regarded as a hero?

Unexpected and remarkable events brought their lives together. Was it possible that life played a joke on them? Will these people overcome their differences?

RUNAWAY ROMANCE
Spoiled Brats Book Series Book Two

TWENTY-TWO-YEAR-OLD Beverly Hills socialite Samantha Isabella St. James is devastated when she learns her father intends to force her to marry the son of a wealthy businessman to pay for his debt. She flees on her wedding day and is unaware of the impact of her actions. Samantha seeks refuge in the stranger's house and reluctantly accepts a job as a nanny for Benjamin McClain, an eccentric, handsome young entrepreneur, after someone steals her wallet and leaves her penniless. There is an immediate and clear affinity between them. Will Samantha's life become more complicated when she has to choose between saving her father and following her heart?

A MAGICAL STORYBOOK SERIES

A Magical Storybook Series tells the amazing adventure of a young boy filled with love, faith, hope, and courage, as well as an incredible experience filled with heartwarming stories that will lift your spirits and warm your hearts.

A RAY OF SUNSHINE
A Magical Storybook Series Book One

THEO AND MARY ARE A deformed husband and wife who are constantly mocked in their small town. The townspeople chased them away from the only home they had ever known. With their meager possessions, Theo and Mary travel to the forest, where they discover a magical and mysterious world of beauty and happiness. Soon God blessed them with a child. To Theo and Mary's surprise, he has healing abilities and a connection with the elements and animals. Will Ray's magical abilities be enough to teach the people of the town the true meaning of unconditional love? Can people accept Theo and Mary despite their unappealing appearances? Come along on the adventures of an amazing family, as they use their special abilities to save others and teach people the power of love and understanding.

RAY AND HALEY
In the Kingdom of the Gobtrolls
A Magical Storybook Series Book Two

THEO AND MARY, TOGETHER with their son Ray and daughter Haley, live peacefully and joyfully in an enchanted forest far from civilization. In this strange and mysterious place, Theo and Mary discover that their children were born with unique gifts. Ray possesses extraordinary powers, including the ability to interact with animals and elements, while Haley has a natural ability to communicate with plants and animals. When Theo learns that the people who drove them away from their homes years ago blame them for the desolation of his old town, he must embark on a journey to prove their innocence. When Theo and Haley disappear, Ray uses his wits and magical abilities to find them in the most polluted and smelliest place in the world!

Thank you for reading!

T hank you for reading *Runaway Romance.* If you enjoyed it, please consider telling your friends or posting a short review. Word of mouth is an author's best friend, and much appreciated.

Please check out the rest of Spoiled Brats Book Series, Mrs. Millionaire Short Story Book Series, and A Magical Storybook Series through various online book retailers and distribution channels available as eBooks and Print. Happy reading!

Marissa Marchan

Don't miss out!

Visit the website below and you can sign up to receive emails whenever Marissa Marchan publishes a new book. There's no charge and no obligation.

https://books2read.com/r/B-A-YPEF-MYHIB

BOOKS 2 READ

Connecting independent readers to independent writers.

Did you love *Runaway Romance: Spoiled Brats Book Series Book Two*? Then you should read *Forbidden Love: Spoiled Brats Book Series Book One*[1] by Marissa Marchan!

Vanessa Florence Grandeville, a Beverly Hills socialite and infamous spoiled brat, celebrated her 21st birthday with her wealthy friends in Honolulu. By chance, she ran into Michael, a fisherman from a nearby island, the same day. Vanessa humiliated him, but Michael fell in love at first sight.

Vanessa and her friends had rented a yacht for a weekend cruise when complications arose. Their boat capsized in a fierce storm and swept them overboard. The Coast Guard rescued

1. https://books2read.com/u/mBGlaD

2. https://books2read.com/u/mBGlaD

everyone except Vanessa, who drifted away. Michael found her at sea suffering from a head injury and amnesia. He saved her life, but did he deserve to be regarded as a hero?

Unexpected and remarkable events brought their lives together. Was it possible that life played a joke on them? Will these people overcome their differences?

Read more at www.marissamarchan.com.

About the Publisher

3 Ways Publishing is an independent publisher established in January 2020 to gain recognition and traction in the publishing world.

Do you ever wonder where the idea for your book came from? Was it from a dream? Perhaps a personal experience or story told by your mother or grandmother? Whatever it is, one important thing is that you have to feel passionate about what you write, which leads to a satisfying ending.

3 Ways Publishing publishes books that they are passionate about—books of fictional and entertaining stories to help children develop a love of reading and learning, young readers, fantasy, romance, and fiction for various age groups with a strong female protagonist.

Visit: https://3wayspublishing.com/

www.ingramcontent.com/pod-product-compliance
Lightning Source LLC
Chambersburg PA
CBHW050358260626
47156CB00003B/779